Don't Go Home

Don't
Go
Home

CAROLYN HART

BERKLEY PRIME CRIME, NEW YORK

THE BERKLEY PUBLISHING GROUP
Published by the Penguin Group
Penguin Group (USA) LLC
375 Hudson Street, New York, New York 10014

USA • Canada • UK • Ireland • Australia • New Zealand • India • South Africa • China

penguin.com

A Penguin Random House Company

This book is an original publication of The Berkley Publishing Group.

Berkley Prime Crime Books are published by The Berkley Publishing Group.
BERKLEY® PRIME CRIME and the PRIME CRIME logo are trademarks of
Penguin Group (USA) LLC.

Library of Congress Cataloging-in-Publication Data

Hart, Carolyn G.
Don't go home / by Carolyn Hart —First edition.
pages ; cm
ISBN 978-0-425-27654-9
I. Title. II. Title: Do not go home.
PS3558.A676D66 2015
813'.54—dc23
2014046280

FIRST EDITION: May 2015

PRINTED IN THE UNITED STATES OF AMERICA

10 9 8 7 6 5 4 3 2 1

Cover photo copyright © by mythja/Shutterstock.
Cover design by George Long.
Interior text design by Laura K. Corless.

In thanks for my daughter, Sarah,
the inspiration for Annie.

Don't Go Home

1

Rae Griffith welcomed the caress of the ocean breeze. Tiny fish formed a dark cloud near her bare feet. Despite the shimmering loveliness of the aquamarine water, she wasn't enchanted. A few years ago to be here with Alex would have been glorious . . .

Alex was farther out. A gentle wave crested near his chest. He turned and was caught in a moment of perfection, chestnut hair golden in the sun, finely chiseled features, deep-set dark brown eyes, muscular and tanned. Extraordinary good looks, boyish charm, and riveting prose had made his novel a smash success.

Descriptive phrases drifted through her mind: *smoldering emotion . . . a hint of danger . . . sex and lies . . . a literary Ryan Gosling . . .* Her lips twisted in wry amusement. She easily churned out apt slogans. Alex had been her first big client, put her on the map of the best Atlanta publicists. She'd crafted plenty of releases for Alex. The one she liked best, the one that now defined him, came in the first flush of their relationship: *The South Rises Again in the Pre-eminence of Alex Griffith, Golden Boy of a New Golden Age in Southern Literature.*

Alex's reckless F. Scott Fitzgerald aura dazzled readers and critics, dimmed those around him to shadowy figures. But the brightest comets burn out and even huge best sellers finally begin a slow slide down the sales charts. The clamor grew. *When will there be a new Alex Griffith novel?*

Alex gave her his old impudent, gonna-knock-'em-dead grin. "Come on, Rae. Look happy. We'll go to the island. The Prodigal returns. All hell breaks loose. The morning shows will go nuts. Like you've always said, sex and lies sell." He was sure of himself and his judgment. For an instant something flickered in his eyes. Not uncertainty. Never uncertainty with Alex. More a suggestion of steel-sharp determination.

She looked at him dispassionately, faced up to a hard reality. Alex was done, finished as a writer. Alex had sucked out the marrow of his life, spun heartbreak and danger and meanness and passion into a sprawling, tumultuous family novel. But he'd been there, done that. Now he was an empty husk. Now she knew the reality. Alex had to have real lives, real people to write about. It was only since they'd begun talking about going to the island that she'd realized his novel was reality in the guise of fiction.

Not like Neil. At this moment, Neil was at his computer, writing, writing, writing, likely unshaven, wearing a T-shirt and shorts, barefoot, maybe hungry, but with too many words to take time for food. She'd persuaded Alex to let Neil live in the sparsely furnished garage apartment behind their house. Behind their mansion. The quarters had once housed a chauffeur in the estate's earlier days. Neil . . .

Alex was talking and much of it she'd heard before. ". . . got the makings of a blockbuster. People rocking along, no threats on their horizon, suddenly everything changes. Once they're scared, every-thing will be new and fresh." He looked triumphant. "I'll get two books out of it."

She said nothing. If he went to the island, there would be turmoil and confrontations, but there would not be the depths of anguish he'd portrayed in his book. He could fashion a novel and the book would sell because best-selling authors have a market, but sour feelings, even gut-wrenching fear, didn't offer the breadth and scope of the lives played out in *Don't Go Home*.

Alex believed he was on the cusp of another huge success, even though she'd told him a nonfiction tell-all wasn't enough. These char-acters weren't famous. They were ordinary people living ordinary lives. For a big success, he needed a new novel. The orders then would be huge, based on the first novel's blockbuster sales.

Instead, in his usual Alex-centric way, he believed he could take what happened on his return and write both a tell-all and a sequel to *Don't Go Home*.

If she approved, they would go to the island. The result would be disrupted lives, anger, fury. Did he understand the consequences? Quite possibly. True to himself, he didn't care. He thought more fame and fortune awaited him. But she knew the limitations of tell-all books unless launched with a sensational twist or sordid revelations about the rich and famous. At Alex's insistence, his agent was trying to get interest in Hollywood. Those calls would go unanswered. Tawdry details about private lives, even those that had inspired famous liter-ary characters, didn't sell in Hollywood. They might get the cable spotlight for a few weeks but that interest was always short, like a sparkler. When the flash ended, there was nothing left but charred wire. Hollywood wanted hot scandal about celebrities, preferably spiced with lust or death or mystery.

Alex reached down, tried to grasp a tiny fish, but the silver sliver swerved and skittered away. He laughed.

She saw him for what he was: handsome, rich, done for as a writer. Not like Neil with his boundless creativity and not a penny to his name. Money made such a huge difference in launching a book. Alex was counting on making old wounds bleed again for another best seller.

If Alex returned to the island, there would be those who would wish him ill.

She'd warned him. If they went to the island . . .

The lead story in the Sunday edition of the *Broward's Rock Gazette* Lifestyle section:

LITERARY BOMBSHELL

by Ginger Harris

Has Martin felt remorse for pressuring Regina before her death? Will Buck keep Louanne's secret? Will Mary Alice ever tell Charles the truth? As he swings a golf club, enjoying power and pleasure, does Kenny think of a wasted form lying on a bed? Does Frances remember choking in the water, flailing to the surface, swimming to safety with no thought for her companion?

Whether in graduate seminars or sophisticated book clubs, readers instantly recognize these characters from the million-plus best seller *Don't Go Home* by Alexander Griffith.

4

In an exclusive to the *Gazette*, Griffith announced plans to reveal the real-life inspirations for characters who cast a spell on readers worldwide. Griffith is included in a short list of exalted Southern writers such as William Faulkner, Thomas Wolfe, Eudora Welty, Tennessee Williams, and Flannery O'Connor.

In an interview Saturday at the Seaside Inn, Griffith revealed for the first time that *Don't Go Home*, which is set in Atlanta's famed Buckhead, is actually based on his boyhood years on Broward's Rock. Critics have marveled at the emotional depths reached in the novel and attributed much of its power to Georgia literary traditions. Griffith has been something of a mysterious literary figure, rarely granting interviews and never discussing his South Carolina roots. Several biographies mistakenly list Augusta as his hometown. He spent summers there with his Georgia grandparents and later attended Emory.

Griffith sounded boyish and eager when he said he was excited to come home. He and his wife, Rae, may spend the remainder of the summer on the island, working on a nonfiction manuscript tentatively entitled *Behind the Page*. "Readers have taken my characters into their hearts, their lives. I have received thousands of requests to share the background of my characters. People want to know if they are based on real people, real lives. For the first time, I intend to be brutally honest about the characters. I owe readers the truth about them."

Griffith said he might reveal some aspects of the book before he finishes the manuscript. "Just enough to give readers a hint of what is coming. Maybe we'll have a pre-publication party while we're here."

Griffith said his agent has spoken with several Hollywood producers about film possibilities. "I expect to hear from some film companies soon." Griffith's smooth tenor voice retains a soft Southern accent, although he has lived in the cosmopolitan Atlanta suburb of Buckhead since he became a literary sensation. Publication of his novel six years ago launched him as a wunderkind of Southern literature. "Drama in ordinary everyday lives matches anything possible in fiction. Reality television exists because of the power of truth. Everyone marvels at the success of *Duck Dynasty*. Not that I watch *Duck Dynasty*." He laughed at that. "The people in my past aren't that wholesome, but Hollywood will find plenty of excitement in the reality behind the characters. As everyone knows, all families are dysfunctional, which warps relationships with classmates and co-workers. Nothing is as powerful as hidden secrets in everyday lives."

When asked if he was concerned about privacy issues, Griffith sounded untroubled. "Libel? Truth is a defense, isn't it? If I honestly discuss my past, who can complain? It's my past. As Burkett says in *Don't Go Home*: 'What is, is.'" The character Jason Burkett is chief of police in the fictional small town in the novel.

Above the headline was a studio photograph of a barefoot man in a black turtleneck and age-whitened jeans leaning against a weathered piling of a dock. He was tanned with reddish-brown hair and brown eyes, handsome with classic features. From beneath a tilted-back slouch hat, a lock of hair drooped—too perfectly?—on a broad forehead. His gaze was level, perhaps with a hint of amusement. There was the aura of a man accustomed to adulation. A second glance noted the supercilious confidence of a slight smile and the swagger of his posture.

Inset in the story was a photograph of a book cover, a starkly white tombstone with black letters—*Don't Go Home*—and the name Alexander Griffith against a crimson background.

The Sunday-morning issue of the *Gazette* was widely read across the island.

The Lifestyle section fluttered to Joan Turner's lap. She stared across the patio but she didn't see the palmetto palms or the white blooms on the honeysuckle or the glitter of sunlight spangling the clear blue water of the pool. The article had torn away the scab of an old wound. Pain bubbled hot and hard just as it had when she'd first read Alex's book. The section on Mary Alice and Charles made every breath a struggle.

Damn Alex.

A core of icy fear had lodged deep inside her ever since. What if Leland read the book? If he read it, he would know. She waited for knowing glances from friends. But so far no one had made the link to her and Leland. The book was set in Atlanta. In several instances the gender of characters had been changed, though not in the scenes with Mary Alice and Charles. None of the names suggested a link to the island. The facts of the incidents were transformed. The character Martin was obviously Lynn, her dead brother's widow. The character Frances was her brother George. She knew. And she knew what Alex knew.

Alex was clever—a woman driver on a foggy night instead of a man, a Scout camp instead of a football game—but she knew who was meant and what. *Names are changed to protect the innocent.* Wasn't that what was always said? But there were no innocents. There were only people whose innermost thoughts and feelings and fears and betrayals and mistakes had been sucked up by Alex and used to make him rich and famous. After he left the island, Alex led a charmed life, acclaimed, lionized, admired. Why did he want to come home and hurt them all?

"What's wrong?" Leland's kind and gentle voice was concerned.

She looked at her husband, thought how perfect they would appear to onlookers, a couple at ease in a sea-island setting, relaxing in wicker furniture with gaily striped cushions on a patio overlooking a glittering pool, she with a pixie haircut and a narrow, fine-boned face, her knit top and linen skirt beautifully tailored, he with a sensitive expression, relaxed in a polo shirt, worn jeans, sandals.

She wanted to rush to Leland and feel his arms around her, a tight hard embrace, but she must never reveal that Alex's return meant anything to her. She managed a bright smile. Leland was innately intuitive with an antenna-like awareness of others clearly apparent in his scholarly face, in the quizzical tufts of his eyebrows, in the depth of his gaze. He would understand. He always understood, but the gossamer bonds of trust would be ripped apart. Love forgives, but love can be maimed like an unsuspecting animal struck without warning.

She brushed back a strand of hair. "I was thinking about the party next week. I haven't decided on the menu yet."

Leland leaned back and laughed. "You looked like you'd had a ransom note for Sugar." His slender hand dropped and he smoothed the golden fur of the cocker resting at his feet. "Go give Mama a kiss, Sugar. Tell her a caterer is the answer to all her worries."

Joan folded the newspaper section into a small, neat square. "Let's go to Savannah." She rose, resolution in every angle of her body. They would take the ferry and stroll on the waterfront, hand in hand, together.

Together . . .

She could not lose Leland.

Head up. Arms back and down. Head down. Dolphin kick. Head up . . . Lynn Griffith reached the end of the pool, made a smooth flip turn. Heyward had never been able to do the butterfly. As Lynn powered through the water, fragments of the *Gazette* feature slid through her mind. Irritating. But unimportant. Alex had never liked her. She kicked, felt as though she flew through the water, washing away all annoyances. Ugly innuendoes have no effect if you ignore them. Her only worry at the time had been the insurance company investigator, who'd been suspicious, hoping to prove Heyward committed suicide. But that was never a danger. No one who knew Heyward would ever believe that was possible. There were rumors that he had chosen to have an "accident" to save Lynn from bankruptcy, but they were spread by people who didn't know him well. And by some who didn't care for her. That didn't bother her a bit. Finally the investigator had had to accept the police conclusion: an accident, a regrettable accident. She, of course, had been sad. Poor Heyward, but how fortunate that he had taken out the insurance, which saved her from penury, made possible all kinds of improvements to the house. She'd used some of the money to refurbish the brown-toned plantation brick home built in 1852. New curtains in the living room, crimson damask lined with ivory silk, patterned after the styles of the 1840s. The room was a gem with cypress paneling and an ebony desk. The money after Heyward's death had saved everything. She still took a cottage in Carmel every August, was a patron of the High Museum, never missed a gala affair there, enjoyed the luxuries that made a good life possible. Her latest pleasure was a red 1952 MG TD in pristine condition, a steal at $26,000.

Alex could spout what he wished, but she was safe and secure.

Head up . . .

The sleek black speedboat came dangerously near tipping as Eddie Olson turned the wheel to catch one of his own waves, spanking over the water with spray peppering his face, plastering his taut T-shirt against his chest. Part of him exulted in the wildness of the ride. A cool sardonic inward voice taunted: *Don't make it easy for the bastard.* No fear. He wasn't going to conveniently crash and plummet to the depths. Maybe he could invite Alex for a ride. He gave a grunt of laughter. Alex was nobody's fool. Alex would take damn good care to keep out of Eddie's way.

He stared out at the wind-flecked waves, slowed a little. If it weren't for his wife, he wouldn't give a damn what Alex wrote. Thank God she wasn't a reader. She knitted, gardened, made his home happy. He'd be glad when she got back from visiting her folks. But if Julie ever heard the accusation, she would come to him, blue eyes wide and grave. She would look at him and she would see the knowledge in his eyes and she would turn and walk away. Forever.

Eddie's lips closed in a tight hard line. It was as if he were back on a football field and the play was beginning. *Bring it on.*

George Griffith leaned back against his desk chair in his study. He sagged back, feeling weak and sick. He had to do something . . . He turned toward his computer, stopped. He'd better not put anything in print. Once inside a computer, information lived on and on, always available if someone looked hard enough. His jaw tightened. The whole damn night was in Alex's book. But no one had ever connected the passage to him.

George's hands tightened into fists. Could he still go to jail? There wasn't any proof. Was Alex's claim enough to start the police checking? Someone might respond if there were stories in the paper asking anyone with information about that night to contact the police. But the night was misty and no one had ever come forward to say they'd seen George drive away with Lucy. At least in the book Alex had turned George into a woman. But that was a nasty dig, too.

Maybe Alex would listen to reason. He had to listen to reason. Would he? Alex had sent him an autographed copy of *Don't Go Home.* George remembered the icy shock when he read the inscription. *You thought no one knew. I saw you come in that night, your clothes wet. I listened to you. Dad said you'd have to keep your mouth shut, that no one would ever know. He also told you what a sorry good-for-nothing shit you were. Read all about it, chapter 14.* He'd flipped to the page and read, the words uneven in his vision: *Frances tried to speak distinctly. "I know the way. Let go of my arm. Don't want to slow down. Down, down, down." She heard the scream as if from far away. Everything seemed to happen in slow motion . . .*

◆ ◆ ◆

Marian Kenyon walked onto the pier, oblivious to the cloying heat, to the squeal of seagulls, to the rattle of her steps on the wood. She didn't have a copy of the *Gazette* with her. She didn't need to see the paper again. The publisher had sent her an e-mail, the subject line a series of stars, acclaim for her last piece in an exposé of a charlatan medical outfit that bilked people in a weight-loss program. The story ran in today's edition, slotted on page 1 above the fold. She was proud of the series. Good stuff.

Sunday morning had started well. The satisfying recollection that she'd excelled, that her boss was pleased, that she'd poked a hole in a mean moneymaking scheme. Then, icing on her personal cake, a happy call from David. "Dad's taking me to a Braves game this afternoon . . ." Her son's young voice was excited. She'd hung up, smiling, happy because David was happy, eager for him to come back to the island, make their house home again with the slam of doors and the thump of running feet. What joy David had brought to her and to Craig as well. She never could have imagined the difference David would make for Craig, that where once there had not seemed to be anything but desolation in her life, the odd pieces had fitted together to create something special.

Sipping her third cup of coffee, she'd picked up the Lifestyle section. Normally she'd have read the paper from cover to cover after the pressrun. The *Gazette* was an afternoon paper except on Sundays. The Sunday edition came off the press about six on Saturday evening. She'd left the office about noon to take David to the airport in Savannah, on his way to Atlanta to spend a week with his dad. So she was, like most on the island, picking up the paper to read on Sunday morning. She didn't have any reason to know about the Lifestyle contents. Ginger Harris, the white-haired, elegant Lifestyle editor, had given her a cheery wave yesterday morning. Marian had waved back, still deep in writing the finale to the series.

It had never occurred to Marian to think that anything Ginger wrote could impact her life.

Water slapped against the pilings. Marian felt hollow inside. She'd read the passages in *Don't Go Home* when it was published, read them with cold, hard fury. One sentence from Ginger's feature ran through her mind in a continuous bitter loop: *Will Buck keep Louanne's secret?*

A nnie Darling tried to pretend nothing was changed, that it was just another Monday morning. She stopped at the railing, even though the air was already heavy with heat, and admired the yachts in the marina, as she usually did when walking to Death on Demand. This was the height of the cruising season. A pearl gray yacht that flew a skull and crossbones was rumored to belong to a famous movie star, and the quartet of pretty girls on board—all blondes, of course, like TV newscasters—were "secretaries." As one fishing boat captain said to another, "Wonder how my wife would feel about me and four pretty little secretaries?"

A V of pelicans began their swift descent toward the wave tops, looking for lunch. Tourists with peeling sunburns moved up the gang plank of the tour boat, another of island mogul Ben Parotti's successful ventures. A catamaran slid through the harbor, steered by a shirtless, well-built thirtysomething in cutoff jeans. A gorgeous girl—blond—held to his side.

Annie wished she were aboard the catamaran or the yacht or even the tour boat. Anything to avoid seeing the dark storefront next to her bookstore. She forced herself to turn and walk up the steps to the wide wooden verandah fronting the marina shops. She kept her eyes sternly focused on the front window of her bookstore. She thought of how she answered the phone: "Death on Demand, finest mystery bookstore north of Delray Beach, Florida," or sometimes, "Death on Demand, the best in thrills, chills, puzzles, and pastries." She was almost smiling when she reached Death on Demand's front window.

Keeping her gaze straight ahead, she checked over the window display. Summer was the time to grab a suitcase and go. Stacked beside a well-worn trunk plastered with travel stickers were five crime novels and five traditional mysteries. She'd picked old favorites, titles by Dashiell Hammett, Raymond Chandler, Lawrence Block, John D. MacDonald, Eric Ambler, Agatha Christie, Mary Roberts Rinehart, Dorothy L. Sayers, Josephine Tey, Ngaio Marsh. A sun hat hung on a corner of a red-and-white-striped beach chair.

Front and center, of course, were some of the best of current wonderful mysteries. She admired the bright covers of the recently published books she had placed upright in a semicircle: *Midnight Crossroad* by Charlaine Harris, *The Wrong Girl* by Hank Phillippi Ryan, *Suspect* by Robert Crais, *Blind Justice* by Anne Perry, *The Kill Room* by Jeffery Deaver, *The Buzzard Table* by Margaret Maron, *Missing You* by Harlan Coben, and *The Sound of Broken Glass* by Deborah Crombie.

She never lost her sense of awe at the outpouring every year of amazing, original, provocative mysteries. As she liked to tell customers, "You'll never run out of good books to read." Certainly not as long as Death on Demand stayed open.

The temporary buoyancy from the bright display beyond the plate glass disappeared as her gaze moved to the right and the dark storefront.

The legend was still there:

Confidential Commissions
Problems?
We can help.

There was no light beyond the door. If she stepped inside, there would be hot musty air instead of a delicious scent of baking wafting from the little back kitchen where Barb created magical desserts—key lime pie or pecan sundrops—when Max had no secretarial duties for her. Barb's computer monitor had a dark screen. Barb was off on a holiday to New England until Max decided the fate of his shop next door to hers. "No more snooping," he'd groused. "Maybe I'll change it to a lifestyle center. 'Come and find out what you really want to do.' That would be fun. I could steer people into new careers."

Annie felt forlorn. Their last talk inside Confidential Commissions had not ended happily. She remembered them standing there, looking at each other across a gulf, Max with his handsome face obdurate, his arms folded. He had shaken his head one final time. "It took a few weeks for it to hit me. I guess I was so relieved at first. It's like getting a kick in your gut and at first you don't realize you're hurt. Then I woke up in the middle of the night and I was still in this dream and you were disappearing. So, no more. I am not a detective and neither are you."

Annie sighed as she unlocked the front door of Death on Demand. As she stepped inside, black fur flashed. Annie bent down and scooped up Agatha, who made the throaty noise that Annie always took as a carol of affection. She nuzzled sweet-smelling fur, hiked Agatha onto her shoulder. Everything was as it should be at Death on Demand. The molty stuffed raven, Edgar, looked down from a perch near the enclave for children's mysteries, which contained every title in the

Boxcar Children mysteries and the Nancy Drew and Hardy Boys series.

Annie flicked on lights and eased Agatha to the floor. Shelves lined the walls and wooden bookcases ranged on either side of the broad center aisle. She still had an hour before the store opened. She'd come in early because the house seemed empty with Max gone. She might as well get some work done before the first customers arrived. A Monday morning in summer was sure to be busy. There were always some tourists who'd arrived on the weekend and frolicked too long in the sun. Wilted and red, smeared with zinc oxide, they came in search of books and a shady spot.

Her first task was fresh dry food for Agatha. Agatha settled at her blue pottery bowl and munched. Annie measured coffee beans and added the just-right amount of water. No weak coffee allowed on the premises. As the coffee brewed, Annie scanned the collection of coffee mugs in the glass shelving behind the coffee bar. Each mug featured the title of a famous mystery in red script. She glanced at *The Fugitive Pigeon* by Donald E. Westlake, *Getaway* by Leslie Charteris, and *Gone, No Forwarding* by Joe Gores, then picked up *Getaway*, thinking obscurely that was what Max had done.

As she filled the mug, a brisk knock sounded at the front of the store. She raised an eyebrow. Some people always believed they were special. The hours were listed on the door: MON.–SAT. 10 TO 9, SUN. 2 TO 6. It was still a good forty-five minutes before ten.

But a sale was a sale.

Annie put the mug on the counter, walked swiftly up the aisle. She unlocked the door.

A slender young woman in her midtwenties didn't give Annie a chance to speak. "I'm hoping you can help me. I'm thrilled to find such a terrific bookstore." She gestured toward the legend on the door.

"I'm sorry to be early, but Alex insisted I come first thing." She spoke as if this intelligence would be immediately understood by Annie.

Annie scrabbled through her mind. Alex? Was she supposed to know someone named Alex? She was certain she didn't know her visitor. Emerald green eyes in an arresting face, features almost too sharp but softened by a mouth that appeared ready to quirk into a smile.

The smile came. "You don't have any idea who I am. Or Alex. I'm sorry. There was a story in yesterday's *Gazette* and I thought you might have seen it. I should have called first, but Alex is always impatient."

"I didn't see the *Gazette*." With Max gone and Ingrid taking care of the store, she'd spent Sunday in Savannah—attended church at St. John's, enjoyed lunch at Paula Deen's, made a round of the antique stores, and devoured oysters on the waterfront. She spent the night at her favorite bed-and-breakfast, returned on the ferry this morning, driven straight to the marina. The Sunday *Gazette* awaited her on their front porch. Ingrid had dropped by morning and evening to feed and pet Dorothy L, the plump white cat who ruled Annie and Max's house.

The visitor brushed back a tangle of soft dark hair that framed her narrow face like a cloud. "I'm Rae Griffith. Alex is my husband. He's the author of—"

Annie clapped her hands together. *"Don't Go Home.* We always stock his book. Is he here? On Broward's Rock?" She knew—who didn't?—that the world-acclaimed novelist had grown up on the island but so far as she was aware he'd not visited in recent years. If she ever thought about it, she assumed his family had moved away and he no longer had ties here. She would have heard if a celebrity of his stature spent time here.

Like the sun going behind a cloud, her visitor's smile slipped away. There was an odd look on her face.

Annie wasn't quite certain whether there was a flash of worry or concern or possibly dismay.

Alex Griffith's wife took a quick breath, as if starting on a path with an unknown destination. "He's here."

Annie was excited. The island had its resident crime novelist, Emma Clyde, but there was no literary author of Alex Griffith's stature. "Would he consider doing a signing?"

"Of course." Again there was an odd note in her voice.

Annie ignored the lack of enthusiasm at the invitation. All right, he was a big deal and maybe a signing at a little store like hers would be more of a bother than a pleasure, but Rae Griffith wanted something and Annie intended to get a quid pro quo: Alex Griffith in person at Death on Demand. "Come in. I've just made coffee. Rich dark Colombian." She beamed at her visitor, held the door wide.

Rae Griffith smiled in return. "Thank you."

As they walked down the central aisle, Rae looked admiringly at the shelves filled with brightly jacketed books. "What a wonderful collection." She pointed at a table with South Carolina authors. "I see you have lots of copies of Alex's book."

"He's one of our top sellers." Annie nodded toward the cluster of tables. "I'll bring coffee."

But Rae followed her to the coffee bar. She looked down at Agatha, now washing her face with a graceful paw. "What a beautiful cat. I admire cats. They never belong to anyone." She described their cat, an orange tabby named Butch.

By the time they settled at a table in the coffee area, Annie felt thoroughly comfortable with Rae Griffith. "What brings you to the island?"

Rae Griffith's face smoothed into blandness. "Alex grew up here. We're back for a visit."

Annie didn't miss the change from relaxation to wariness. Interesting. Why the sudden reserve? "Does your husband have family here still?" With the continuing influx of new residents, Annie no longer counted on knowing most people in town. Annie had grown up in Amarillo, but she had often visited her uncle on the beautiful sea island off the coast of South Carolina. A couple of years out of college, she'd inherited his bookstore. Max Darling had soon followed and on a beautiful June day they'd married. They'd been here long enough to feel a part of the island, but they didn't know all the family connections as did those born and bred on Broward's Rock.

There was a slight hesitation, then Rae said without any hint of enthusiasm, "His sister, Joan Turner, and brother, George. And his late brother Heyward's widow, Lynn."

Faces flickered in Annie's mind. She did know these Griffiths, though she'd never associated them with the novelist. Max's mother, Laurel, had consulted Joan Turner when she redecorated her home. Annie had been fascinated at the interchange between crisp, no-nonsense Joan and Laurel, who was, to put it charitably, a free spirit rarely constrained by conventional ideas. The result—ethereal surroundings evocative of misty clouds and moonlight—surprised everyone except possibly Joan and Laurel. Joan's clear-cut features were accented by ebony hair in a jagged cut that emphasized the depth of her violet eyes. Pudgy George Griffith, fleshy and faintly dissolute, always held Annie a little too close at the club dances. Bourbon laced his breath when he exhaled. Annie liked his wife, Susan, wondered why she'd married him. Lynn Griffith was always beautifully coiffed, perfect silver blond hair cupping a rounded face with wide-spaced blue eyes, a several-thousand-dollar complexion enhanced by every expensive emollient available, lips that curved in a social smile. It always faintly surprised her that Lynn was an accomplished long-distance swimmer, competed in Masters events. But why shouldn't an athletic woman also enjoy perfection in her appearance?

Annie tried to remember always to be kind to Lynn because she'd heard the rumors: Heyward's drowning death was awfully convenient after his investment firm collapsed . . . a huge life insurance payoff saved Lynn from bankruptcy. Annie had sat next to her at a couple of Friends of the Library luncheons. Whatever the conversation, Lynn soon swung like a magnet to the wonderful antique she'd just bought, a cameo, a cut-glass vase, a silver tea urn, a serving tray in old English Davenport china, a Sèvres figurine of a Napoleonic soldier . . .

"How nice. Are you staying with Joan?" The Turner home was one of the loveliest on the island, not pretentious but perfect, a three-story white frame with front and back verandahs and a magnificent pool framed by palmettos.

Rae's tone was just a shade too bright. "Alex is a great believer in Benjamin Franklin's edict: Guests, like fish, begin to smell after three days. Since we may be here all summer, we're at the Seaside Inn. We're hoping you'll help us put together a really grand evening there." She reached into an oversized catchall cloth bag, pulled out several sheets of paper. "Here's what we have in mind . . ."

2

The storeroom door opened. Ingrid Webb poked her head inside. "I brought lunch."

Annie swung around from her computer, frazzled and stressed. She pulled her mind away from orders and logistics and the challenge of setting up an extravagant book event in little more than forty-eight hours. As soon as Ingrid arrived that morning, she'd turned the store over to her, explaining in staccato bursts that she was under the gun—huge event, Alex Griffith, Wednesday night—and withdrawn to the storeroom to set everything in motion. "Lunch?" She blinked. "Oh hey, lunch. That's wonderful."

Ingrid stepped inside, used her free elbow to push the door shut behind her. "Making progress?"

"Three hundred books are promised. They'll arrive on tomorrow's ferry. I had to pull out all the stops to get them that quickly."

Ingrid was calm. "Duane can pick them up and schlep them over to the inn."

Annie looked at her thin, tireless, wonderful clerk, short brown hair frizzed by the summer humidity, brown eyes that observed carefully, a calm, comforting presence whether a hurricane was coming or a visiting author turned out to be truculent as a warthog. "I'll fix Duane a basket of books." Ingrid's husband loved thrillers, especially those by Lee Child, Joseph Finder, Brad Meltzer, Michael Connelly, L. J. Sellers, and Michael Sears.

Ingrid plopped the sack from Parotti's Bar and Grill on the worktable. "Fried oysters on an onion bun with Thousand Island dressing, plus coleslaw. Slice of key lime pie on the house. I told Ben you were lit up like a pinball machine calculating how many books you can sell if you manage to arrange a Force Five blowout by Wednesday night."

Annie realized she was ravenous. She fumbled with the sack, pulled out her favorite meal from Parotti's Bar and Grill, and, indistinctly, between mouthfuls, brought Ingrid up-to-date. "Gazebo rented, check. Hotel catering, coffee, cash bars, check. Seating for one hundred and fifty, check. Mic, sound equipment, speaker stand for gazebo, check. Two tables behind the rows of chairs, one for the author, one for book sales, check." She ran over the list in her mind, nodded. "It should be really neat. There are lots of weddings in the gazebo so the inn's used to setting up folding chairs. The event opens at seven, he'll speak at eight. It will be pretty because they have strings of lights in the live oak trees on either side of the gazebo and around the pool. The weather will still be steamy but with the sun sliding behind the pines it won't seem as hot." She hoped. But islanders who stayed here in summer were acclimated to heavy hot air.

Ingrid hesitated, then asked abruptly, "What did you think about the piece in the *Gazette*?"

Annie wiped a smudge of Thousand Island from her chin. Ben's sandwiches dripped. "I haven't seen the *Gazette*. I've worked the phone and the computer nonstop since Rae Griffith left. Can you think of anything I've missed?"

Ingrid looked thoughtful. "A fire brigade might come in handy."

Annie went on alert. "Fire brigade? Why?"

Ingrid was blunt. "To put out the blazes when he tosses Molotov cocktails at the natives."

"Blazes?" Annie heard the hollow tone in her voice.

"Did his wife tell you what he had in mind?"

Annie looked at her clerk in apprehension. "I assume he's going to talk about his book."

"The book and the people whose lives he used to write a 'sprawling family epic about sex and lies and treachery.' I thought you knew what was coming or I would have said something earlier."

A nnie settled in a rocker on the screened-in porch. Tuesday night. It seemed an eon since Rae Griffith had walked into Death on Demand Monday morning. The hours had passed in a blur, calling, arranging, planning.

Worrying.

She loved dusk and listening to rustles and calls as the night brimmed with life and movement. Cicadas sang their song of summer. Crickets trilled. A distant owl whooed, always a lonely cry to Annie. Virile frogs trumpeted a hot time in the old pond tonight to listening lady frogs. As shadows thickened, the vivid blaze of summer softened to impressionistic hints of color, indistinct splotches of orange, violet, and red hibiscus, golden daffodils, crimson roses. Pink crape myrtle flowered near the gazebo. This time tomorrow night Alex Griffith would look out at an eager audience.

She took a deep breath of the usually soothing scents of pittosporum blossoms and honeysuckle. If Max were here, they would wander hand in hand to the gazebo and sit in the swing and she'd tell him about her frantic two days. She'd not realized how much she would miss him. They usually traveled together, but when an old friend invited him and three other college chums for a week of deep-sea fishing in the gulf, she'd been glad he decided to go.

For one thing, his absence put on hold the final demise of Confidential Commissions. For another, they were determinedly bright and cheerful but there was a shadow between them.

She gave a little push and the rocker creaked. Not that she believed there was a chance he would change his mind. He'd made himself absolutely, irrevocably clear. "No more delving into other people's problems, Annie. Period. End of story. Since I'm not a politician, when I say 'period,' I mean 'period.'"

As he pointed out, if she wanted to help people, she could volunteer at a hospice, make food for Mobile Meals, tutor at the elementary school.

Her face softened. She understood. He'd demanded her promise: Hands Off. No More Nancy Drew. Keep Crime on the Shelves. Because, as he put it, his face grim, "You scared the ever-living hell out of me. How do you think I felt when your cell didn't answer? And didn't answer? And then we knew you were there with a killer . . ."

She felt an uneven lurch deep inside. Max had been scared for her. So had she. She'd not been stupid. She'd been on her way to the police station, sure she knew the truth behind the murder of a reckless young second wife who'd disappeared after a Fourth of July dance. Instead Annie had answered her cell phone and turned another way. At road's end, she'd faced death.

Her brush with death had occurred only a few weeks before. The very next week, Max woke up in the middle of the night and rolled over to take her in his arms and hold her in a bone-tight grip. After that, he had wasted no time deciding to close down Confidential Commissions, which had no real purpose other than, as he inelegantly phrased it, screwing around in other people's lives. No more.

She'd protested. Confidential Commissions helped people; it made a difference to their lives in ways both great and small. There had been those caught up in fear and despair and Max had helped right their world. He'd said, "Yeah. But one of these days, you'll poke that snub nose into the wrong mess. No more danger, Annie." She'd pointed out that Confidential Commissions wasn't always involved in messes, that Max did all sorts of interesting things that made people happy. He'd helped a woman find a long-lost sister, found the rightful owners of a small Remington sculpture discovered in an abandoned well, put together a history of the Class of '46 at the local high school, proved the provenance of a baseball signed by Babe Ruth, uncovered the final hours of a corporal who died in the Battle of the Bulge. She'd told him, "You've made a lot of people happy."

He hadn't been swayed. "You were a short walk away from dying."

He was right. Her escape had been a very near thing. She thought of Max's life without her or hers without Max. They would live because the living must do what they must do, but light would be leached from the world, leaving gray days without vibrancy, without music, without warmth.

He'd extracted her promise:

"I will not engage in any activities that could put me in danger. Period."

When she dropped her raised hand after completing the pledge, he'd given her his wonderful, terrific, all-American grin—to her mind, tall, blond, handsome Max was always Joe Hardy all grown up—and tilted her face up and bent down for his warm lips to touch hers. From there . . . She felt a glow at the remembrance.

She wished Max was here, that she could reach out and take his hand. He was only going to be gone a week, but she hadn't realized how accustomed she was to the ping of her cell and texts from Max—"Meet me at Parotti's for lunch." "Hey, how about some afternoon delight?" "Missing you." "Look under the cushion in the gazebo swing." He was always fun. Besides, he had very good judgment. Maybe he would reassure her that the Griffith event was no big deal. But he and the guys had left their cells onshore, sworn to a week on the boat untethered to the world. She hoped they were having fun— fish and beer and rowdy buddy talk on the gulf without a link to land.

Annie gave herself an impatient shake. Okay. Max wasn't here. What was, was.

The phrase reminded her abruptly of the quote in the *Gazette* feature on Alex Griffith. A character had observed grimly, "What is, is."

Since Ingrid had alerted her, Annie had read the article a half dozen times. Last night and in snatches today, she'd reread *Don't Go Home*. This time she read the book with the *Gazette* story clear in her mind and with an understanding of how Griffith's past was revealed in the story. The characters were based on people she knew. Okay, fine. If he wanted to write a nonfiction book claiming people he knew were the real-life counterparts to fictional characters in compromising situations, that was his right. What he wrote was up to him. But did he intend to divulge the gritty details at a talk sponsored by Death on Demand?

The more she thought about the reception, the edgier she felt. She glanced at the book lying in her lap. Previously she'd found the stark black letters on the alabaster white tombstone hugely effective. Now she loathed looking at the book. She didn't have good vibes about tomorrow night. If Griffith spoke about writing, his stature as a Southern author, anything on the book business, that would be fine. But a hard cold kernel of worry lodged in her gut. What if he used the talk, sponsored by her bookstore, to name names? What if he revealed the inspirations for the characters, many quite unsavory? What if he blatantly linked people on the island to several episodes that hinged on criminal conduct?

Rae Griffith had insisted on a Wednesday-night event, making it clear that was a good night for news to break, both for TV and for print.

Was Rae expecting a scandal-laced story that would make the tabloids, land on TMZ?

Annie gave a push with her foot and the rocker moved. She looked again at the Sunday *Gazette*, reread Ginger Harris's opening paragraph:

> Has Martin felt remorse for pressuring Regina before her death? Will Buck keep Louanne's secret? Will Mary Alice ever tell Charles the truth? As he swings a golf club, enjoying power and pleasure, does Kenny think of a wasted form lying on a bed? Does Frances remember choking in the water, flailing to the surface, swimming to safety with no thought for her companion?

Annie pressed her lips together. She would not be complicit in an attack on people she knew. Tomorrow she would confront Alex Griffith. If he intended to publicly embarrass island residents, she would withdraw. Death on Demand would not be involved.

◆　◆　◆

Annie parked her Thunderbird in the shade of a towering rhododendron. She left the windows down in hopes the red leather seat that matched the red exterior didn't feel like a griddle on her return. The late-July morning was as humid as a sweat bath. Her once crisp candy-striped blouse was wilting. She was glad she'd opted for linen Bermudas rather than a skirt. Anything to be a little cooler. She walked swiftly on the crushed oyster shell path toward the entrance to the Seaside Inn. The inn looked like an old Southern plantation in front with inviting wicker rockers on a wide verandah. Huge blue urns on either side of the broad steps overflowed with sweet-smelling hibiscus.

In the lobby, Annie threaded her way around clumps of wicker chairs and potted ferns. Island visitors, uniformly casual in tees and shorts, were beginning another day in paradise, some heading for the golf courses, others ready to fish or sail, many lugging beach umbrellas, chairs, and coolers. Elderly ladies rocked placidly.

She curved around the broad sweep of central steps that led up to the second and third floors. Behind the stairway stretched a short hall with several shops. She paused for an instant to look through the window of a women's casual wear store, Her Best. She admired a pristine white hip-length cotton blouse with ornate lace on either side of a V-neck and three-quarter-length sleeves with lacy cuffs. Maybe she'd stop and shop on her way out. She reached the door that opened to the terrace. She stepped out into the heavy heat and passed umbrella-shaded tables and deck chairs by a long pool. The springboard snapped. The diver executed a back one-and-a-half somersault. Although it was still early, the pool was perhaps a third full of swimmers, side clingers, and relaxed inhabitants of assorted floats. The pool water shimmered in the brilliant sunlight. To one side was a basketball hoop and a small paved area. A woman jumped rope with a steady rhythm, face creased in concentration. Annie recognized Rae Griffith. There was no sign of her husband. Rae looked like a woman engaged in a serious exercise program, oblivious to her surroundings.

Annie didn't try to attract her attention. She wasn't here to see Rae. She was here to see Alex Griffith. Annie continued to the end of the terrace. She shaded her eyes and admired a sweep of grass framed by pines. An oyster shell path up the middle led to a white gazebo. She nodded in approval at the rows of folding chairs on either side of the path. These would be perfect for tonight. She walked up the path and climbed the gazebo steps. The lectern was in place and tonight a portable mic would be available. She looked out at the empty chairs and pictured the scene, dusk falling, cash bars set up. Before the program began, there would be plenty of room for people to mill around, say hello to friends, enjoy the small bright white lights twinkling in the live oaks.

The inn was shaped like a square-edged U, with a wing on either side. Some ground-floor rooms looked out on the patio and pool. Ground-floor rooms in the outer west wing faced a side parking lot. The more desirable outer rooms, in the east wing, had individual patios that looked out on a thick cluster of loblolly pines.

Annie started down the gazebo steps, then paused as she recognized a trim figure coming around the end of the west wing. Marian Kenyon's thin shoulders were hunched. She was moving fast, canvas shoulder bag banging against one hip. Marian was always in a hurry, with a story to cover, a deadline to meet, quick to pick up on the unusual, the dramatic, sometimes the poignant, sometimes the heartbreaking. Marian talked in fast, staccato bursts, brown eyes bright in a gamine face beneath a mop of unruly dark hair.

As Annie watched, Marian covered half the space between the end of the wing and the expanse of the patio, clearly on her way to the crushed oyster shell path on the far side of the east wing.

Annie's partially lifted hand fell. She'd been ready to call out, but now she had a clear view of Marian's face in bright sunlight, a face Annie had never seen, pale, set, hard. Usually Marian exuded life. She brimmed with vitality. The woman striding toward the end of the wing looked bleak and driven, with hollow eyes, jutting cheekbones, lips pressed together.

Annie hurried down the steps. Scarcely formed thoughts flitted in her mind . . . *something wrong . . . Marian's face . . . a look of fury, dread, implacable resolve . . . what had happened? . . . why is Marian here? . . . have to help her . . .*

Annie reached the path that ran behind the east wing. Ground-floor rooms had small private patios separated by head-high, stuccoed walls. She recalled the number of the Griffith room and thought it was at the end of the east wing, a corner suite.

Annie reached the beginning of the path.

"Alex, please." The husky voice belonged to Marian. It rose from beyond the patio wall.

Annie took one step, another, came close to the wall that extended from the corner.

A man spoke. "I thought you were a free spirit . . . Louanne." The tone was easy, amused.

"Don't call me Louanne." Marian's voice was harsh.

"Would you rather"—the voice was silky—"have me call you Mom? Is that what the kid—"

"Shut up, Alex. Someone might hear you."

A careless laugh. "They might. They'll hear me tonight. I trust you'll be on the front row."

30

"Why are you doing this?" The words were sharp, insistent.

"For my art, darling. Readers have asked and asked about the characters and now it's time for me—"

"You can't."

"I can." He sounded untroubled. "But maybe I won't tell everything about you. For now. Just enough to give a hint of good old-fashioned scandal to come. I have to keep some spicy parts for the book. But I can mention enough to get everyone talking. That will make the book sell."

"It won't sell." Marian's voice was flat. "Nobody cares about any of us."

"Sorry about that. But people care about me. The last time I was on *The Diane Rehm Show*, the phones rang off the hook."

"Alex"—she sounded like a woman holding on to a lifeline as a huge wave loomed—"don't do it. Leave us alone."

"Trying to make me feel bad? It won't work. You know the old saying, take what you want and pay for it. Afraid you've got a bill coming due. You've always been tough. We'll see how tough you are. Will Louanne jut out that sharp little chin and spit in the wind? Or will she throw her bags in a trunk and ride out of town, leaving everything behind?"

Annie touched the smooth stucco of the wall. She felt frozen in place. She wanted to help but there was no help she could give. Louanne was one of the characters . . .

"Did I ever tell you how much I hate you—"

"You didn't always hate me."

The note of amusement and satisfaction jarred Annie.

He continued in that light, faintly mocking tone. "Once, you couldn't get enough of me. Do you know why I bothered with you? I owed Craig one. He shot me down with the boss. I damn near lost

31

my job. How do you think I liked it when a slobbering drunk got all righteous about my getting a free weekend at a casino, girls included? Do you think I won't enjoy his finding out the truth?"

"Craig pulled himself together. Because of David. He's been sober for years. Alex, please—"

"Good for him. It's even better that he's sober. Cold, hard truth packs a punch when there's nothing to dull the edges. His reaction should be interesting. Maybe I'll pay him a visit, tell him how the cookie crumbled, how his wife—"

There was the sound of a slap.

Annie pressed against the intervening wall. She hadn't seen Marian, small, desperate, at-bay Marian, lift a hand and strike Alex Griffith, but she knew what she had heard.

"Not the way to win friends, Marian."

"You have no friends. You will never have friends. Everyone knows who you are, what you are." Marian's husky voice was cold, scathing. "You'll poke and prod and stab until we all bleed and then you can write another book, be richer and richer. When you were a kid, did you tear the wings off butterflies to see what they'd do, how they'd writhe and struggle until they died?" Her voice grated like a car fender scraping a wall.

"I like watching people." There was no stress in his voice, merely amusement.

"Sure you do. More fun than a Saturday-night dogfight. Lots of blood and death at the end." The words came out in spurts as Marian struggled to breathe. "Here's something to watch." There was a crash and the sound of splintering glass. Running steps sounded and Marian burst from behind the patio wall.

She skidded to a stop inches from Annie and stared at her, eyes glazed. Marian's chest heaved. Her face twisted in fury. Bright patches of red stained chalk white cheeks. She hurled out the words, "I wish I'd killed him." She ducked around Annie and flew down the oyster shell path.

Annie stood rooted for an instant, then bolted forward and came around the patio wall.

Alex Griffith stood with his hands on his hips, gazing down at the wreckage, a twisted hurricane lamp and a cracked glass patio door.

"You're all right." Annie's voice was shaky. She was shaky.

He looked at her with a rueful expression. One cheek was still reddened from Marian's slap. "Never better. Can't say the same for the patio door. I'll tell the inn to send the bill to Marian." His gaze focused on Annie. There was a flicker of approval and interest. "This seems to be my morning for women to arrive unannounced on my small terrace. I hope you don't throw things." His tone was whimsical. He pointed at the shards of red-and-green glass scattered on the patio tiles.

"You were horrid to Marian."

He raised a sandy eyebrow. "Ah, you don't throw hurricane lamps but you have no objections to insults. Didn't your mama tell you it isn't nice to eavesdrop?" But there was no rancor, simply mild inquiry. "I don't believe we've met. I'm Alex Griffith."

He spoke with assurance, a man who was accustomed to instant recognition by Four Seasons Hotel clerks—*Mr. Griffith, we have your favorite suite ready . . . Mr. Griffith, the Krug 1990 is cooled and awaiting you . . . Mr. Griffith, we know you prefer fresh papaya with your cereal.* A man who led a charmed life, sucking like a vampire on everyone around him.

He smoothed back a tangle of reddish-brown hair, his handsome features relaxed. Shirtless and barefoot, he wore gray gym shorts. He was a little over six feet tall, well built and muscular, the kind of man any woman on a beach would note with interest.

Annie was aware of his appeal. If she hadn't overheard him and Marian—casual disdain and cruelty on his part, desperation and despair on Marian's part—she might have responded to his amused confidence, his undeniable good looks.

Not now. Not ever.

"I'm Annie Darling." She knew her voice was thin and strained. "Your wife came to my store and asked me to arrange everything for your talk tonight. I didn't know what you intended. I hadn't read the *Gazette*. I've read the article now. I don't like bullies. So forget it. I won't be here tonight. Nor will there be any copies of your book." With that she turned and moved toward the path.

She turned at the end of the wing, realized her face was flaming. She felt a whipping anger. What a complete and total jerk. She was still fuming when she reached the lobby. She turned and charged up the stairs to the second floor. She burst into the catering office.

A plump woman with dark hair looked up with a smile that stopped midway in its formation. "Annie, what's wrong?" Rita White was a mainstay in Friends of the Library. She handled volatile personalities on the board with the same aplomb she'd gained from years of arranging events at the Seaside Inn.

Annie took a deep breath. Rita was going to think she was unhinged. There was no good way to announce that the store was no longer involved and that any and all questions about the reception should be directed to Rae Griffith. It was important that Annie not say anything about why she was distraught. That would be the last thing Marian would want.

Annie stood at the door with one hand gripping the knob.

"What's wrong?" Rita pushed up from her chair, came around the side of her desk.

Annie managed to sound crisp. "I'm no longer involved in the event planned for tonight." It seemed an eon ago that she and Rita had worked out the number of chairs, the positioning of the lectern, the location of the cash bars. "Death on Demand isn't participating."

Rita looked shocked. "Has the staff—"

"It has nothing to do with the hotel. I have withdrawn as a sponsor of anything connected with Alex Griffith. Whatever the Griffiths do has nothing to do with me or Death on Demand."

"Why?"

Why, indeed. "Let's just say I decided it wasn't an appropriate event for Death on Demand."

"But, Annie—"

Annie held up a hand. "Alex Griffith has a program in mind that wouldn't be helpful to the bookstore. I don't want to get into details. Let's leave it at that. Now, if you'll call a bellman, I'll retrieve the boxes of books that Duane brought over."

Rita turned to her desk, lifted a phone. "Ask the bellman to bring the boxes of books stored for tonight's event to the front desk . . . Thank you." She looked at Annie. "The boxes will be there for you." Her face creased in concern. "Will his talk go on as planned?"

"I suggest," Annie said carefully, "that you speak to the Griffiths."

Annie handed the bellman a twenty-dollar tip after he slid the last box of books into the Thunderbird's trunk. She would be happiest if she could take Griffith's damnable books and toss them from Fish Haul Pier, watch the boxes sink into green water. The next best thing was to return them to the wholesaler. Her lips pressed together as she slid behind the wheel. Alex Griffith was going to cost her money—the shipping costs for special quick delivery, the returns—but she didn't care. She drove straight to the FedEx office, smiled at

Carolyn Hart

the freckle-faced teenager who carried the boxes inside for her, filled out address labels. Good riddance.

Annie carried the last copies of *Don't Go Home* from the South Carolina authors table to the storeroom. She filled out forms for their return and boxed the books. When they were gone—she could drop them at FedEx—there would be no trace of Alex Griffith or his books at Death on Demand.

Annie felt like she was swimming through heated molasses as she walked from her car up the back steps of the house. The sunlight now slanted through the pines but beginning shadows offered no respite from the humid air. She stepped into the kitchen, welcomed the cool blast of air-conditioning.

Dorothy L, their gorgeous white cat, Max's special gal, gave a plaintive mew.

Annie understood. Max wasn't here and he should be, so far as Dorothy L was concerned. He was often immersed in creating dinner when Annie arrived home. This evening there were no delicious smells, no pans on the range.

"Sorry, sweetie. Just you and me." She bent and stroked Dorothy L's thick, long fur, only a little thinned from summer shedding.

Dorothy L gazed up at her with China blue eyes, then, almost as if shrugging in sadness, turned and padded slowly away.

Annie fixed a tall glass of ice water. She felt at loose ends. Ingrid had already lined up Duane to help at the store tonight so she insisted Annie leave. "Take a break. Go down to the beach. There's a new fish shack that deep-fries breaded jumbo shrimp. Without the food gendarme along, you can indulge."

Annie smiled as she imagined Max's response when she told him he was now officially known as the food gendarme. Served him right for his raised eyebrow when she ordered her usual fried oyster sandwich or chose fried flounder instead of grilled. But tonight she had little appetite. She fixed cold smoked salmon with cream cheese on a bagel with onions and capers, added potato chips and coleslaw, and carried a paper plate onto the screened-in porch. As she ate, the sun sank behind tall pines and shadows stretched across the backyard.

She tried to think of other things—the drought that threatened the Southwest, the fetching video on YouTube of a sleeping Great Dane with a bright-eyed kitten jumping back and forth over its recumbent form, a reprise of the famous tennis match between Billie Jean King and Bobby Riggs—but remembered voices sounded over and over in her mind, one amused and taunting, the other despairing. Marian had been her friend and Max's for years, cocky, funny, bright, quick, always lively, never bitter or angry or despairing.

Annie pulled her cell from her pocket. Marian was in her Favorites list. She swiped the name and listened as the phone rang and rang. When voice mail came on, she hesitated, then said uncertainly, "Marian, you know if I can help, I will."

She put the cell back in her pocket. Had Marian seen caller ID and chosen not to answer? Was Marian on her way to the Seaside Inn?

Annie looked out at the thickening shadows. Was there anything she could do? Would it help or hurt if she asked Alex for the sake of decency to leave people in peace? Annie jumped to her feet. She couldn't sit here, listening to the cicadas and the frogs, and do nothing to help Marian. At least, whatever happened, Annie could be there for Marian.

3

The parking lot on the west side of the inn was almost full. Annie found an empty space at the end of the third row. She could easily have walked over to the inn. Their house was only a half mile distant on a path that wound through a thick forest of live oaks, slash pine, bayberry, ferns, and saw palmettos. The night forest was cheerful, crickets and cicadas serenading, greenery rustling in a slight breeze, birds chattering in the treetops, but the night also hosted foxes, raccoons, cotton rats, possibly even a wild boar. Most fearsome to Annie was the possibility of stumbling over an alligator. A lagoon, home to several of the huge creatures, lay midway between their house and the inn. Alligators might look like logs with legs but they could outrun humans, and mama alligators didn't take kindly to any perceived threat to their babies.

Annie crossed the parking lot in deepening shadows as the sun continued to slip behind majestic pines. At the back of the inn, she made a slow circuit of the terrace, looking for Marian. She spotted her in the shadows of the gazebo. Even dimly seen, the stiffness of her posture was evident; it said, *Don't come near, leave me alone.*

A great majority of seats were taken but people still streamed toward the rows of white folding chairs. There was a festive air. Free entertainment was always a hit. That afternoon's *Gazette* had carried a half-page ad apparently placed by Rae. Either it had been too late for Rae to cancel the ad or she didn't mind leaving Death on Demand on the hook as a sponsor. There was nothing Annie could do about that.

DEATH ON DEMAND
Presents

ALEX GRIFFITH

Famous Southern Author

GRIFFITH'S Promise:
You Won't Be Bored
True Facts Behind Double-Dealing,
Freewheeling, Scandalous Lives
8 P.M. Wednesday, Free Admission,
Seaside Inn Gazebo

Annie stopped and scanned the crowd. She knew many of those attending. She watched as guests found seats, turned to talk to friends. Convivial groups clustered near two cash bars. Laughter rose on the night air amid the light high sound of women talking and the deeper rumble of men's voices.

She looked for particular faces, found them. Her careful rereading of *Don't Go Home*, now that she knew Alex's connection to Joan Turner, opened doors these islanders had surely thought closed to the world at large. Those in the family and connected to Alex were well aware what a careful reading revealed. They dared not stay away. What if Alex told everyone? That possibility brought them. They knew at terrible personal cost the truth behind Alex Griffith's characters. She saw that knowledge as she studied them, one by one. Each made an effort to appear as usual, but perhaps no one can face disgrace, embarrassment, perhaps criminal accusations, and maintain a bright and comfortable facade. Deep inside she felt a sickening realization that they would also associate this night with her and Death on Demand. Tomorrow she'd put an ad in the *Gazette*, disclaim all responsibility.

Annie felt enormous sympathy as well as a disturbing frisson of threat and darkness as she looked from face to face.

The provocative sentences in Ginger Harris's lead floated in her mind.

Has Martin felt remorse?

A fatal car wreck in the novel, not a sailing accident, a woman who died, not a man. In the book, Martin ran through the money that his wife, Regina, inherited, then pressured her until she took out an insurance policy. Her death was accidental but perhaps there was a sense that Regina welcomed death, that she drove fast and recklessly, angry with her husband. The kernel of the story was true here, an accidental death and the payoff of a huge insurance policy, a spouse saved from financial ruin, a speculator saved from disgrace. Martin and Regina in the novel represented Lynn Griffith and her late husband, Heyward. Lynn was Heyward's well-heeled widow after his sailboat was found drifting. Heyward's body floated to shore three days later.

Tonight Lynn was a vision of elegance in a pale green silk jacket with oversized shimmering abalone-shell buttons. Lynn stared at the empty gazebo. There was no social smile this evening.

Will Buck keep Louanne's secret?

Alex Griffith wasn't onstage yet. Would he appear in a white planter's suit, shades of Tom Wolfe? Had Rae arranged for a spot to illuminate him? A TV camera crew moved a little restively near one side of the gazebo. The comely reporter, swirling black hair, smoothly made-up face, checked her watch, tapped an impatient foot.

When Alex appeared, he would be handsome, virile, exuding charm just as the rumpled ad exec Buck did in Alex's book. Alex's self-portrait was admiring. Buck was the eye through which everyone in the novel was viewed, including Louanne, who was unhappily married to a feckless alcoholic. An impetuous affair. An unexpected pregnancy. A cuckolded husband who never knew. Annie thought about Marian's freckle-faced son, not dark like Marian and her ex-husband, but fair like Alex Griffith, a sunny kid with golden brown hair.

Marian still lurked in the shadows on the far side of the gazebo, close to a path that led to the rooms in the east wing. She would see Alex as soon as he reached the terrace.

Will Mary Alice ever tell Charles the truth?

Joan Turner, Alex's sister, rested a sharply pointed chin on the back of a fist. She was undoubtedly attractive, the pale blue linen dress perfect for her coal black hair, but her rigid posture betrayed her. She sat stiff and still, her thin face expressionless in the fading light. The passage in the novel detailing a sister's affair had been explicit. Now Joan's husband, Leland, looked toward the gazebo, but he radiated awareness of his wife beside him. Abruptly, Joan came to her feet. She bent, murmured something, then moved out into the aisle. She walked swiftly toward the back of the inn. Leland Turner twisted in his seat and watched as she disappeared inside the inn.

As he swings a golf club, enjoying power and pleasure, does Kenny think of a wasted form lying on a bed?

Annie recalled the narrative and the evocation of a powerful alpha

42

male. The fact that Eddie Olson was here revealed him as Kenny in the book. This gathering wasn't loud, brash Eddie Olson's milieu. In her occasional chats with him at parties or charity golf tournaments, he never mentioned books or reading, which usually came up since she was a bookseller. He never evinced any interest in Death on Demand. He could describe play by play the Citadel football games for the last twenty years. He talked about football, his latest golf score, football, the odds on the Kentucky Derby, football . . . He stood near a cash bar, gripping a drink. His heavy face was impassive. Burly and muscular, he stood with his feet apart, like a boxer balancing. Abruptly, he lifted the glass, drank the contents down, turned back toward the bar.

Does Frances remember choking in the water . . .

Another gender change, but Frances in the book was clearly a feminized George Griffith, fairly unkempt dark hair in loose curls, a little too much lipstick. George's shaggy hair was dark and curly. He might have been a handsome teenager, but too many drinks over too many years had coarsened his features. Oddly he didn't hold a glass in his hand tonight. Annie thought it might be the first time in a social situation with alcohol available that she had not seen a glass in his plump hand. He stood to one side of the path, his expression brooding. In the book Frances had been the lushly beautiful teenage girl, drunk, unsteady, clothes sopping, crying, "It wasn't my fault. The mist. The bicycle came out of nowhere . . ."

All of them were here to find out what Alex Griffith was going to say in his well-modulated, expressive voice. Would he read passages from the book, toy with those who were afraid, or did he intend to talk about himself? Annie suspected that in Alex's world it was always all about him: how he saw everything, how nothing escaped him, how delicately and perfectly he could wring laughter or tears.

A smug voice at her shoulder oozed pleasure. "I always wished

I'd lived in first-century Rome. What could be more thrilling than watching lions devour those tiresome Christians? This is the next-best thing. Love Lynn's face. Pure Ibsen. Not quite as supercilious as she was at the last Friends meeting." Two little sniffs followed. The sniffs were habitual, an annoying accompaniment that always concluded breathy observations.

Annie didn't turn to look. She knew the voice and the sniffs. "Hello, Warren." Warren Foster was the kind of person who couldn't be avoided in a small town. In his early thirties, though his fussy manner made him seem older, he lived on inherited money. He was ubiquitous on boards, at charity events, never missed a meeting of Friends of the Library. He knew everyone and absorbed gossip, innuendo, and outright slander with the delight of a connoisseur. His pale green eyes roved every gathering as he looked for hints of discord, acrimony, lust, or fear.

"Now, now, Annie, don't pretend you don't know what I mean. This may be the most exciting evening our little island has enjoyed in a long time. You may have missed the best part of the show, a delicious riff on foreplay. I've been watching them come and go for quite a while. Nervous as cats on a hot sidewalk." Sniff sniff.

Warren Foster moved nearer, leaned to murmur in her ear.

Annie's nose wrinkled at the heavy scent of peppermint.

"Joan's hopped up and down a half dozen times. Leland sits there and looks after her and I'll bet a penny to a farthing—"

Weedy Warren Foster was tall and a little stooped. Ever since a summer at Oxford, he'd affected day cravats (even Warren wouldn't dare an ascot with a tweed jacket) and sprinkled Britishisms with abandon: *mum* for mother, *biscuit* for cookie, *bonnet* for hood. From the corner of her eye, she noted the day cravat was a deep purple, his shirt gray, and thought longingly how nice the cravat would look stuffed between his thin lips or tied around his long, thin nose, possibly muting those inevitable sniffs.

"—he knows all about her fling. Husbands can sense these things. At least that's what I've been told. As for Eddie Olson"—a slight shudder—"he's as appalling now as he was in high school. I avoided meeting him in a hallway. What a brute. Looked at me like I was a palmetto bug. But I didn't know until I read the book that he was the one who hurt Michael Smith. I knew he was sullen that Michael beat him in tennis. Never a good idea to beat someone like Eddie. Of course, he relished football. Physical, you know. Star turns for bullies. I didn't go to football games, my dear. Savagery, that's what football is. Everyone said, 'Oh well, too bad, these things happen.' Eddie still has that tough-guy glare but he's restless tonight, too. He can't stand still for long. First he's here, then there." Sniff sniff. "Then there's poor George Griffith." The light high malicious voice was regretful. "He used to be much better looking, but he's let himself go. A definite potbelly. Cute on pigs and babies. Someone should tell—"

"Oh golly, Warren, I see a customer I need to say hello to. Excuse me. Good to see you." She didn't want to spend another instant listening to that soft trickle of venom, but Warren's patter was a harsh reminder that she wasn't alone in connecting islanders to Alex's book. At least Warren hadn't mentioned Marian.

She strode firmly away, skirting those who had yet to take seats, until she reached a favorite customer, SueLee Douglas. "Margaret Maron's new book will arrive next week. Do you want me to hold a copy?"

They chatted for a moment, then Annie edged nearer the gazebo, though she made no effort to make eye contact with Marian, whose thin face was turned toward the steps.

Near the steps, the TV reporter shrugged her shoulders impatiently.

Her photogenic face was abruptly not quite so lovely, perfect brows drawn in a frown, lips pressed together. She glanced at her watch. Likely the crew intended to film a portion of Alex Griffith's talk, then leave to catch the nine o'clock ferry back to the mainland.

Annie looked at her watch. Five minutes after eight. Abruptly she made up her mind. Maybe it wouldn't matter but she was going to find Alex Griffith, try to stop him. She knew she had to move fast. Maybe Alex was waiting for the lights to dim, intending a dramatic entrance up the center aisle.

Annie was painfully aware of Marian's hunched figure a few feet away. Annie knew that she was helpless to prevent misery for Marian. Nothing stopped an avalanche. But she could try. She started toward the far side of the terrace.

The TV reporter, who had forgotten to smile, huffed, moved with a grim face, dark hair swinging. In two long-legged strides, she reached Rae Griffith. The reporter's gestures were clear. One bright nail tapped the wrist with a watch, a slender hand swept toward the gazebo.

Annie had no difficulty imagining the cool, modulated tone as the reporter pointed out they had a ferry to catch, and where was the speaker?

Rae brushed back a strand of silky black hair, her expression ingratiating. She said something, then quickly ducked around the reporter and walked fast toward the inn. She passed within a few feet of Marian.

Marian's face . . .

Annie hurried after Rae.

Rae was at the corner of the inn.

"Rae," Annie called out, starting to run, her steps loud on the terrace. Maybe Rae would help.

Rae Griffith half turned, frowned, looked both impatient and irritated. "A little late, aren't you? Did you change your mind?"

Annie skidded to a stop. "I'm not here about books. I wouldn't bring books for him ever. I'm here about people. Can't you stop him?"

Rae's irritated look slid away, replaced by a mixture of regret and uneasiness. Her expressive face was suddenly forlorn, weary. "I've tried." She pressed her lips together for an instant, then blurted out, "Everything's a mess. Look, I don't have time to talk now, the TV crew's about to leave. I have to get him."

As she started to turn away, Annie talked fast. "He can make something up. He doesn't have to hurt people."

Rae paused. "I'm afraid that's what he wants to do. I told him—Oh, it doesn't matter now." She shook her head, started up the oyster shell path.

Annie hesitated, then followed Rae. Annie made up her mind. She would warn Alex Griffith. Before he spoke, she was going to climb up on the gazebo steps and face the audience first. He wasn't going to have everything his way. She had a lot of friends here tonight. She didn't relish making a scene, but she and Death on Demand were not going to be associated with Alex Griffith. Phrases tumbled through her mind . . . *can't stand by and see cruelty . . . Griffith's book belongs to him but people's lives aren't his property . . . you know what he plans, he's told the world . . . don't help him destroy people you know . . . get up . . . walk out . . . now* . . . Then she'd sail down the steps. She hoped she wouldn't leave alone. Some would stay and she would have made a spectacle of herself and the TV crew wouldn't have missed a bit of it and probably the reporter would be following her, mic outstretched, asking, "What do you mean by cruelty?"

As she came around the corner of the building, she heard a sliding door open. She reached the patio. A drape billowed out through the partially open door. Black industrial tape covered the gash in the glass made earlier in the day by the hurricane lamp. Light streamed across the flagstones. Someone had swept up the shards of brightly colored glass. A new hurricane lamp sat on the patio table.

A strangled cry, deep, wrenching, came from beyond the partially open door. A hand with bright red fingernails gripped the drape, pulled the soft yellow cloth aside. Rae Griffith stumbled out onto the patio, eyes staring, mouth working, face ashen. "Alex. Help me. Alex . . ." She careened into the table, both hands outstretched. The new lamp wobbled, toppled on its side, crashed onto the cement. Rae shuddered and scarcely breathed the words. "Alex . . . someone hurt him . . . help . . . we need help."

Annie looked from her to the open doorway, took one step, another. She pulled aside the drape. She stopped, stared in shock.

Alex Griffith lay on his back at an awkward angle on the wicker sofa, his torso twisted as if he had fallen to his left. A yellow throw pillow rested atop his face. Blood had seeped from beneath the pillow. His left arm hung limply, part of one grayish hand resting on the parquet flooring.

Behind her came an unsteady step. "We need to get help."
Annie turned.
Rae stood just inside the room.
Annie struggled to breathe. "I'm afraid no one can help him."
Rae lifted her hands to her face, began to make soft whimpering sounds.

Annie moved toward her, gripped one arm, tried to steer her to a chair.

Rae jerked away. "I can't bear to be in here." She pulled aside the drape and stepped onto the patio. She looked diminished, still with the same flyaway silky dark hair but her face sharp and pointed, her shoulders bowed.

Annie followed, glad to be out of the room, trying not to remember with such clarity the stillness, that pillow, the blood. She yanked her cell phone from her pocket. She swiped a familiar name.

Rae collapsed onto a patio chair. She gripped the arms with fingers like claws.

Police Chief Billy Cameron's wife, Mavis, answered. "Hey, Annie." Mavis sounded relaxed. She was at home, enjoying a summer evening. When she responded to a call at the police station, she spoke formally, as a dispatcher should.

Annie spoke carefully, kept her voice steady. "Billy needs to come to Seaside Inn. Suite 130. Alex Griffith—the author—back on the island—is dead. I'm afraid—" Annie felt shaky. Was there any doubt? That blood . . . "—he's been murdered."

"Stay on the line." Mavis was crisp, all business. Mavis also doubled as a crime scene tech. There was the sound of brisk steps, Mavis's muffled call. "Billy. Trouble." Mavis's words drifted to her. ". . . writer dead. Annie says murder. Suite 130, Seaside Inn."

Annie was painfully aware of Rae, huddled in a brightly striped canvas chair, staring emptily at nothing, the muscles of her face slack. How awful to sit alone, her world transformed from golden days to numbing horror.

Billy's deep voice was brisk. "On my way. Stay on the line." Billy always sounded calm. The island's police chief had grown up on Broward's Rock, beginning as a young patrolman, moving up through the ranks. His sandy hair was now touched by silver, his broad face seamed with lines of good humor but bulldog toughness as well. "Start at the beginning."

She was still talking when she heard the wail of sirens. Possibly Billy had arrived. He lived not far from the inn. And likely Mavis had summoned off-duty officers to join him. Annie kept talking. She hoped Billy didn't sense that she was parsing her words. Perhaps Billy thought her simple, unelaborated sentences reflected her status as a bystander. *Famous author supposed to speak . . . didn't show up at the podium . . . wife went to get him . . .* Here was where she avoided full disclosure . . . *I was coming up behind her . . . she went into the room . . . out in an instant . . . said he'd been hurt . . . went in and I knew he was dead . . .*

She said nothing about her determination to disrupt Alex's evening. She simply reported facts. Implicit was the message that the sudden death had nothing to do with her. She was a bystander. She pushed deep inside the achy feeling that she owed Billy better. But she was torn. The law or Marian. People who could be hurt . . . And she knew nothing for a fact, only inferences drawn from a book, except for the quarrel she'd heard between Marian and Alex. The law or Marian . . . Otherwise, she was only a bystander, not involved.

Annie held fast to that thought. She had no real connection to Alex Griffith or his wife. What she surmised, well, she was under no obligation to point fingers. Let Rae Griffith fill that role. Annie pushed away the memory of morning heat and standing on the other side of the patio wall and Marian's husky, desperate voice.

The fact that Annie had come to the Seaside Inn tonight didn't involve her in anything, and definitely not an investigation. She would contribute what she knew of this evening, which was very little. She would keep her answers simple.

". . . so I called you—"

"We're here. Wait for us." Billy ended the call.

More sirens rose and fell, growing nearer and nearer, abruptly cut off in midsqueal. Even from this small patio at the end of the wing, she saw the flash of red lights at the far end of the wing, knew patrol cars had arrived in front of the inn. Car doors slammed.

Billy knew his island, knew the inn, knew where to park for quickest access to a patio in the east wing. Footsteps crunched on oyster shells. Light from lampposts illuminated the walk.

Billy Cameron was in the lead. He had not taken time to change clothes. Instead of his usual short-sleeved white shirt and dress slacks, he wore a blue polo, jeans, and sneakers. Close behind followed two officers, dark-haired, stocky Lou Pirelli and thin, angular Hyla Harrison. Lou was in casual dress. Annie didn't know if Hyla had also been summoned from home. No matter, she was trim in her uniform: khaki blouse with her name tag—Officer H. Harrison—khaki trousers, black shoes. Her reddish-brown hair was drawn back in a ponytail, her pale, freckled face impassive, but her eyes moved back and forth, noting the partially open sliding door marred by crisscrossing black tape, the yellow drape that wavered in the breeze. Mavis Cameron and three patrolmen waited a few feet from the patio. Mavis carried a rectangular black plastic evidence case.

Billy took in the patio at a glance, the stricken young woman in the webbed patio chair, Annie standing at her side, the partially open door with the splotch of tape, the room, the drape that blocked a view of the interior. Careful not to touch any surface, Billy edged past the drape. He was back in only a moment. Death confirmed. Murder apparent. He and his officers could secure the perimeter of the crime scene, but investigation had to await the arrival of the medical examiner and an official confirmation of death. He glanced at Hyla Harrison. "Take a quick look. Tell me if anything indicates robbery."

Hyla slipped into the room.

Billy walked to Rae's chair. "Mrs. Griffith?" His tone was gentle. "I'm Police Chief Billy Cameron."

Rae looked up, her lips trembling. "Someone killed Alex. I found him . . ."

Oyster shells crackled. Doc Burford loomed up out of the dusk, unkempt shaggy white hair, probably not combed since morning, white long-sleeved shirt open at the throat, a smear of mustard near the third button likely a reminder of a hot dog lunch grabbed in the hospital cafeteria, wrinkled black trousers dulled with age, thick-soled running shoes. He was not only chief of hospital, he also served as the island medical examiner. His heavy face was lined by years of hard work, unremitting effort to save lives. He had an abiding hatred for murder and lives cut short. Bristly gray brows drawn down in a tight frown, he looked only at Billy.

Billy turned a thumb toward the partially open sliding door. "Inside, Doc."

After a nod from Billy, Mavis followed Doc Burford, careful not to touch any surface.

Rae looked even more stricken. She kept her gaze away from the entrance to the suite.

Rapid footsteps sounded. Annie looked toward the walk.

"Hey, what's going on?" The dark-haired TV reporter strode up to the patio, thrust a mic toward Billy. "We heard sirens." Marian Kenyon was right behind her.

Billy gave the reporter a cold stare. "Crime scene. You are requested to remain on the terrace."

Marian Kenyon peered around the taller woman. "Chief?"

"No press now. Wait on the terrace. We'll brief you when we can." Billy nodded toward Lou Pirelli, who moved purposefully toward the TV reporter and Marian.

Rae's head turned. She frowned at Marian.

Hyla stepped out onto the patio. "No evidence of a search. A man's billfold on the dresser, along with coins and cell phone. Woman's purse on the hall table. Mavis will check to see if the billfold belongs to the deceased and the purse to his widow."

"Who's dead?" the TV reporter shouted as she backpedaled away from Lou.

Billy ignored the question, spoke quietly to Rae. "Mrs. Griffith, as soon as we secure the scene, I'll be with you." He turned to Annie, gestured toward the terrace. "Has an announcement been made?"

"Not yet."

Billy walked to the path. "Officers Harrison and Pirelli will come with me."

Billy, Hyla, and Lou moved fast and were swiftly out of sight, the TV reporter and Marian close behind. The patio with its embracing walls was only a few feet from the rear rows of chairs.

There was a cessation of sound from the waiting audience and Annie knew the officers had been seen. She wondered if the earlier sound of sirens had been noticed or unheard in the crowd noise. Conversations broke off. Puzzled faces turned to watch as the obvious harbingers of something gone wrong strode onto the terrace and moved up the central aisle.

There was the hollow knocking sound of a microphone being handled, then Billy's voice was clear and distinct. "Ladies and gentlemen, Mr. Griffith will be unable to speak this evening. I am sorry to report that his body was discovered shortly after eight P.M. He is apparently the victim of a homicide. It is important for us to know who was at the inn tonight. I ask everyone to remain seated until Officers Harrison and Pirelli have spoken to each of you and obtained your name and address. I'm sure everyone wants to cooperate. In addition, will anyone who feels that he or she may have information important to our investigation or any knowledge of Alex Griffith's movements this evening please remain until an officer can speak with you."

Annie pictured Hyla and Lou setting about their task, impassive, professional, quick.

Doc Burford shouldered his way past the drape, stopped on the patio.

Billy came around the patio wall.

Rae rose, moved toward the ME. "What did they do to him? What happened?"

Doc Burford spoke carefully. "I can't be certain of the cause of death until I complete an autopsy. My preliminary finding"—he glanced toward Billy—"is severe head trauma, which either stunned him or resulted in loss of consciousness. There are signs of asphyxia, which suggests the sofa pillow was used to suffocate him. The supposition is that he was struck down, toppled onto the sofa, then someone pressed the pillow against his face until he stopped breathing." He moved heavily toward the path, looked back at Billy. "There's a heavy, thick piece of wood, maybe a foot and a half long, at least two-inch circumference, lying near the sofa. Probably the weapon. I'll see if I find fragments of bark."

Rae clasped her hands tightly together. Her face held a look of horror.

Annie knew Rae was creating a scene in her mind: her husband, handsome, alive, leaning back on the sofa, someone moving behind him, raising an arm to bring down a piece of wood with brute, final force.

A bloodied piece of heavy wood.

Annie hadn't seen the weapon in the short space of time she was in the sitting room, but the presence of a weapon meant someone came prepared. Annie visualized a heavy stick as described by the

ME. A foot and a half in length was half again as long as a ruler. More than a two-inch circumference was larger than a blackjack. A weapon that size could be slipped beneath a loose shirt, held tight against one side by the pressure of an arm. A weapon that size could be tucked in a woman's oversized purse. That afternoon someone must have walked along a forest path, looking, searching, until the right broken-off piece of wood was spotted. Hard wood, nothing soft or rotten. A brilliant choice for a bludgeon. The rough bark would probably hold no fingerprints. To be certain, a handkerchief or soft cloth likely had been used to protect the hand.

Doc Burford was across the patio and stepping onto the oyster shell path.

"Doc." Marian Kenyon moved out of a shadow on the far side of the path.

Annie wondered how she'd slipped unnoticed from the terrace. But her presence would not surprise Billy. Marian was always on the spot with breaking news, rules be damned.

Marian held a pen above her notebook. "Can I quote you on the preliminary finding?"

Burford nodded, moved past her without another word.

Annie thought Marian's always white face was paler than usual, but she spoke in her usual rapid staccato. "Chief, can you confirm the victim's identity?"

Billy shot her an irritated look. "The victim has been identified as Alex Griffith. This is a crime scene and it is closed to everyone except police and witnesses. Please wait on the terrace for an update."

Marian looked straight at Annie. Instead of her usual bright, inquisitive, intent expression, her face was drawn, eyes bleak, cheeks sunken. There was no plea, only hopeless resignation. She turned away.

Annie felt hollow inside. Marian believed Annie would tell Billy about the damning conversation she had overheard and the smashing of the hurricane lamp. Perhaps Marian assumed Annie had already informed Billy. But no, Marian must realize her secret was still safe or Billy would not have treated Marian as a reporter doing her job. He had yet to discover that Marian had any connection to Alex Griffith.

Annie's thoughts skittered like marbles flung on a table. No one except Marian knew what Annie had overheard. However, it seemed almost certain Alex would have told Rae about Marian's visit and the smashing of the hurricane lamp. But—

"Annie, hey, Annie." Billy sounded impatient.

She realized Billy must have spoken to her several times. "Sorry. I was thinking." Was that a giveaway that she knew more than she had revealed?

But Billy was focused on the moment. "Do you have any information you didn't tell me on the phone?"

"I don't know anything else about this evening." That was true.

"You're free to go."

Annie gained the path with a sense of escape. But Billy was thorough. He would interview hotel staff. Rita White would tell him that Annie had withdrawn from the program. Billy would want to know why. She could say she'd had further thoughts after reading the *Gazette* feature and decided it wouldn't be a wise move for an island merchant to be involved in a program that might upset some islanders. Was that answer good enough? It would have to be.

She came around the end of the wing. She wasn't surprised to see that the pool was empty of swimmers and no one lounged in deck chairs. An announcement of murder was enough to encourage guests to leave the scene along with those in the audience who could offer nothing to the investigation. But she was a little surprised that only Joan and Leland

Turner had remained behind. After all, George Griffith was now the only surviving brother in the family and Lynn Griffith had been Alex's sister-in-law. Obviously neither had chosen to remain. She was not surprised that heavy-faced, muscular Eddie Olson had left.

Joan Turner and her husband stood a few feet from the last empty row of chairs. Marian Kenyon, stiff and still, stood a dozen yards away. Joan stared toward the oyster shell path that led to Alex and Rae's room. Marian, too, watched. The TV camera crew roamed restlessly back and forth on the end of the terrace. They'd missed their ferry but they had a murder to cover.

Joan saw Annie and took a step forward.

Lou Pirelli, managing to look official despite his baggy Braves T-shirt and shabby jeans, immediately held up a broad hand. "Ma'am, I'm sorry. Please remain here. The chief will come and speak with you as soon as the preliminary investigation is complete." Preliminary investigation—a sanitized description of the careful survey, measurements, markings of a death scene, and all the while the body remained, growing colder, very dead. Alex Griffith wouldn't be lifted onto a gurney, transported to the morgue, until every scrap of information was gleaned from his position, making it possible to estimate just how he had been sitting when the unexpected blow came.

The gentle night breeze stirred Joan's dark hair. Her aristocratic face twisted in a spasm of emotion.

Alex Griffith had been her younger brother. They'd grown up on the island, knew island joys. Did she have a sudden memory of a laughing boy running across the sand, perhaps holding a starfish?

"I know." Her voice broke. "But it seems wrong that I'm standing here, doing nothing. No one is helping his wife. I don't know what happened but if she's there and Alex is dead . . . This is dreadful. Someone needs to be with her." She looked past Lou. "Annie, can you help? Can you go and tell her that we'll wait for her, take her home with us?"

Lou's usually genial face struggled between official displeasure and human kindness. "Ma'am, witnesses are requested not to speak to each other." He shot a hopeful glance at Annie. "Are you supposed to wait here, too?"

Annie spoke to Lou, but she looked for a long instant directly into Marian's dark eyes. "I'm free to go. As I told Billy, I don't know anything about Alex Griffith or what he did this evening. My only contact with him this morning was to discuss the event tonight. I don't know anything else."

Marian took an unsteady breath. She pressed a tight fist against one cheek.

"I'm sorry I don't know anything helpful. This was just a business connection for me." Again Annie looked directly at Marian.

Marian gave an almost infinitesimal nod.

Annie contrived to look earnest. "Lou, I know you need to stay with Joan and Leland since you are by yourself." Hyla hadn't come back to the Griffiths' room so she must be inside the inn. "I'll be glad to go and tell Billy that Joan wants to help Rae." A pause. "If that's all right."

Lou looked appreciative. Order had been maintained as he had been directed but compassion could be facilitated. "Yeah. Thanks, Annie."

Annie didn't look toward Marian as she turned to retrace her steps, but she felt she could sense relief. Eventually Billy would discover whether Alex had told Rae about Marian's angry visit, but that would be hearsay, not the direct testimony of someone who'd heard the bitter exchange.

Annie realized as she reached the oyster shell path that she had made a decision to protect Marian. She knew why. She wouldn't believe—couldn't believe—didn't believe—Marian could kill anyone, not even a man she obviously hated.

Annie tried to hide her inner turmoil as she neared the patio. She'd promised Max she would never, ever again be involved in any crime investigation. But that was all right. She wasn't involved in an investigation. She was removing herself from an investigation. As Max pointed out, Billy Cameron was a good, effective, careful policeman. Leave the work to him. Gladly. She was on the far side of the patio wall when she heard Billy's voice.

"What happened to the patio door?"

Annie stopped. Marian was now feeling relief, but perhaps she felt safe too soon. She wanted to hear Rae's response.

". . . actually he laughed. He didn't say what happened, just that he intended to send the bill for the patio door to someone he knew rather well a long time ago. He said"—Rae paused—"the animals were getting restless, which suited him just fine. I think he'd been on the phone with people today. He went off early this morning and didn't get back until four. I sat in a cabana at the pool and read and tried not to think about tonight. He didn't tell me where he went or who he talked to. I know he saw some people. When he came back late this afternoon, he was keyed up, like something unexpected had happened. But he knew I didn't want him to dump on people so maybe that's why he didn't have a lot to say. I asked him one last time not to talk about people tonight. He told me I was trying to keep him from writing a book that would outsell *Don't Go Home*."

"I thought you organized tonight's event."

A slight whistle of sound, a sigh. "I set up everything for Alex. I do—I did—publicity and talked to booksellers, everything he needed. He was stubborn. He went his own way. I knew he was going to go ahead no matter what I said, so I thought I'd get it done, we'd get past the evening, and maybe it wouldn't be as bad as I imagined."

That accounted for Rae's odd manner when she came to Death

on Demand Monday. She was doing what her husband asked. She opposed the plan, but she did as he asked.

Her voice was thin, strained, hollow. "I didn't want to come to the island. I told him from the first that I didn't think that kind of book worked and he was going to upset a lot of people. He didn't care." A pause. "That makes him sound mean. He wasn't mean. But he didn't feel things. I guess I should have known that from the first, the way he never got in touch with his family, didn't talk about them. But we were having fun and were busy and I didn't think about it. He always liked to watch people. He watched and listened and was able to take what he saw and write this raw, hot story. He wrote with incredible power. I think he was able to write that way because everything was true. That's why he couldn't just write another book. All he could write was what he knew. So he came back to see—" She broke off.

"If the animals would provide enough misery for a best seller." Billy spoke with no emphasis. "Can you tell me who he threatened?"

Annie moved forward. She had learned what mattered to her. Marian wasn't a suspect yet. Perhaps Rae knew the source of the characters. Perhaps she didn't. In any event, Annie didn't want to know more than she had guessed from her reading of *Don't Go Home*. She wanted to deliver Joan's message and walk swiftly across the terrace and hurry to her car, sever her connection to Alex Griffith, keep her promise to Max.

4

Officer Hyla Harrison nodded her thanks. "This will do for a start." She pocketed her pencil, held a small notebook in her hand.

The night clerk was college age, likely thrilled to land a summer job enhanced by sun, surf, and sand. At the moment, rounded, fearful brown eyes stared from a plump face. The girl swallowed. "I'm scared."

Hyla appraised her with clear green eyes. "I won't say there is never danger to bystanders when a murder has been committed. But the suite did not appear to be ransacked. There was no evidence of disarray. The position of the body indicates the victim wasn't expecting an attack, which suggests he knew his attacker." Aware the clerk hung on every word, she added in a reassuring tone, "Barring drug deals and gang violence, most murders are committed by someone known to a victim. This appears to be the case here, which means it's unlikely a deranged killer threatens danger to ordinary people. Did you know the victim?"

The girl shook her head violently, short brown hair rippling.

"I wouldn't worry, then." Hyla turned and walked swiftly across the lobby. As always, she looked about her as she moved, noting who was near, attitude, appearance, posture, expression. She saw nothing out of the ordinary, though obviously most of the guests had heard there was a problem and eyed her with sharp interest.

She walked past the central stairway and into the hallway of shops. When she reached the east wing, she paused in thought for an instant. The nearer the scene of the crime, the likelier something interesting might have been observed by a fellow guest. She walked to the end of the corridor, knocked on the door of 128, next to the Griffith corner suite. She glanced at her pad. The clerk had given her the names and arrival and expected departure dates. Room 128, Robert Haws, checked in Tuesday, scheduled to check out Thursday.

She waited to a count of five, knocked again. No answer.

She moved to the next even-numbered room, looked at the pad, knocked.

The door opened. "Bring—Oh." The thirtyish sandy-haired woman with a peeling nose looked surprised. Behind her a television blared and a boy shouted, "I don't care. It's mine. Give it—" The woman swung around. "Roger, hush," she said and turned apologetically back to Hyla. "Can I help you?"

Hyla saw a room with two double beds, clothing strewn on chairs, and wet towels wadded in a corner along with a stack of sand buckets. The drapes were open though the night was now dark beyond the glass of the patio door. "Mrs. Carey?" At her nod, Hyla continued, "Officer Hyla Harrison, Broward's Rock Police. Have you been on your patio this evening . . ."

◆　◆　◆

The air-conditioning was cranked. Dorothy L rested in the curve of Annie's arm beneath a light cover. The plump cat's cheerful purr, the warmth of her furry body, made the bed a little less lonely. Annie was comfortable, her shorty nightgown light as froth, but sleep seemed impossible. She could not push away images of the day. Or the night. If Max were here, she could share with him and everything would be better. Finally, to Dorothy L's dismay, she turned to the edge of the bed and got up. She slipped into house shoes, turned on lights as she went. Downstairs, she poured a glass of milk and zapped one of Max's incredible peanut butter cookies in the microwave. She carried her snack out on the porch, welcoming the heat and the familiar night sounds, the incessant chatter of the frogs, the distant whoo of an owl, the rasp of the cicadas. She sank onto the soft cushions of the swing, gave a push with her foot. The familiar creak was reassuring. All was well . . .

Well for her. Not for others this sultry summer night. What was Marian doing tonight? Annie recalled the searing passage in *Don't Go Home* when Louanne called Buck. But Annie knew the truth. It was Marian who gripped a phone, called her lover; Marian who was unfaithful to her husband, Craig; Marian who cried out in her husky voice, "I waited for you. I waited until dawn." It was Alex who answered in a light, untroubled tenor, "I didn't come. I won't be coming." "You said we could run away together." "Thought about it. Not a good idea." "You said you loved me." "That's what I always tell married women. Married women make the best—" "Alex, I left a message for you. I'm pregnant." "Yeah, you did. I'm sure everything will work out for the best. Won't Craig be surprised?" The phone went dead.

Annie knew abruptly that Marian was awake this moment, too.

Marian and her son, David, lived in a modest one-story stucco home on a crooked lane not far from downtown. Marian always joked that she could hop on a bike and be at the *Gazette* in four minutes, sooner than she could drive.

Annie knew she was pushing away from the reality of Marian's heartbreak, thinking instead of Marian as she knew her: brusque, funny, acerbic, smart, a mom who went to baseball games and sold popcorn to raise money for uniforms, a mom who was proud of her sandy-haired, freckle-faced, fun kid who struggled with algebra but worked on the school newspaper and wanted to go to Clemson and major in journalism, and an ex-wife who often spoke admiringly of what a great dad Craig was and how he'd started going to AA after David was born and how proud he was of his son.

Yes, Marian was awake.

Annie took a last bite of cookie, finished the milk, heard the distant sad cry of a mourning dove, oh-wah-oh-who-who. Perhaps no one else connected Marian to Louanne. In the novel, Louanne was a round-faced blonde. Louanne wasn't a reporter, she was a copywriter in an advertising agency in Atlanta, a long, long way from the island. Annie wouldn't have made the connection if she hadn't overheard the exchange between Marian and Alex.

It was almost as if Max were there beside her. *Be her friend. Be there for her. That's how you help Marian. Leave murder to Billy.*

Slowly she began to relax. Whatever happened, she was out of it. She had promised. She sent a little message across the forest and out onto the ocean to Max. Was he on deck watching the stars? Drinking a beer? Laughing? He would be pleased at how she'd handled everything tonight. She'd kept free of all entanglements—

A siren shrilled.

Her hand tightened on the cool glass.

The siren came nearer and nearer. She gauged its progress, knew when it—patrol car? ambulance? fire truck?—turned into the broad avenue that led to the Seaside Inn. The shrill wail cut off. In the distance sounded another siren, again coming nearer and nearer. Two sirens. Not more, not the cacophony of cars converging as they had in the early evening. Still, something had happened and she was sure the sirens led to the Seaside Inn.

Annie came to her feet, moved across the porch, stared across the darkness of the garden. A golden glow from the lamppost near the gazebo illuminated the path that curved into the woods, the path to the inn.

Maybe someone had a heart attack. Not that she wished illness on anyone, but help would come. That would be a single siren. Didn't two sirens spell police?

She knew what she feared in a dark recess of her mind. Was Alex Griffith's murderer afraid of how much Rae knew? But Joan Turner had invited Rae to come to the Turner home, leave the physical surroundings where Alex died. Even if Rae had declined the offer, surely she had relocated to another room in the inn. Annie had a swift memory of Rae huddled in the webbed chair on the patio just the other side of the cracked glass door and the room where her husband lay twisted in death.

Rae had huddled alone. All alone. No one to care. No one to help.

It was far too late at night to call the Turner house, ask if Rae was there. Annie whirled and hurried across the porch, flinging open the door, running with her slippers slapping softly on the wooden floor, taking the stairs two at a time. It took only a couple of minutes to step out of her nightie, put on a cotton top and slacks, tug on running shoes.

She raced down the stairs and into the kitchen, where she grabbed a flashlight. Outside, she crossed the yard and reached the path. When she plunged into the woods, the canopy of trees closed overhead, blocking out the stars and the glow of the moon. The flashlight beam offered a reassuring tunnel of light in the pitch darkness. Ferns and vines poked into her path. Movement and rustles in dense thickets brought the hair up on the back of her neck. She knew what was out there—raccoons, deer, rats, porcupines, foxes—but surely they would stay out of her way. As she ran, she murmured in almost a conversational tone, "Max, I'm not being stupid. I'm going to be careful. I just don't want Rae to be alone, if she's there. She may not be there, so then I can come home and all is well, and I promise I am not getting involved in anything." She slowed and peered at the farthest reach of the light. Worse than upsetting Max would be coming nose to snout with an alligator lounging on the path. If she saw a long dark blotch across the trail, she would skid to a terrified stop, inch her way back. But the path was the quickest way to the inn. Her heart was thudding by the time she plunged out of the woods into the west parking lot. Immediately she felt better. She'd sent ESP vibes to Max and she hadn't confronted an alligator. She crossed the terrace, the untenanted swimming pool emphasizing the late hour. She heard voices before she reached the east wing.

As she came around the corner, she saw beams from Maglites dancing in the forest west of the inn. There were sounds of movement, twigs breaking, men calling to each other.

Several dark figures clustered near the first patio.

Rae Griffith stood by an overturned patio chair. Her dark hair was tousled, her pale blue cotton nightgown pulled low on one shoulder. At some point in whatever had occurred, she'd pulled on running shoes and they were an odd contrast to the delicate nightgown.

Officer Harrison, as crisp as always, was listening, her face intent.

". . . never saw him," Rae was saying. Her voice was strained.

"Him?" Hyla asked.

In the grass a few feet from the patio, a college-age girl in a white peasant blouse and blue denim skirt watched anxiously. Her name tag read: Night Clerk Judith Reilly. At a shout from the woods, she looked even more scared, edged closer to Hyla.

Rae massaged the bare shoulder, grimaced. "It could have been a woman. Everything happened so fast."

Running steps sounded. Marian Kenyon skidded to a stop by Annie, notebook in one hand, Leica in the other. "Scanner," she explained to Annie before turning to Hyla Harrison. "You caught anybody?" Marian was middle-of-the-night frowsy in a too-large orange T-shirt and faded jeans and worn huaraches.

Hyla jerked a thumb toward the woods. "Search under way," she answered, but her eyes never moved from Rae's pale face. "You were in the bedroom"—a slight upward inflection—"here?"

Rae brushed back tangled hair, looked defiant. "I know what you're thinking." Her voice was ragged. "You think I should have moved. Alex's sister asked me. The hotel offered another room." Her lips quivered. "His things are here."

Annie pressed her nails into her palms. The room was all Rae had now of Alex. *His things are here* . . . Annie understood. Even with the memory of that twisted body, utterly still and limp in death, Rae wanted to be where she felt nearest to him.

Hyla continued to watch Rae, her face impassive, then pressed on. "You were in the bedroom."

Rae blinked and her face furrowed in concentration. "I'd taken a sleeping pill. If I sound groggy, that's why." Her voice was dull, dragging. "I heard noise, something out in the sitting room. I wasn't thinking. At first I thought Alex was up—and then I remembered. I got up but I was dizzy. I hung on to the headboard for a minute. There were thumps, little noises. I knew something was wrong, somebody out there who shouldn't be. I wasn't thinking straight or I would have stayed where I was—the bedroom door was locked—and called the police. But I was mad and upset. I started across the room, kind of stumbling. I got to the door and pulled it open. I saw a shaft of light and all of a sudden the light was in my eyes. I couldn't see anything. I screamed. But I don't think I made much noise. Somebody rushed at me and I saw the light swing up and I knew I was going to be hit. I tried to get out of the way and the flashlight slammed down onto my shoulder and I fell. By the time I got up, it was dark in the sitting room. The only light came from the lantern on the patio. I saw that light and the curtain blowing and knew the patio door was open. I turned on all the lights and called 911."

The sounds of the search were distant now. There were no warning shouts, no harsh orders to raise hands and remain still. Annie knew no one had been spotted. By now the intruder was likely long gone.

Hyla was brisk. "Did your assailant's footsteps sound loud?"

Rae stared at the slender officer. "Loud?"

"The level of noise might indicate whether your assailant was a man or woman. Loud steps, a man. Light steps, a woman."

Rae shook her head. "I don't know."

Marian was at the edge of the patio, leaning forward. In the light from the lantern at the end of the dividing wall, she looked tense. "What do you have that someone wants? Or what did your husband have?"

Annie noticed that Marian did not call the dead man by his first name.

Rae looked past Hyla, apparently seeing Marian for the first time. Rae's face twisted in uncertainty. "I don't know."

Hyla shot Marian a squelching look, said to Rae, "How do you think the intruder gained entry?"

Rae gestured toward the patio door.

Instead of industrial tape masking a crack, the pane was now shattered. Shards of glass littered the patio floor. A gaping hole by the handle easily provided enough space for a gloved hand to reach inside, loosen the lock, delve down carefully past jagged edges to toss aside the security bar. The intruder's entry had been made easier by the previous damage. The thick crisscross of tape muffled the sound of further cracking.

Rae's eyes narrowed. She took a step toward Marian. "How come you're here? Alex said he used to know you."

Hyla looked from one to the other, absorbing every nuance, every breath, every flicker of expression.

Marian returned Rae's stare. "I heard the alert on the scanner. I cover the news. I don't know anything about your husband's activities."

Rae took another step forward. "You used to know a lot about him. He said he knew you in the old days, before I met him. What did that mean? Are you the one who threw the hurricane lamp at him?"

Annie wondered if Rae, in her shocked state, was attuned to fear and desperation. She had somehow connected the violence that morning with Marian.

Marian managed a strained laugh. "If someone threw a hurricane lamp at him, I'd think there are a lot of people who might have wanted to smash things around him. As for me, I can't explain why the lamp was thrown."

Annie wished she could turn and leave. Marian, her friend Marian, Marian, who was light and funny and clever and eager, was picking words as delicately as a scam artist. Marian said she couldn't explain why the lamp was thrown. If she explained, she would have to admit she'd thrown the lamp at Alex in a rage.

"The lamp doesn't matter." Marian talked fast. "What matters is why someone came here tonight. Did your husband have something somebody wanted?"

Rae rubbed knuckles against one cheek, like a tired child. "The policeman asked me if Alex had papers that might be connected to his murder. Alex brought his briefcase when we came to the island. He was carrying it yesterday, but he left it in the car when he got back to the inn. I went out to Alex's car and got it."

Hyla's eyes narrowed. "Where's the briefcase now?"

Rae pointed inside. "I put it on the counter." She turned, walked wearily into the suite.

Hyla followed.

Marian stepped to the open doorway, rose on tiptoe to watch. Annie joined her. The hotel clerk scurried to be near them.

"What was in the briefcase?" Marian's voice was taut.

Rae looked back at her. "Things about people on the island. And a letter, something to do with his brother. He was talking about the letter after he got back today but I didn't pay much attention. The letter and some old friend."

Hyla stood next to the counter by the wet bar. The empty counter.

Rae stared. "The briefcase is gone. That's where I put it."

Every light burned. A green tarp covered the sofa and a portion of the floor. Had the police covered the sofa to hide the bloodstains when Rae insisted on remaining in the suite? The crime scene survey had been completed or Billy would not have permitted Rae to stay. But traces of the crime would be evident from dark splotches of dried blood on the sofa and floor.

A stool near the coffee bar had been toppled. A lamp had been knocked to the floor from the table by the bedroom door.

Rae pointed at the wet bar. "The briefcase was lying on the counter."

Hyla moved swiftly. She searched the room, even lifted the tarp to flash her light beneath it.

Annie averted her gaze, but not before she saw a grisly blackish stain.

Hyla said briefly to Rae, "Stay here." She came toward the patio.

Marian and Annie moved out of the way and the plump girl remained within a foot of Annie.

Hyla flashed the Maglite over the patio, walked out ten feet toward the woods. Finally, she shook her head and strode back.

Rae stood in the opening. "They—he—whoever—took the briefcase."

Hyla nodded. "Looks like that's what the intruder wanted. Description?"

Rae rubbed her eyes. "I got it for him for Christmas. A man's brief-case. Small. Tan leather. His initials on the front in gold letters." She sagged a little against the upright metal rod of the patio door. "That man, the big one, he asked me if Alex had brought any papers with him to the island. I looked around and didn't see his briefcase and so I went out and the policeman went with me and I got the briefcase out of Alex's car. We brought it in here and he looked through it."

Marian stood quite still. "You said there was information about people on the island?"

Annie saw fear in Marian's dark eyes.

Rae massaged her right temple. "We didn't find anything that looked important." Her voice was weary. "The police chief and I looked. A woman took pictures of stuff. There wasn't much."

Annie saw Marian swallow.

There was thrashing in the woods, coming nearer. Lights flickered, became brighter. Lou Pirelli thudded out of the woods, followed by two other officers. He strode to Hyla. "No luck. We went all the way through the woods to the main road. Fifty people could be hiding in there. If the perp knew the terrain, he probably got clear before we arrived." He looked at the gathering, noted Rae Griffith, and saw, with a slight look of inquiry, Annie standing by the wall and Marian at the edge of the patio. "What have you got?"

Hyla was precise. "Unauthorized entry into corner suite. Bedroom occupied by Rae Griffith. Intrusion awakened her. She went out into the sitting room. Intruder struck her. She fell. Intruder escaped. No injury beyond bruised shoulder. Intruder apparently removed a briefcase belonging to the dead man. The intruder did not gain access to contents of bedroom. No description." She turned back to Rae. "Anything of value in the sitting room?"

Rae looked exhausted. "I'd taken our things out after the policewoman finished. She was nice enough but she warned me not to go into the sitting room, that the site shouldn't be disturbed. Site." Rae's voice was uneven. "Site of murder? That's what she meant. But I wasn't going to be driven away. She watched while I took my things into the bedroom. She told me to go in and out through the bedroom door into the hall, not to come into the sitting room. As if I'd want to go in there."

Hyla's gaze flickered toward the broken patio door. "I'm sure the hotel will provide another room—"

"No." Rae's response was sharp. "I'm staying here."

Hyla nodded. "Tomorrow we'll check the sitting room and surroundings for fingerprints. Most perps who come prepared to break in, especially to this kind of scene, wear gloves so it's unlikely we'll find anything useful. We'll look. I suggest you lock the bedroom door. I'll wait here until you are safely in the bedroom." She watched as

Rae picked her way through the broken glass. Her running shoes looked odd beneath the bare legs and shorty nightgown.

Lou spoke quietly to Hyla, the words indistinguishable.

Annie knew Marian strained to hear, just as she herself did, but he spoke with his back to the two women, his voice a murmur, as was Hyla's reply. Lou gave a nod, turned to leave the patio, gesturing to the officers standing a few feet away. They moved toward the front of the inn.

Hyla stepped to the threshold of the sitting room, head cocked, apparently charting Rae's progress to the bedroom.

Lou passed close to Annie and Marian. He knew them both well, but his gaze was neither friendly nor unfriendly. He was a cop, observing, thinking, wondering.

Apparently satisfied that Rae was in the bedroom, Hyla turned and walked toward them. She stopped a scant foot away, looked from Annie to Marian and back at Annie. "You have a scanner?" The words were pleasant, but the skeptical look in her eyes told Annie that her presence there was definitely suspect.

"I was on the back porch. I heard sirens."

"You always go out to see about sirens"—Hyla glanced at her watch—"you hear close to two A.M.?"

"I knew the sirens stopped at the inn. It's only a half mile through the woods to our house. And after what happened tonight . . ." She trailed off, aware that Hyla and Marian both watched her. "I was afraid something else had happened to Rae and I was afraid she was all alone. I just came to see."

Hyla's pale green eyes still looked skeptical. "Right. Well, I'd say there's nothing to see now."

Annie was dismissed. She left silence behind her as she rounded the wall and walked toward the terrace. Hyla obviously intended to wait until she was out of earshot, but Annie caught a scrap of Hyla's question to Marian.

"Is your car in the front . . ."

Hyla Harrison consciously elevated her chin. There would be no evidence of fatigue in her demeanor this morning. From a history of World War II, she remembered a dictum favored by General George C. Marshall: An officer is responsible for his own morale. In war, officers as well as their men were hungry or exhausted or in peril but it was their duty to remain positive, forceful, and commanding. Hyla liked that thought. No matter how tired she might be after the late-night alarm, she reported for work on schedule at eight A.M., ready for the day, makeup fresh, hair neatly brushed, uniform crisp.

Now she was once again in the east wing of the Seaside Inn next door to the suite where Alex Griffith violently died. Last night, she'd checked each occupied room, spoken to all but three guests. None reported seeing anything useful to the investigation from their patios.

She ignored the Do Not Disturb placard hung on the knob and knocked firmly on the door to Room 128, guest Robert Haws.

No answer.

Rap. Rap. Rap.

No answer.

Hyla knocked again, waited a minute, knocked, waited, knocked. She checked a page in her small notebook, slid it back into a pocket, pulled out her cell phone, swiped a number.

"Seaside Inn. How may I help you?"

"Police Officer H. Harrison. Will you ring Room 128, inform Mr. Haws that a police officer is at the door and wishes to speak to him."

"Yes, ma'am." The tone was breathy, excited.

Hyla held until the recording function switched on. She ended the call, frowned. She walked swiftly up the hall, into the small arcade, past the shops, and into the main lobby.

The clerk at the desk was tall, willowy, in her forties, with an old-fashioned upswept hairdo. With a worried frown, she watched Hyla approach. "Is anything wrong?"

"I'd like information about the guest in Room 128."

The clerk, Mrs. Childers, turned to her workstation. Her fingers flew over the keyboard. Relief was evident when she turned back to Hyla. "Mr. Haws checked out via the hotel television channel this morning."

"He didn't come to the desk?"

"No, ma'am."

"I'd like his credit card information."

Mrs. Childers tapped again, gave Hyla a bright smile. "He didn't use a credit card. He paid cash."

Hyla stiffened, much like a dog on point. Anomalies were warning flags. "Did he have a reservation when he arrived?"

Dark eyes turned back to the screen. "Yes. The reservation was made on Monday."

"Don't you require a credit card?"

"Yes."

"The number, please."

Mrs. Childers complied. Hyla wrote down the number for a Visa card. If the number checked out to a Robert Haws, that would allay her suspicion, but if the number was fake . . . "What time Tuesday did he check in?"

The clerk peered at the screen. "Ten oh seven A.M."

"Why did he get Room 128?"

The clerk looked back at the screen. "Special request. He asked for a room as near the end of the east wing as possible."

Special request. Hyla was quick. "Instruct housekeeping not to enter Room 128 until further notice."

Mrs. Childers looked shocked. "I don't know if—"

Hyla's gaze was commanding. "This is part of the investigation into the murder of Mr. Griffith, who was killed in the suite next door to Room 128. The manager assured Chief Cameron that the inn will cooperate in all matters. Since Mr. Haws has checked out, the room is currently unoccupied and permission to enter is at the prerogative of the hotel." Hyla was bluffing, but she felt confident some such agreement had been reached between the manager and Chief Cameron.

Mrs. Childers picked up the house phone and dialed. "Jesse, the police don't want housekeeping in either 130 or 128. Will you please see to that? . . . Good. Thanks." Her look at Hyla was bright. "Housekeeping won't clean the rooms."

Hyla held out her hand. "A key to 128, please."

When she held the card in her hand, she nodded. "Now I need to speak to the manager."

Annie scanned the rows of gorgeous—to her—white mugs that lined the glass shelves behind the coffee bar. She chose *A Close Call* by Eden Phillpotts and poured a steaming mug of double-strong dark Colombian brew. She'd never read his mysteries but anyone who wrote a hundred books deserved the minor acclaim afforded by her mugs. She carried the mug, warm in her fingers, to a table and settled into a chair. She glanced again at the title in red script. Last night had been a near thing, definitely a close call. She had promised Max she would mind her own business. She had little doubt that Max would not be delighted that she'd run through the dark woods at two in the morning. It was time to keep her promise to Max and not do anything that might put her in danger. Rae Griffith had chosen to remain at the hotel. Annie could do nothing to ease her grief or her anger. Rae would cope as best she could. Certainly she should be safe enough in her bedroom. It was unlikely anyone would try to gain access to the suite now because enough time had passed that anything incriminating among Alex's papers would have been found and turned over to the police.

The mug remained poised halfway from the table to Annie's lips.

Annie's conclusion was swift. There might not be papers that incriminated anyone, but surely Rae knew the identities of the family and friends Alex exploited in his novel . . .

"Stop." She spoke aloud. What Rae Griffith knew or didn't know, did or didn't do, was no concern of Annie's. Last night was over and done. She was a bookseller. Period.

She drank her hot, strong coffee and gazed determinedly at the watercolors mounted above the fireplace mantel. Every month a local artist provided her with five paintings based on significant scenes in five mysteries. Bookstore visitors were invited to identify the scenes by title and author. The first reader to come up with five correct answers received a free month's worth of coffee and one free book (not a collectible). This month, at Annie's direction, the artist included in the bottom right-hand corner the year of publication. Fair was fair. Some of the books were from long ago.

In the first painting, a tall blond man in a blue beret fired a huge pearl-handled automatic at a coral snake as the snake leapt from a wicker basket onto the tiled floor of a restaurant. A dark-haired woman stared down in horror. A tall, angular woman clutched the arm of an unshaven middle-aged man in a crumpled gray suit and vest. (1937)

In the second painting, a blue-eyed, brown-haired young woman in a patterned brown-and-white silk dress stood in the compartment of a moving train, a vast treeless plain visible through the window. She stared down in horror at the body of a dark-haired young man resting on a train seat. The body was partially covered by a white sheet. (1944)

In the third painting, a disheveled middle-aged woman in a purple dress sat on the edge of a bed in a dim room. Tortoiseshell combs were askew in her upswept hair. Lying beside her was an old handmade quilt with a log cabin pattern. Her feet rested on a rag rug. A man sat in a chair across the room. He wore a Halloween mask, which hid his face. (2010)

In the fourth painting, a tall, attractive man with an intelligent, civilized expression stood before a mirror, appraising the effect of his costume, a wool suit in the style of the 1930s with a heavy linen shirt and a silk waistcoat, finished off by a thick cravat. A tidy black mustache that appeared artificial adorned his upper lip. A huge Maine coon cat watched. The cat appeared puzzled. (2013)

In the fifth painting, a neglected sunken garden featured Greek statues set into alcoves. Tiny shells and fragments of colored glass paved the paths. A grand country house with crumbling cornices and a roof in disrepair was visible in the distance. An appealing young woman with thick, waist-length chestnut hair, dressed in a white shirt and jeans, looked down at a little boy wearing a World War I Biggles flying helmet and goggles. He held a toy Merrythought mouse. (2014)

Annie relaxed against the chair, sipped coffee, and enjoyed silence. Death on Demand would open soon, customers would flock in, and it would be another busy summer day. Unpacking books, placing orders, sharing tips with customers—*Don't miss the new Mark Pryor . . . Carola Dunn's historical mysteries are a delight . . . Kerry Greenwood has a new series set in Egypt*—would make the day happy and soon the darkness from Seaside Inn would begin to recede.

A firm knock sounded at the front door.

5

Hyla Harrison's eyes adjusted to the dimness. The hotel meeting room on the second floor was set up for a film to be shown. Rows of chairs separated by a middle aisle stretched behind her. She was the only viewer. She half turned to watch as the manager adjusted the projector. Bud Crane was new to the island. In the future, Hyla would know him at a glance. Around six foot four with the aura of an old athlete gone a bit soft. Perhaps thirty-five or thirty-six. Reddish hair cut short, light brown eyes alert for trouble, a crooked nose, likely once broken, a smile that didn't reach his gaze. Not a man to trifle with. Probably been around some tough blocks in his time. Right now he was eager to cooperate.

He talked fast as an image flickered on the screen. "We run the cameras on a twenty-four-hour cycle. I'm fast-forwarding. Here we are. Tuesday morning." Abruptly the film slowed. Images slipped across the screen with time noted below in numerals: 10:02, 10:03, 10:04 . . .

Hyla leaned forward, held up her hand at 10:07.

The film stopped.

Hyla's eyes scoured the image. She committed every detail to memory.

A young man faced the counter. Approximately five foot ten. An oversized straw hat with a brim shadowed his face, hid his hair except for a fringe of thick blond curls on either side. Large aviator sunglasses, puffy cheeks, a bushy black mustache, smooth unlined skin. A Hawaiian shirt hung outside worn jeans, a bulge near the waistline. Lean, muscular arms extended below the short sleeves of the shirt. The arms looked fit, no stranger to weight bands at the gym, belying the soft rounding beneath the shirt. Worn Adidas running shoes. The left shoe had a tear along one side. Weight? A beer belly would add ten, fifteen pounds, make it one eighty-five. Was the belly authentic or artfully managed by a strapped-on pillow? Subtract the bulge, likely one seventy.

Billy Cameron declined a mug of coffee and a Danish. He looked fit and fresh in a short-sleeved white shirt, tan trousers, and brown leather loafers. His blond hair, flecked with white, was bleached a light gold by the summer sun. His face was tanned by the unrelenting sun of the late-summer afternoons that he and Mavis spent watching their son, Kevin, play baseball. The tan emphasized the deep blue of his eyes. He remained standing by the coffee bar, big and impressive, and those startlingly blue eyes studied Annie.

"Midmorning yesterday you alerted the inn that Death on Demand was no longer associated with the Griffith book event." It was a statement.

Annie had expected this moment to come. Of course he had spoken to Rita White. "Yes."

For an instant, Billy's broad mouth quirked in a slight grin. "Can't you do a little better than that? For starters, had you told Alex Griffith that you were withdrawing?"

"Yes."

Billy folded his arms, waited.

Annie took a quick breath. "The whole thing came without warning. I mean, when I came to work Monday morning I didn't know much about Alex Griffith except that he was a huge author and he'd grown up here. I didn't see the Sunday paper because I was gone this weekend. Max—"

Billy nodded. "Fishing."

A small town at work. Billy knew them, knew charter captains, loved to fish; likely he and Max had talked about the old-friends-on-a-boat outing.

"Right. So I went to Savannah for the weekend." She was filling in more than he wanted but she had to make the point about the *Gazette* story. "I drove straight to the store when I got off the ferry Monday morning. Rae Griffith came to see me. That's when I realized I knew some of his family." Billy was an island boy born and bred. She looked at him curiously. "Did you know Alex Griffith grew up here?"

He nodded. "He's years younger than I am. Alex was in the same class as my brother Ben."

At her blank look, another slight smile. "Ben went to West Point, career military, stationed at Wiesbaden in Germany right now."

Annie once again realized the gulf between native islanders and outsiders like her and Max. They were part of the community but . . .

there would always be a *but*. "Anyway, I knew he was from here and famous and I was thrilled that his wife wanted Death on Demand to host a talk. I didn't know about the article in the *Gazette*"—she looked inquiringly at Billy and he nodded—"until Monday afternoon and by then I was committed. At least that's how I felt. But I read the article several times and then I reread *Don't Go Home*. When I looked at those questions in the *Gazette* and thought about the characters in the book, I didn't like the idea he was going to name names last night."

"But you didn't do anything about it until Wednesday morning?"

Here's where the ice thinned. How long would it take Billy to decide something in particular Wednesday morning prompted Annie to withdraw? Or had that thought already occurred to him? The best defense . . . "I kept dithering." Her tone was self-critical. "I didn't like the article. The idea of tying particular characters to actual people here on the island was revolting. But I was in the middle of arranging the program and I'd promised. But the more I thought about it, the worse I felt. I didn't want Death on Demand connected to that kind of spectacle. So I had a bright idea. I decided I'd talk to him, ask him to change the tenor of the evening, focus on talking about writing. But when I spoke to him Wednesday morning"—and she was being accurate, changing the focus to her morning encounter with Alex, though a taunting imp in her mind chanted, *Sophism, sophism*—"I told him I didn't know what he intended to do but I wasn't going to be a party to it." She turned both hands palms up. "I walked out, went upstairs, told Rita that Death on Demand was out."

"Did you discuss the *Gazette* article with him?"

"I told him I'd read it." Oh happy day, she was going to succeed in skirting past the dangerous moments of her talk with Alex Griffith, the dangerous moments for Marian. "I told him I don't like bullies."

"Did he identify anyone he intended to discuss?"

"No."

"What was his demeanor?"

"Pleased with himself. Impervious."

"Do you know if he had spoken with anyone else about the article?"

"I have no idea if he discussed the article with anyone." Again the choice of words saved her. "I told him what I had to say and I left. I didn't wait for him to answer."

Billy's gaze narrowed. "Yet you came to the inn even though you weren't going to participate."

"I wanted people to know that Death on Demand wasn't involved. I hadn't quite decided what to do. I thought maybe I'd go up onstage just before he started and announce that Death on Demand had withdrawn from the program."

Billy's blue eyes never left her face. "You showed up at the inn last night after someone broke in to the Griffith suite."

Annie felt tension ease from her body, hoped Billy's watchful gaze didn't pick up on her relief. She was happy to talk about anything but the moments she'd spent near the Griffith patio. "I was on our porch. I heard the sirens. I knew Rae Griffith was invited to the Turner house but I worried that she might still be by herself at the inn."

Billy's gaze was searching. "A couple of weeks ago you set out to prove a suicide was murder. You got the proof but a killer almost got you. Max told me you'd promised to stay out of other people's troubles. But last night you showed up at the inn."

"Not at all the same thing. Last night I was worried about Rae Griffith being alone. Obviously she's decided to stay at the inn no matter what happens, but she'll be all right. If there was anything in his papers, the briefcase is gone now. The word will get out. She doesn't need my help. I'm not involved."

"Good to know." His voice was mild. "Max will be proud of you."

Hyla Harrison ignored the glare of the midmorning sun. She felt a trickle of sweat down her back and legs. Summer on a sea island. The thought was fleeting, dismissed. It didn't matter if it was hot or if rare sleet whistled, she would keep after a trail until she reached the end or the trail disappeared. When she was back in the office, she'd make some calls, find out more about the widow. She was always suspicious of family members. Most crimes were committed, as she'd told the clerk, by someone who knew the victim. There was no doubt in Hyla's mind that when they eventually discovered Alex's killer, the killer would be known to him. The blow had come from behind, likely as he was relaxed on the sofa, catching him across the back of the head. Another strike and the stick bludgeoned the side of his face. The two together were enough to stun him. Then the pillow jammed against his face until there was no more breath. The killer could be a hulking man or a petite woman. Hyla pictured the widow. Looked like there was plenty of strength in her arms; obviously she was in good physical shape.

What kind of shape had her marriage been in?

Ingrid understood her meaning when Annie pointed toward the back room, then turned her thumb down. It was a do-not-disturb, I'm-not-here signal. No one would knock on that door until Annie reemerged. The center aisle was clogged with shoppers. Annie was stopped twice on her way to the back room to respond to questions.

"A book about a ship going down and an old champion swimmer? You may be thinking of *The Poseidon Adventure* by Paul Gallico." "John Marquand is the author of *Ming Yellow*." She declared herself baffled about a book that was either set in a garden or where the murderer was a gardener . . . "Sorry. Urgent call I have to take," she said and slid past the customer to reach the door to the back room.

Annie closed the door behind her, shutting out the noise and bustle of the store. On the worktable, Agatha stretched in utter abandon on her back, four paws elevated. Annie gave the lightest of strokes to the sleek soft fur of her tummy. Annie understood the great compliment. Agatha's relaxed posture said to all the world, *I'm safe. I'm loved.*

Annie unlocked the rear door that opened to the alley, then settled in her swivel chair by the computer. She clicked on an order form, shook her head, made no effort to work. She waited, dreading the coming moments. When Marian had called, her voice was grim, strained.

The expected knock at the door sounded in only a few minutes. The knob turned.

Marian Kenyon stepped inside, black curls mussed by the breeze off the harbor, dark eyes huge in a set, pale face. She was neatly attired in a short-sleeved cream linen blouse with a twisted drape collar and slim-leg gray slacks, stylishly short at the ankles with side slits at the hem, and gray sandals. She leaned back against the door. "You didn't tell Billy. But I can't ask you to lie for me." Her voice was dull, hopeless.

Annie jumped up and hurried around the table. She took one thin elbow, steered Marian to the rickety wooden chair by the worktable. "I'll never tell him."

Marian looked up; her face worked. Tears spilled down her cheeks. "David gets home Sunday. I can't bear it if he ever knows. He mustn't know. Craig is his father. Craig's been a wonderful dad to him. Having David turned Craig's life around. If either of them ever finds out, everything will be ruined." She used both hands to brush away the tears. "Billy's suspicious. He looks at me and he knows I know something. He doesn't know what it is. So far, he hasn't connected me to Alex. But if he keeps looking, he'll put it together. Craig and I were both reporters in Atlanta when Alex was hired. Craig was a mess. Drunk most of the time. But"—and now her gaze was earnest—"Craig was a good reporter and he never took a dime from anybody for anything. I never knew until later that he turned Alex in for being on the take." Her face twisted. "I should have known Alex didn't come after me because he thought I was—" She broke off, didn't finish.

Annie understood. Alex didn't make love to Marian because she was appealing or fun or smart or kind. He came after her to get back at Craig.

"Funny." Marian's lips quivered. "I thought it was the end of the world when he dumped me because I was pregnant. Craig never realized he wasn't the dad. Craig—"

Annie knew it caused Marian pain to remember.

"—was too drunk too much of the time to know whether he'd slept with me or not. I wasn't trying to take advantage of Craig. That's one reason I divorced him. I refused child support. But later, he came to see me and David was about eight months old and I saw it happen. He picked David up and I saw him fall in love and that's when Craig got it all together. He stopped drinking and he insisted I take some money for David and I couldn't tell him that David wasn't his, not when I saw his face whenever David was in the room. Oh God, I don't know what's right or wrong. I only know I messed up everything but I don't want to mess up Craig's life or David's. That's what will happen if Billy burrows into those days in Atlanta. Somebody will have seen Alex and me together and Billy will look at dates and then he'll push me to answer questions and he'll know I had a hell of a reason to kill Alex. I didn't kill him. But there's no way I can prove that." There was defeat in her voice.

"Why not?" Annie heard her own words with surprise. "You can ask questions. You can try to find out what's going on."

Marian twined thin fingers together. "Billy's already given me the word. No tips from the cop shop until he's figured out how I knew Alex and when and whether it mattered. The door's barred. I can drop by, pick up news releases, attend press conferences. Otherwise, nada, zip, zero." She took a deep breath, pushed to her feet. "I got to get back to the newsroom, pretend I'm Marian Kenyon, girl reporter, pretend my world isn't crashing into bloody little bits."

She was at the door when Annie called out, "Marian, wait."

Hyla Harrison was untroubled by the tense atmosphere in the gleaming kitchen, all stainless steel and white surfaces, and by the banging of pots, sharp quick exchanges between white-aproned figures ranging in age from late teens to late sixties, and hurried footsteps. She stood next to a battered oak desk and repeated patiently, "The call to room service from Suite 130 came in at seventeen minutes past seven."

"Yes, ma'am." A matronly woman pointed at a computer. "All orders are put into the computer."

"Who took the order?"

"J. T. Lewis. One of our summer workers. I talked to J. T. later. He said the man sounded—"

"The speaker was a man?"

A vigorous nod. "According to J. T. He'll come on duty about four. But I know how he answered. He would have said, 'Room service. How may I help you?' I checked the order: one gin and tonic, one rum collins. Some peanuts. J. T. said the man—he called him Mr. Griffith—was in a hurry, wanted quick service, said he had to be somewhere pretty soon."

Hyla considered the possibilities. The caller could have been Alex Griffith. The caller could have been an unknown man. "What time was the order delivered?"

The plump-faced older woman frowned. "As I said, I saw the order. We made a special effort. The delivery left the bar at seven thirty-one, went directly to the suite. The waiter knocked three times, returned to the bar, said delivery attempted at thirty-four minutes after the hour, no response. J. T. said he called the room at"—she glanced toward the screen—"seven thirty-seven. No answer."

As the alley door closed after Marian, Annie felt surrounded by silence, silence that amplified the clamor in her mind. She'd promised Max . . . Marian was desperate . . . If she didn't help Marian, Billy would keep looking and he'd make the connection. If Marian was arrested, everything would come out. David would struggle with two realities: His mother had lived a lie, the man he loved as his father wasn't his father . . . Marian's life would be torn and twisted, the fodder for sensational stories in the papers and on TV . . .

Annie pushed up from her swivel chair, began to pace. She'd promised Max that she'd stay out of other people's troubles. Now she'd promised Marian that she would help. Brave words. What could Annie do by herself? She wouldn't have Max at Confidential Commissions. He was superb at trolling the Internet for information, uncovering odd facts that revealed the inner truth about people. She wouldn't have the unusual and sometimes inspired assistance of the Intrepid Trio: Max's mother, Laurel Darling Roethke; island mystery writer Emma Clyde; and Death on Demand's best customer, Henny Brawley. Elegant, patrician, and incredibly beautiful, Laurel was always spacey but her Nordic blue eyes could be surprisingly observant and her insights as unexpected and on point as pronouncements by Pam North in Frances and Richard Lockridge's Pam and Jerry North series. Didactic as her fictional heroine Marigold Rembrandt, Emma nonetheless was ferociously bright and once she set out on a trail nothing would deter her. Henny Brawley flew experimental planes during World War II, knew the anguish of two lost loves, was steeped in the best of English literature, and was a connoisseur of mysteries, fictional and real. Henny delighted in recounting examples from Agatha Christie's Miss Marple as she used parallels from everyday life to unmask evil.

Annie rued the fact that she'd been delighted that the Trio would be gone for several weeks. Laurel's penchant for new enthusiasms, which she hoped everyone would enjoy, had a tendency to unnerve Annie. There had been her infatuation with saints, her dandelion period, the cat photographs with trenchant captions (sure, Annie loved cats but why did the photos have to be displayed in her bookstore?), her delight in quoting Byron at his most provocative at somewhat inappropriate moments. As for Emma, the mercurial author kept entirely too sharp an eye on the displays of her books at Death on Demand. If she didn't have the front endcap, her glare was formidable. As soon as the Trio departed on their journey, Annie redid the front endcap to hold nine Robert Crais titles. And if the endcap returned to Emma Clyde mode just before they returned to the island, well, Annie made it a point not to provoke either Emma or any of the island alligators. Henny was always positive. In addition to being a world-class mystery reader, Henny was fun, energetic, perceptive, a true friend always.

Annie pulled out her cell phone, deflecting for the moment her painful dilemma: two promises made, each mutually exclusive. Missing the Intrepid Trio reminded her of a daily treat since they'd been gone: trenchant texts sent from a Mark Twain–style steamboat on the Mississippi River.

From Laurel: *Do the right thing. It will gratify some people and astonish the rest. Mark Twain.*

From Henny: *Did you know Phoebe Atwood Taylor wrote a novelette, The Disappearing Hermit, where Asey Mayo is detecting in Boston?*

From Emma: *The steamboat is perfect for murder but Marigold's turned her back on me.*

Annie sighed. *Do the right thing?* A true friend . . . a true love . . . she wanted to serve both. She shook her head impatiently, tapped Favorites. Max's phone rested in a locker. He wouldn't hear this message until he returned to land. But she owed him honesty. They'd always been honest with each other. The recorder came on. She didn't know how she'd planned to start, but the words tumbled out. "Max, I love you . . ."

Hyla Harrison sat perfectly straight in the chair facing Billy Cameron's desk, shoulders back, feet aligned, hands planted firmly on her thighs. "I smell fear."

"Not grief?" Billy looked at her intently. Hyla was a good cop, smart, quick, careful, honest. She'd never palm a twenty to let a driver off a ticket or fix evidence to prove a case. When Hyla spoke, he listened.

She took her time in answering, green eyes narrowing, lips pursing. Finally: "Not sure. Definitely shocked. That's at odds with fear. If she killed him, sure, she'd be scared we'd find out. But would she be shocked? If she was actually shocked, that knocks out the idea of prior knowledge. All I know is, she's hiding something." Hyla spoke with more assurance. "Don't know what it is. Maybe she bashed him. Maybe somebody else bashed him and she knows but she didn't know how rough it would be to walk in on a corpse. She's scared spitless. I want to find out more about the Griffiths. A lot more."

"Something funny? I'd suggest Rhys Bowen's Royal Spyness books or Hannah Dennison's Vicky Hill series or a Pamela Branch title." The shopper, rotund and cheerful in a muumuu, murmured her thanks.

Annie turned and stopped in surprise.

Rae Griffith hesitated in the center aisle. "I wish I was looking for something funny." Rae's thin face had aged. She looked drawn, tired. "I guess no one knows how lucky they are when all they are thinking about is finding a funny book or drinking a cup of coffee or going to a movie. I guess they don't know until they stop being lucky."

The encounter was so unexpected Annie simply stood and waited.

"You're wondering why I'm here." The words were jerky. "Could I talk to you? For a minute?" Her voice was shaky, the plea in her eyes unmistakable.

"Of course. Let's go back to my office. It's pretty noisy in the coffee area." Annie led the way down the aisle and held open the door to the back room.

As the door closed behind them, the silence was sudden.

Rae clasped her hands tightly together, blurted out, "I need help. I don't know where to get it. I asked at the inn and a guy told me about this place called Confidential Commissions. I came but it's all closed up. Then I realized it was next door to your store." She stopped, swallowed. "You were nice to me when I came Monday."

"Confidential Commissions," Annie repeated.

"Do you know who runs it? Maybe if I paid enough, I could get some help."

"He's gone fishing. Why don't you sit down." Annie gestured toward the chair as she settled into her swivel chair. "Tell me what you're looking for."

Rae sank into the chair. She looked very young in a blue T-shirt and white slacks and white sandals. Her soft black hair was glossy but her eyes had the uneasiness of a startled fawn. "Do you know that police-woman? She has reddish hair and pale green eyes, cold eyes."

Annie nodded. "Officer Harrison."

"She thinks I killed Alex." There was a look of panic on Rae's face. "She didn't say so straight out, but I could tell. She kept asking questions. When did I leave the room? What did Alex look like when I left? What did he say? Had we quarreled? What time exactly did I get to the gazebo? Did I come back to the room? Where was I between seventeen minutes after seven and thirty-four minutes after seven? Do I drink gin and tonic? Rum collins? Why does she care what I drink? I always order a margarita. Did I leave the terrace at any point during that time? How could I know it made any difference? I went to get raspberry iced tea for that reporter from Savannah. Nothing from the bar was good enough, had to be raspberry. I don't know how long it took. Could I have stopped by the suite? I guess. But I didn't. I swear I didn't."

"They always ask a lot of questions. I wouldn't worry—"

"She looked at me like I was scum." Rae's voice shook.

Annie was struck by the difference in Marian's demeanor and Rae's. Marian was terrified at what would happen if her son and the man he knew as his father ever learned the truth about Marian and Alex, agonizing about the pain they would suffer. Rae was terrified that the police suspected her.

"What did you want Confidential Commissions to do?"

"The guy told me the owner would find out things for people, that he wasn't a detective but he took on all kinds of commissions."

"What do you want to find out?"

Rae leaned forward. "I need to find out who killed Alex." There was a look of doom in her eyes, a conviction that if she didn't discover the truth, the police would arrest her. "I don't know anyone here. I don't know who wanted him dead."

Annie looked at her in disbelief. "You helped set up the evening. Wednesday you all but admitted he was going to tie the characters in the book to people he'd known on the island."

"How does that help me? I've never been here. I never met any of his family until now. I wanted to ask them to the wedding but Alex decided we'd get married in Tahiti and he said that wouldn't be right for any of them. I know that's odd, but lots of people leave family behind. I thought maybe they were strange or mean or low-class. I didn't know he'd used real people until a few weeks ago. He never said who any of them were. I guess some of them are obvious, like, I guess his sister screwed around on her husband, but I don't know who the rest of the characters are."

There was silence between them.

Rae's eyes were huge, filled with fear and uncertainty. Then her gaze sharpened. "You know who they are. You've read the book. You live here. That's why you didn't want to have anything to do with his talk. You've got to help me. Tell me who wanted him dead."

Images from the night before flickered in Annie's memory. Lynn Griffith, Heyward's widow, had the waxen appearance of a prisoner in the dock. Amid the cheery conversations, Joan Turner, Alex's sister, sat stiff and silent, her face empty. Big, burly Eddie Olson downed a drink and looked mean. George Griffith was soft and puffy from too many years of too many drinks, but last night he didn't hold a drink in his hand. And there was Marian, her features set and hard as she lurked in the shadows near the gazebo.

Rae came to her feet. "Tell me who they are."

Annie knew there were some things she could not do. She was not going to give a possibly unbalanced woman the names of those she could use to divert the police from herself. "I'm in no position to talk about anyone on the island. You're scared of the police. Am I supposed to accuse other people of having motives? How do you think they'd feel?"

Rae's breaths came in jerky gasps. "I'm the outsider. That makes it easy, doesn't it? Isn't that what they say about small-town police? They look for somebody from out of town?"

Annie stood, too. "Not here." Her tone was sharp. "Billy Cameron will look at everybody."

"Who is everybody? Who will they look at besides me?" Rae sounded frantic. "You know and you won't tell me."

Marian was desperate to know what had happened to Alex.

Marian, who loved her son . . .

Rae was the outsider, scared, desperate, vulnerable. She thought she didn't know anything, but surely she did. Surely she had some idea of what Alex had done the day he died.

Annie was blunt. "I won't talk about people on the island but I'll find out what I can for you. I don't know that anything I can do will make a difference, but I promise"—when would she learn not to make promises?—"that if I find out anything the police should know, I will tell them. Sit down. Let's talk."

Rae sank onto the chair, waited. Her gaze clung to Annie, hopeful but uncertain.

Annie picked up a notebook and pen, perched on the edge of the worktable. "What did Alex do yesterday?"

An odd look came on Rae's face, as if she'd been asked about a moment so distant in time that it held no reality. "Yesterday. He had room service. He liked steak for breakfast. We always traveled with some caviar. He added the caviar to scrambled eggs. A big pot of coffee. I don't like breakfast. I just have a yogurt. He was in a good humor, said he was going to add some spice to his family's day, high-five some old friends. When I left to go jump rope, he was leaning back on the couch. I saw him reach for the phone. I guess he called his sister and brother and sister-in-law. I don't know who else he called. When I came back, there was broken glass all over the patio and he said someone he'd known a long time ago heaved the hurricane lamp at him but he seemed to think it was funny so I guess nobody tried to hit him. He sure wasn't scared or upset. Then he told me to relax, spend the afternoon at the pool, go shopping, walk on the beach. I asked him what he was going to do. He laughed and said he planned to roll around town, that he'd set up quite a few meetings. For auld lang syne. He was gone until late afternoon. I wasn't paying much attention, I was still checking on everything for the event. I had to make sure the catering was set up, the mic ready, everything. Alex was different when he got back that afternoon. I think he was excited about something that had happened, but we mostly talked about the schedule for that night. We had an early dinner by the pool. I had a salad. Alex ordered a shrimp cocktail and a gin and tonic. I told him he'd better not drink too much before he spoke but he said he was fine." She averted her eyes from Annie.

Annie had a cold sense that Rae was upset not by her husband's death but by her fear that the police would suspect her of his murder.

"Do you remember anything he said about the people he saw Wednesday?"

She gave a hopeless shrug. "Not a lot. He said nobody'd changed much and they didn't seem to have the welcome mat out. He laughed about that. He said something about now he really knew what happened . . ." Her voice trailed off. "I don't know. He said he wished he'd talked to someone he saw before he'd written *Don't Go Home*." She pressed fingertips against each temple. "It was someone he hadn't seen in years, somebody with a funny name. I got the idea he found out something that changed his mind about something in the book."

6

Hyla Harrison used the landline, knew the recipient's caller ID would display *Broward's Rock Police*, a whiff of official to pave the way. Phone numbers were easy to obtain from a cross directory. She'd been to Atlanta several times, knew the area. The addresses signaled one of the more exclusive streets in Buckhead. She made two calls, learned a disgruntled next-door neighbor disliked the flock of geese kept on the Griffiths' property. "You think they pick up the geese potty? Can't be bothered and the nasty things are all over my front lawn. I don't have any use for the Griffiths, either one of them. Nouveau."

The third call was to the house across the street.

"Townsend residence."

"Mrs. Townsend, please."

"May I ask who's calling?"

Hyla grew up in Florida. She recognized the smooth, uninflected tone of a housekeeper. "Officer H. Harrison, Broward's Rock Police Department. Official business."

"Yes, ma'am. One moment, please."

It was a bit longer than a moment and this time the voice was full and throaty. "I always knew my lurid past would catch up with me." There was raucous amusement and the utter confidence of a certain kind of Southern belle, rowdy, unconventional, ready to hike up a satin skirt and slide down a banister or start a morning with champagne. "What can I do for you, Officer H. Harrison?"

"Alex and Rae Griffith live across the street from you."

"I saw the morning news. So the handsome laddie met his match." There was a tinge of regret in the husky voice.

"Did you know the Griffiths?"

"I recognized them going in and out. He drove a red Porsche. She has a black Mercedes."

"Do you have any idea whether the Griffiths were on good terms?"

"Lord, woman, I'd be the last to chide my neighbors for their marital woes. I just booted out my third. Good in bed but too prone"— a hoot of laughter—"to sliding between the sheets with other married women. As for the Griffiths, I don't know anything firsthand but my Miriam knows the Griffiths' housekeeper, Ella, and according to Miriam . . ."

nnie sat gingerly on the hot leather, turned the air-conditioning on full blast. She remembered her frugal mother's warning not to sit in the car and run the motor and waste gas. They watched pennies and dollars when she grew up in Amarillo. Funny how an unexpected memory could be so clear and distinct; it felt almost as if she could reach out and touch her mother, who died when she was in college. Frugal, yes, but generous and warm and caring, always there for her daughter and her friends. Her mom would have liked Marian.

Annie touched the steering wheel, yanked her hands away. Cars around here heated up like volcanoes in July. Firmly she punched the ignition, gripped the wheel. Her thoughts were skittering, focusing on heat and steering wheels and long ago because she didn't have a single idea what to do next. It was easy to tell Marian that of course they could figure out who killed Alex Griffith. At least Marian had specific tasks: cover Billy Cameron's news conference, write the *Gazette*'s lead story, check out unsolved crimes when George Griffith was in high school, track down how someone named Michael Smith became a paraplegic when Warren Foster, Eddie Olson, and Alex Griffith were teenagers.

As for Annie, she had a list, too: other islanders who'd waited in dread last night for Alex to speak. Had one of them known he would never speak?

Annie rolled up the windows, pulled out her cell. Joan Turner had offered a haven to Rae Griffith. Annie found Joan's home number, called.

"Hello." Leland's voice was pleasant though a bit weary.

"This is Annie Darling. May I speak to Joan?"

"She's at the shop. Do you have that number?"

"Yes. Thanks." Annie dropped the cell back in her purse. It was interesting that Leland answered the phone, not a friend from church. Usually when a family is bereaved, ladies show up, handle phone calls, bring food, offer comfort. Instead Leland answered the phone and Joan had gone to work, though her brother was lying in a mortuary, a murder victim.

Annie backed from the slot, turned toward the main drive to town. She knew the way to Joan Turner's shop. She'd gone there often with Laurel, watched with amazement when her mother-in-law murmured about the sea at night, waved a graceful hand, and Joan Turner immediately suggested a wall of photographs by William Hartshorn, turning Laurel's family room into a spectacular evocation of moonlight and ocean.

Joan's shop was in a small frame cottage overlooking the harbor. Annie hurried up the steps, admired the massive brass knob as she opened the door and stepped inside.

Joan was seated at a sleek and simple Danish modern white desk, hand poised over a sketch pad. Two crimson molded chairs that faced the desk made it appear even whiter. The desktop held only a framed photograph of Leland and a seashell. Joan looked up with the beginning of a smile. Her face froze for an instant before she managed a pleasant expression. "Hello, Annie. What can I do for you?"

Annie walked across the floor, knew that Joan's gaze was wary, possibly frightened. As she'd driven toward town, Annie grappled with how to approach people who had every reason to hate a murdered man.

She realized that truth is always best.

Annie didn't sit down. She wasn't sure she would be welcome to sit down. "Death on Demand initially agreed to sponsor your brother's talk last night."

Joan's face was now carefully empty. She made no response.

Annie continued despite that resistant silence. "Rae Griffith came to the store Monday and invited me to sponsor Alex's talk. I was excited. He was a famous author. I thought I'd sell a lot of books." She saw understanding in a fellow shopkeeper's eyes, a good project, a good return on time and effort. "I hadn't seen the article in the *Gazette*. I read the article. Yesterday morning I withdrew."

"That was kind of you." Joan's tone was cautious.

"I don't like cruelty."

"I don't either." Joan gestured toward the molded chairs that faced the desk. "It's awfully nice of you to explain the connection."

Annie perched on the edge of a red chair.

Joan took a deep breath. "Very thoughtful of you." A pause. "I hadn't seen Alex in years."

"That's what his wife said. She came to see me this morning. She doesn't know any of you. I felt sorry for her." Sorry for Rae, scared for Marian. "Rae hoped someone he spoke to yesterday might know if he quarreled with anyone." Annie gambled. She didn't know specifically who Alex called, but family seemed likely. "Alex came to see you."

Joan picked up a letter opener with a turquoise handle, turned it over and over. "Did Alex tell her what he said to me?"

"I can't speak to that."

Joan's face was tight, her words clipped. "I offered hospitality to her. She's Alex's widow. I invited her to come home with us last night. And this is how she repays me. I gather she doesn't want to have anything to do with us. There won't be a funeral." Her voice was empty. "She said Alex didn't believe in funerals." Joan glanced toward the window that overlooked the harbor.

Annie knew she wasn't seeing the *Miss Jolene* at her berth or dolphins curving above a placid sea or the distant shape of a passing freighter.

Joan looked at Annie. "You've read *Don't Go Home.*" She didn't wait for an answer. "The funeral scene. That was how it was when Alex's mother died. She was Dad's second wife. He already had Heyward and George and me. Our mother left when George and I were eight and ten. Heyward was already in college. I always wondered whether Dad had something on her, if that's why she didn't get custody. Maybe she didn't give a damn." Joan's voice reflected nothing more than mild curiosity, as if she were chatting about someone she'd scarcely known. "About a year later, she died somewhere in Italy, we never knew exactly how. Dad married Jessica. She died—cancer—when Alex was seven. To George and me, he was a pest, always hanging around, butting in." Her gaze at Annie was rueful. "Looking back, I can see George and I ignored Alex. Heyward had a soft spot for him, kept in touch with him. Even years later. Maybe because Heyward and Lynn never had kids. George and I both were busy with our kids. Dad was remote from all of us. He died the summer after Alex finished high school. Heyward and George and I were all married. We sold the house. Alex went to Augusta to stay with Jessica's parents, then he went to Emory." Her face was thoughtful. "I wondered later, after the book came out, if Heyward talked about George and me with Alex. Heyward was always stiff and formal. He thought George drank too much. And . . ." Her gaze fell. "Heyward disapproved of"—a pulse flickered in her throat—"some of my friends."

Joan lifted a graceful hand to brush back a sprig of dark hair. "Ever since the story in the *Gazette*, I've wondered why Alex wanted to come back and tear lives apart, like an Aztec priest yanking out a living heart. Vindictive? Maybe. Heedless? Maybe. Or maybe he was willing to do whatever he had to do to get another book. What made him the way he was—handsome, brilliant, able to make any sentence sing? Why do people turn out the way they do? A twist of genes, choices. Sins of omission and commission. People are who they are. Heyward was judgmental. George drinks too much, runs around on his wife; his kids are a mess. Alex sucked the life out of everything around him. Maybe he couldn't feel other people's pain; maybe he had so much pain bottled up inside that he had to write to survive. I don't know. Heyward demanded too much of everyone around him. George was reckless and unstable. And Alex was watching . . ."

Joan made no mention of herself. Annie recalled the action in the novel. A drunken teenager hid a crime. A high school sports "accident" resulted in paraplegia. A fatal car accident after the money was gone. An unhappily married copywriter's affair led to a surprise pregnancy. A sister was unfaithful to her husband. Alex had indeed been watchful, learning secrets, keeping them until one day he took those lives and used them in his novel.

Joan's gaze challenged her. "However, all of this is hypothetical. People can say what they wish, believe what they wish. Death changes everything." She spoke without expression, as if merely stating a fact. Slowly tension eased out of her body. "No one now can make any claims about what may or may not have been in Alex's mind when he wrote the book. As for my conversation with Alex, I don't recall anything of interest to anyone else. If he offered lurid accusations to his wife about yesterday"—a shrug—"well, Alex dramatized everything. She should remember he wrote fiction."

"Miss Ella Peabody?"

"Yes'm."

"Officer H. Harrison, Broward's Rock Police. I'm calling to confirm that Neil Kelly resides in the garage apartment, formerly chauffeur's quarters, behind the home of Mr. and Mrs. Alex Griffith."

"Yes, ma'am."

"Miss Peabody, I am asking you to confirm information received from a confidential source. On the night of July eight, your car turned into the drive of the Griffith home in Buckhead—"

"I forgot my purse. That's the reason I came back."

"—and you followed the drive to the back. The drive curves around a line of pines. The garage isn't visible from the street. Lights were on in the bedroom of **the garage** apartment. The renter, Neil Kelly, reached up to close the curtains. He was embracing Rae Griffith. He was bare chested, apparently wearing only boxer shorts. Before the curtains closed, they were seen in a passionate embrace. Can you confirm this information?"

Her voice was small and tight. "It isn't any business of mine what—"

"Miss Peabody"—Hyla's voice was stern—"there is a criminal investigation under way into the murder of your employer, Alex Griffith. Are you aware Mr. Griffith was killed last night?"

A quick gasp. "Yes'm. I saw the story this morning on Channel 46. They had pictures of this real pretty place with pillars in front and rocking chairs, then they showed this smashed sliding glass door and a picture of Mr. Griffith in that white suit he liked to wear sometimes. I never been so shocked. He was always real nice to me, gave me a special bonus every Christmas."

"You understand that every citizen has an obligation to answer police inquiries honestly?"

"Yes'm, I do."

"All we are asking is for you to confirm or deny information received from a confidential source." Hyla suspected Ella was amazed at the call. Did she wonder who else might have been observing the garage apartment that night or did she link the information to her friend and confidante who worked across the street? Whichever, the request simply to confirm or deny freed her from feeling that she was betraying her mistress. "Did you observe the scene I have described?"

"Yes'm."

"Mr. Griffith was out of town that night."

"Yes'm."

"Mr. Kelly drives a red 2009 Mustang. Do you know if the car is currently at the address?"

"No'm. It hasn't been here since Tuesday. I saw Mr. Kelly put a suitcase in his trunk on Tuesday morning."

Marian held up her Leica, framed Billy Cameron standing on the steps in front of the police station. The light onshore breeze stirred his short, silvered blond hair. He was imposing, broad face with a strong jaw, solidly muscular in a short-sleeved white shirt and khaki trousers.

Reporters stood as near the steps as possible. Cameramen held videocams. A small crowd had gathered: curious residents, tourists enjoying proximity to drama.

Billy spoke slowly, clearly. ". . . and the autopsy confirms the initial report. Alex Griffith died from suffocation after he was either stunned or rendered unconscious by a crushing blow to the back of his head. The blow cracked the cranium and blood seeped into the interior of the brain. Another blow struck the right side of his face. Griffith was seated on a sofa. He was struck by a heavy piece of wood approximately two inches in circumference, a piece of live oak, which is a hardwood. Griffith slumped to his left. A cushion from the sofa was pressed against his face. The ME estimates he was dead within two minutes after he suffered the brain injury. No fingerprints were found on the stick or the pillow."

Two camera crews from Savannah jostled for advantage. A smooth-faced young woman with blond hair held out a mic. "Time of death?"

"Mr. Griffith died between approximately six thirty P.M. and eight oh nine P.M., when his body was—"

Marian edged even with the TV crew. "Chief, when was he last seen?"

Billy's gaze touched her, impersonal and professional. "His wife says she left Griffith alive at a quarter to seven. No one has admitted seeing him since then. Room service received a call from Suite 130 at seven seventeen—"

The TV reporters brightened. Something new. Maybe a good sound bite.

"—and attempted to deliver an order at seven thirty-four. Room service waiter knocked, received no answer."

A TV reporter called out, "Did Griffith make the call?"

"A man called from Suite 130." Billy was precise. "Room service greeted the caller as Mr. Griffith. The caller ordered one gin and tonic, one rum collins. Either Griffith placed the call or another man placed the call."

A rotund, balding reporter swiped sweat from his face. "Is the assumption that Griffith was entertaining a guest?"

"No assumptions. These are the possibilities: The order was placed by Griffith, which suggests he had a guest, who could have been either male or female. The fact that there was no answer when the order arrived makes it likely that Griffith was dead by that point. Or the order was placed by an unknown male, which could indicate that Griffith was already dead when the call was made. Or a male guest placed the order at Griffith's request. Any hotel guests, employees, or members of the public who observed anyone in the hallway of the east wing or near the patio of Suite 130 are asked to contact police."

"Chief"—the TV reporter poked a shoulder in front of Marian—"any evidence of robbery?"

"No."

Marian knew that nothing had been taken at the time of Alex's murder, but Billy apparently didn't intend to mention the briefcase that was stolen from the suite later that night.

The TV reporter pressed. "Drug deal gone wrong?"

Billy shook his head. "No drug paraphernalia was found at the scene. There is no evidence Griffith used drugs. According to his wife, he drank wine and gin, did not take drugs of any sort. Toxicology tests are being run to complete the record. Those findings will be released when they are available . . ."

Marian made notes, knew that any minute the question would be asked—

The sweaty reporter looked wilted in the midday heat, but his brown eyes bored into Billy's. "Looks like you've knocked out robbery and drugs as motives. Griffith ordering up drinks suggests he had company. Is this homicide considered personal?"

"It is possible that Mr. Griffith was acquainted with his killer."

The reporter was irritable. "Come on, Chief. Griffith—or somebody—ordered drinks. That sounds like Griffith knew his guest."

Billy nodded. "That is one possibility."

The reporter persisted. "Last week the local paper carried a story suggesting Griffith planned to tag people on the island as the 'inspiration' for his characters. Some of the characters in the novel are pretty tawdry. Are you checking out people who knew Griffith when he lived on the island?"

"We are making inquiries into Griffith's past."

The blond TV reporter thrust out her mic, a predatory expression on her lovely face. "Do you have a person of interest?"

Billy looked especially stolid.

Marian knew this indicated knowledge he had no intention of sharing. Her gut tightened. He wasn't looking her way. Was that deliberate?

Billy's voice was uninflected. "At this point we are pursuing information about individuals who may have been connected in some manner to Mr. Griffith. Thank you for your attention, ladies and gentlemen. We will offer an update tomorrow morning at ten." He gave a brisk nod, turned away.

As the front door closed behind him, the TV reporter smiled into the videocam. "Broward's Rock police today revealed that the murder of Southern author Alex Griffith may be linked to steamy scenes in his world-famous novel, scenes reportedly based on real individuals on this idyllic sea island where Griffith was brutally slain last night. Police have declined . . ."

Hyla Harrison studied the Georgia driver's license for Neil B. Kelly. Address: 107½ Ginger Lily Lane. DOB: May 6, 1986. Eyes: Brown. Height: 5'10". Weight: 146 lbs. For an instant photo, the likeness was good. Narrow forehead beneath curly hair. Thin, straight nose. Pointed cheekbones and chin. A bony face, eyes deep set.

Hyla squinted, imagining a wide-brimmed straw hat, a blond curly wig, aviator sunglasses, a fake mustache, and a couple of small gauze pads stuffed in each cheek.

Slowly, she nodded. She'd check the photo from the inn's security cam but those high cheekbones couldn't be disguised. She reached for her desk phone, glanced at a small pad with the description of the car registered to Neil B. Kelly. "Mavis, send out an alert for a red 2009 Mustang." Hyla's smile was satisfied. "Vanity license plate: CHARIOT. If found, do not stop or apprehend unless attempting to leave island. Maintain surveillance. Ascertain activities. Do not alarm suspect. Kelly may be a person of interest in the Griffith kill."

◆ ◆ ◆

Annie pushed the bell, smelled the cloying sweetness of a gardenia shrub flowering in a waist-tall blue vase on the front verandah. Gardenia shrubs flanked both sides of Lynn Griffith's porch. The fanlight over the Greek Revival front door sparkled with cleanliness.

The door swung in. Lynn Griffith stood in the shadowy hall. As always she was immaculately dressed. A gold-and-ivory-striped tunic hung loose over white narrow-legged slacks. Already tall with an imposing appearance, wearing jute and rope wedges gave her an added inch of height so that her wide blue eyes looked down on Annie.

"Annie, I wasn't expecting you." The voice was light and pleasant.

Annie knew she had been pleasantly but firmly reproved. One called before one came. There seemed to be a distinct distance between them.

"Lynn, I hope you can spare a moment. I promised Rae Griffith I would find out more about what Alex did yesterday." Annie had scored when she blandly announced Alex had visited his sister. Now for his sister-in-law . . . "We know he came to see you."

Lynn's face molded into a conventional expression of sorrow. "Such a shock." Her voice rose. "I couldn't believe it when that policeman made the announcement. I didn't know what to do. I thought perhaps I should stay"—her tone was earnest—"then I thought I didn't know anything that would matter to authorities and I didn't want to be in the way. I am still reeling. I can't believe Alex was killed at the Seaside Inn. That's not the kind of thing we expect here. Why, you'd think we were in Chicago. Though I understand he wasn't shot. I turned off the television this morning as I just knew it was going to be too graphic. Heyward always kept that kind of thing from me.

Won't you come in?" She held the door wide. "I doubt I can help, but, of course, I want to do everything I can for his widow. Not that we've ever met. Alex hadn't kept up with family in recent years. Poor, poor Alex. I was saddened—"

Annie stepped inside. Lynn closed the door. Their reflections wavered in the graying depths of an old mirror in an ornate gilded frame as Annie followed her through a wide doorway into the drawing room. Gold hangings added color to oyster gray walls. Lynn led the way to a brocaded sofa in a warm apricot tone, sank gracefully at one end, patted the sofa beside her.

"—truly saddened when I spoke to Joan and she told me there won't be a service. I don't think ashes scattered from a boat is the least bit fitting. But Alex has been gone for so many years and people do follow different paths, don't they?" The last was offered with a pitying shake of those perfect silver blond curls.

Annie felt overwhelmed by the scent of gardenia, obviously Lynn's perfume of choice. "You saw Alex yesterday?"

Lynn folded her hands together. "Wasn't that nice of him?"

Annie had a sense of bewilderment. According to Rae, Alex set out to taunt his prospective victims, make certain they were among the listeners at his evening event. "Nice?"

Lynn nodded energetically. "Of course, Heyward was so much older that we spent very little time with Alex. I almost feel as though I scarcely knew him. Still, I thought it showed a proper family feeling that he came by to visit with me." There was the slightest tinge of satisfaction in her sweet voice.

"I understand Alex used family background in writing his novel. Did he talk about that with you?"

Lynn's laughter was a trill of amusement. "Oh, I have to confess. I hope you won't hold it against me, being a bookseller, but I don't bother with books. I have so many interests. I've started a collection of cameos. Sometime I will have to show you my newest, though of course it isn't new. It's a carving in high relief of the goddess Ceres and the coral is the most glowing delicate peach color. By the famous Chicago jeweler Peacock in about 1910. The craftsmanship is exquisite. I simply adore her. I would have shown it to Alex, but he didn't stay long. As I say, just a little family hello, so kind of him." She came to her feet. "I don't know a thing about his book. Such a shame he didn't have a chance to give his talk. We all could have learned so much."

Marian did a little math, figured out when George was in high school. Marian's fingers flew over the keyboard as she accessed an index. It was very helpful that all the *Gazette*s back to 1980 were available online. It took time, almost an hour, before she found the stories.

TEENAGER REPORTED MISSING

Police announced this morning that the family of Lucy Galloway, 16, is seeking information about the teen, who was last seen by her parents Friday evening when she left home to spend the night with a friend.

Lucy told her mother, Jane Galloway, that she would be home midmorning Saturday. When she did not return as expected, Mrs. Galloway called the friend's home and was told that Lucy had not spent the night. Lucy was among a group of girls attending a movie at the Rialto Theater.

Lucy's friend said she slipped in and out of her seat several times to go out to the concession area. The last time she returned she told her friend she'd changed her mind about spending the night and she was going home early because the movie was boring.

Mrs. Galloway called a number of Lucy's friends but no one admitted seeing her after the movie. Lucy was driving a green 1994 Oldsmobile sedan. The island was experiencing occasional mist and there were patches of heavy fog.

Mrs. Galloway insists Lucy would not run away from home and that she was happy and looking forward to her junior year in high school.

Anyone with information as to her whereabouts is asked to contact the Broward's Rock Police Department or the Galloway family.

DEATH IN A LAGOON

According to police reports, Lucy Galloway, 16, apparently drowned in Ghost Lagoon sometime last Friday night. Police recovered the car Monday afternoon. The deep lagoon is in a remote area of a forest preserve. Miss Galloway was reported missing by her parents on Saturday.

John Elliot, 165 Crescent Drive, notified police when he saw tire tracks in the mud at a boat ramp. Elliot was jogging on a path that passed by the ramp. He jogs every morning and said the tire tracks weren't there Friday morning.

Police Chief Frank Saulter examined the tire tracks and knew the missing teenager's car had not been found. Saulter ordered an exploration of the lagoon. A dragging operation indicated a vehicle was submerged at a depth of twenty feet. The car, which proved to be the missing Oldsmobile, was pulled from the lagoon at 4:09 P.M. Monday.

According to police, the car, traveling at a high rate of speed, traveled onto the boat ramp, became airborne, and entered the water hood down. The car windows were open. Lucy Galloway's body was found in a second search. Police indicated she was not wearing a seat belt. Police cannot explain why the teen would have driven onto the boat ramp. However, the lane that leads to the ramp forks off another road through the preserve that has a reputation as a drag strip as it runs straight for about fifty yards.

NO EVIDENCE OF ALCOHOL

The drowning death of high school rising junior Lucy Galloway remains a mystery. Police today said toxicology tests revealed no traces of alcohol or drugs. How the teenager came to drive her car onto a boat ramp and into a remote lagoon is unknown.

A friend of Galloway's, who declined to be named, said she has no idea what caused the accident but she remembers Lucy was always up for a dare and liked to drive fast and often didn't wear a seat belt. "It's real sad. I thought something was up that night at the movie because she sounded kind of excited when she said she was leaving."

Marian had covered a lot of stories. More than that, she was the mom of a teenager. She could write this script. How about a stroll into the lobby and a good-looking senior—George Griffith wasn't paunchy and red-faced when he was young—swaggered up to Lucy. Maybe he was already half drunk, slipping bourbon into a tall Coke. Maybe he said, *How about we split this place, go out and take a drive.* Somehow they went in her car, not his, and he was the macho man—*Hell, I'll drive, I'll show you some fun*—and off they went . . .

7

Hyla Harrison tried to look like a tourist, laid-back and unofficial, but it was hard to shed the impassive face and shoulders-back posture she presented when in uniform. Her casual clothes definitely weren't tourist flamboyant: a crisp lemon blouse, khaki Bermudas, well-kept running shoes. She rode her secondhand Harley Street 500 with competence and in compliance with all rules of the road. She rode sedately but she quivered with excitement at her assignment. She carried with her a proud memory of Billy Cameron's praise. "Excellent work, Officer. You'll be pleased to know fresh fingerprints were found in Room 128. Light switches. Toilet handle and seat. TV remote. Bedside radio alarm. You sense a connection to the murder. They will be checked against unidentified prints from the murder scene. If there is a match, we are going to have evidence, thanks to you. Moreover, thanks to you, we may have a suspect in Neil Kelly. He could be on the island. All officers have been alerted to be on the lookout for the car. See if you can find him."

As she steered the small Harley down Main Street in the momentary clog of traffic that indicated the ferry had just docked, Hyla checked out parked cars. She slowed near Coble's Drugstore but the red car turned out to be a Dodge. It took twenty minutes to explore every nook and cranny near the harbor, including the parking areas near Fish Haul Pier and the Pavilion Park and the small lot near the lone hotel. She eased off onto a graveled path in the park, straddled the bike, and considered. If she were a stranger to the island, running scared, trying to avoid notice, where would she go?

M arian hit pay dirt as soon as she opened the 2001 Broward's Rock High School yearbook. The dedication read:

> *To Michael Smith*
> *In admiration for his courage*

The cheers ended on a foggy Friday night in November as classmates watched in shock when Michael Smith was unable to get up after a play ended in the football game against Chastain High School.

Michael suffered a neck injury that resulted in paralysis. His classmates have worked all year to raise money for his care. Soft-spoken and gentle, Michael says he has no memory of the play that brought him down.

Marian found the football page, noted names of players, including Alex Griffith and Eddie Olson. Turning to the *Gazette*'s database, she found several stories about the injured player. Cheerleader Kristin Akers described the moment: "It was a huge dog pile and all these players climbed on and I think Michael was near the bottom, but it was so foggy you could barely make out the players. We are all brokenhearted for Michael. He was our best tennis player. He'd been accepted to switch to a tennis academy on Hilton Head for juniors. We were all excited for him."

A soft ping announced a text. Marian glanced at her cell. *Meet me for lunch, Parotti's. A.*

W arren Foster took a tiny sip. Perfection. He'd adored daiquiris ever since he and Mother made that cruise to the Caribbean. Cuba was off-limits then and everything he'd heard about the tours people now took didn't sound appealing. He did so dislike run-down cities and apparently Havana was just as drab as an old house shoe. But it might be soulful to go to Cuba, a pilgrimage to daiquiris and, of course, to Hemingway, who loved daiquiris, too. To visit Hemingway's home would be splendid, so easy to picture him there. Such a virile man.

Warren carried the chilled flute with its golden contents to a sumptuous white sofa in his ruby-walled living room. Mother, may her soul R.I.P., would likely have objected to the color scheme, but ruby simply spoke to his imagination and Mother always admired his imagination. He hummed a little tune, almost giddy with delight as he contemplated the evening ahead. But he must remain practical. As soon as he finished his libation, he would reconnoiter.

A nnie loved Parotti's Bar and Grill whether on a bleak winter day when the wind whistled and the most excitement would be a long table with retirees playing checkers or, as now, jammed with customers in the height of the season. She eased her way past a gaggle of sunburned tourists, smelled coconut oil and sweat. The old-fashioned jukebox blared Glenn Miller's "In the Mood." Owner Ben Parotti had inherited the 1940s jukebox from an uncle and what was good enough for Uncle Travis was good enough for Ben.

Marian waved from a table for two near the entrance to the bait shop. Off-islanders experienced a qualm when they saw—and smelled—the bait shop, which offered coolers filled with chicken necks and chunks of black bass, squid, grouper, and snapper. A well-smeared blackboard behind the bar proclaimed: SPECIAL TODAY—SALTED EEL—$3 PER LB. Inch-deep sawdust covered the floor. The bait shop was much as it had been for the past fifty years, but after Ben married a tea shop owner on the mainland and brought her to the sea island, she transformed the main eating area into a genteel replica of her shop, with cloth-covered tables and bright menus.

Annie dropped into the chair opposite Marian.

The reporter gave her a searching look. "No luck?"

Annie wondered if it was that apparent that she was discouraged. Maybe it was time to try for a little inscrutability, the quality author John Marquand celebrated in his imperturbable Mr. Moto. But Marian knew her too well to try for false cheer. "I talked to Joan Turner and Lynn Griffith." Quickly she recounted the conversations.

Marian's smile was grim. "I'm not surprised that Joan Turner figured out she's in the catbird seat—all of them are." At Annie's blank look, Marian elaborated. "You never hung around a sports desk in a newsroom. Old baseball term. At least, that's what I was told. Used by Red Barber to describe a batter who's seeing the ball like it's a slow-motion grapefruit. Anyway, I'd say the catbird seat's pretty damn crowded right now. They're all home free—Joan and George and Lynn and Eddie. It's not like Alex had already written his tell-all. If he knew things, saw things that could louse up people's lives, well, he's dead now."

But there was no lift in Marian's voice.

Annie was afraid she understood. The only claim that could ever be proved beyond question was the paternity of the child resulting from a love affair. Marian could not rest easy as long as a search continued for Alex's killer. If suspicion ever turned on her, if there was a hint that Marian was Louanne in *Don't Go Home*, the question could be asked, "Who is David's father?"

Annie reached across the table, gripped her friend's arm.

Marian turned her hand, gave Annie a reassuring squeeze, managed a gallant bright smile. She looked past Annie. "Yo, Ben. Full house today."

Ben Parotti skidded to a stop by their table. Five feet, four inches tall on a good day, he looked like a harried gnome but he was expansive. "Three fishing charters, plus some eco-specialists—that's what they called themselves—over here to ponder sea turtle eggs, and I told them we keep the island dark as a witch's hat at night. We love the bloomin' sea turtles. What's good for you today?"

Marian ordered spinach quiche and sweet tea. Annie selected the grilled flounder sandwich with Thousand Island dressing, plain tea.

As Ben turned away, Marian raised an eyebrow. "I won't tell Max if you order a fried fish sandwich."

Max encouraged healthy eating and she'd chosen the grilled fillet because it made her feel in an obscure way that at least she was doing something he approved of. Usually, as Marian well knew, she ordered crisply fried flounder. Annie loved the cornmeal crust, which was seasoned with a dash of paprika. She met Marian's concerned gaze with a bright smile. "Can't be in a rut."

Marian said, almost angrily, "I heard about your promise to Max. You shouldn't have agreed to help me."

Annie spoke firmly. "You are *our* friend." She emphasized the possessive. "He'll be glad if I can help. Though"—she sighed—"right now I don't see I've made any headway at all."

Marian reached across the table, gave Annie's arm a squeeze. "I'll tell Max it's all my fault. But you know how much it means to me that you're standing by me. And maybe between the two of us, we will find out what happened. I'm hoping what I found will lead somewhere. The tip from Warren Foster was right on. Here." She pushed several sheets of paper toward Annie.

Annie first read the stories about Lucy Galloway. She was almost finished with Marian's factual summary of Michael Smith's injury when Ben returned with their orders.

She took several bites of the sandwich and realized grilled was good, too. *Max, I wish you were here. Or at least, if not right this minute, soon. I mean, I have to keep helping Marian* . . . She read the last sentence about Michael, looked up at Marian. "Warren Foster claimed as soon as he read *Don't Go Home*, he immediately knew it was Eddie Olson who hurt Michael Smith. I'll use that when I talk to Eddie. And I think I can rattle George Griffith."

Marian looked uneasy. "I don't have a good feeling about you taunting somebody who may have killed Alex."

"I'll be careful. I promise." *Max, I won't be stupid.*

"Max will kill me if anything happens to you."

"Then I better make sure nothing does."

Hyla made several calls. Four single males, none using the names of either Neil Kelly or Robert Haws, had checked into some of the seedier accommodations on the north end of the island that morning. Two matched the description of Neil Kelly. Hyla headed out on her Harley.

At her first stop, the manager glanced at Hyla's printout of Kelly's driver's license. "You just called? A guy by himself, you said? Sorry, sweetie, his honey just showed up with a couple of kids and they're out by the pool."

Hyla was thorough. She strolled around a clump of palmetto shrubs, glanced at the blondish man, in his late twenties, who was pulling a toddler holding on to a plastic ring, hoped the murky green water had enough chlorine to keep it safe, and turned away.

It was a quarter mile farther to Mickey's Fish Camp, which boasted a half dozen ramshackle cabins on stilts. The balding, portly manager took a look at the photo, nodded. "Eight." He studied Hyla. "Seen you around. No uniform today. There gonna be any trouble?"

"Surveillance only. You never talked to me, right?"

The manager nodded. "I'm in my office, watching bass fishing on my black-and-white, sipping a cool one. Speaking of cool, just kind of talking to myself, there's a clump of pines next to 8. Plenty of shade in there. Got a good view."

Warren Foster didn't relish the heat, nudging ninety-five. The languorous air steamed, could be seen shimmering in sunlight. The tabby ruins of the old plantation home only hinted at the magnificent 1790s home that had once stood there. A portion of the walls of the central house remained almost intact. Behind the main house were tumbled walls of an overseer's home and slave cabins. The sun was high so the tall pines that rimmed the ruins offered no shade.

The local historical preservation society kept the grounds cleared and maintained the oyster shell paths. Warren wallowed in the haunting quality of the ruins, imagining the sound of a harpsichord, a melody played by fingers long since turned to dust. The low cry of a mourning dove mingled with the shrill caw of a crow. There were tales of loves lost, duels fought, a fortune frittered away. The ruins were called Widow's Haunt. Theodosia Ryan's husband was lost at sea in 1910. She became a recluse, dressed always in black with a large black hat and veil. She was found dead one winter morning half submerged in a lagoon. It was discovered after her death that the long black flowing clothing covered an emaciated body. There were no survivors and the house and grounds fell into disrepair.

Warren nodded in pleasure. The site was perfect. Except, of course, for ever-present swirls of no-see-ums, the little biting midges that made outdoors a misery in areas not heavily impregnated with insecticides. But an artist sacrifices comfort for perfection. Tonight there would be a full moon, light enough for visitors to find their way. Now to find just the right spot . . .

He walked several yards to a huge spreading live oak. Spanish moss hung from the limbs, delicate and fragile. Leaves crackled underfoot. He shook his head, turned away, gazed again at the portion that remained of the main structure. Ah . . . Moving quickly despite the heat, he came around the corner of a tabby wall. A large square opening had once been a window. If he stood behind the wall, he could see anyone who approached but he would be out of sight.

Annie squinted against the brilliant sun, wished she had thought to wear her floppy brimmed hat. Her sleeveless lacy white blouse and pale yellow linen skirt were perfect for the store, not so great in the afternoon glare.

Eddie Olson, face red beneath a worn ball cap, was caulking a seam in a dingy wooden boat elevated on blocks. With a sharp-edged tool in his right hand, he jammed a strand of looped cotton into the boat's seam.

Annie came within a few feet.

His head jerked toward her. The hand with the tool remained pressed against the strand of cotton.

Annie knew she'd made very little noise as she worked her way through the boatyard. Did he have unusually acute hearing to pick up muted footsteps over the squeal of gulls and the slap of water against the pilings of a pier? Or was he tuned to a high pitch of awareness, alert for any hint of danger?

His dark eyes were unreadable. Sweat slid down his heavy face. His T-shirt clung to him. He loomed beside the boat, strength evident in bulky shoulders, massive chest, powerful legs. "Yeah?" His tone was brusque.

She stopped only two feet away. "Alex Griffith came to see you yesterday."

"If you got a boat to be fixed, I can help you. Otherwise I'm busy."

"Alex was on the football field the night Michael Smith was hurt."

He looked back at the boat, pushed, and another cotton loop was locked into the seam.

Gulls screamed. In the distance, a blast from the horn of the *Miss Jolene* signaled her departure from the dock.

Annie took a step nearer, close enough to see the thickness of his neck, the shoulder muscles evident beneath the sweaty shirt. "In Alex's book, a Scout fell from a rope swing. Kenny had sawed on the rope, weakened it so that it broke when the Scout was at the highest point of the swing."

"Yeah." He spoke over his shoulder. "But that happened in a book."

"I did some research and found out what happened to Michael.

But you and I know his injury wasn't an accident. You grabbed Michael's face mask, yanked, broke his neck, made him a paraplegic."

The big head slowly turned.

She stared at that blunt, formidable face.

Full lips moved in the slightest trace of a smile. "Who says?"

"Warren Foster. He knew immediately when he read the book that you were Kenny and the Scout was Michael."

"Warren." His tone was musing. "I haven't seen him in a while. He was always sniveling about something. Nobody paid any attention to him."

"Alex was on the field. Did he warn you he was going to describe that night at his talk?"

"Funny." There was no laughter in his eyes. "I was surprised when Alex dropped by. I guess we talked about old times. But I'm not much to think about the past. And now"—his big body relaxed—"Alex isn't thinking at all."

As Marian drove to Warren's, she passed the small cottage she shared with her son. Three bedrooms, combo living-dining room, small kitchen. They used one bedroom as a study for her and a work space for David, plenty of room for his watercolors and easel and a good, plain deal table where he was always working on a sketch. David would be home Sunday. He would know something was wrong. Kids always knew. She felt a wrench deep inside. Would Billy Cameron call her or come by the newsroom? Maybe he'd be waiting when she got home tonight. If he knew about Alex, if that information ever made its way into a report, somehow, someway, word would slip out. Word always did.

Whether anyone on the island had any inkling of her connection to Alex was one of the reasons she wanted to talk to Warren. If anyone would know of the tiniest whispers, it would be Warren.

Oh, David . . .

She was pleased to see Warren's low-slung cobalt blue Bugatti parked in the shade of a live oak. Ever since his mother's death a few years ago, Warren had spent money with abandon. She'd heard rumors that he indulged himself in various unsavory pursuits off island, murmuring to a mutual friend, "Ah, the ennui. I am always seeking a new experience."

The front door opened before she was halfway up the immaculate steps of the Greek Revival mansion. The Foster family had known wealth since time immemorial: indigo, cotton, several times an infusion of money from Northern heiresses.

Marian had attended several soirees, as Warren billed them, in the spacious drawing room. The ruby walls, quite different from the pale gray when his mother was alive, reminded her of the interior of a fortune-teller's tent, vaguely oppressive, suggestive of hooded glances, faintly heard whispers. She didn't contrast the opulence of the Foster house with her small home. She was comfortable with her world. Warren Foster was wealthy. She was not quite poor, but bills could be a struggle. She never envied anyone. She had David. She had her work. At least that was true for now . . .

Warren waited in the doorway. "Marian, my dear. What a delightful surprise. Won't you have a drink with me? Or are you tracking me down for a tabloid exposé?" His tone was arch.

He reminded Marian of a stork—sharp head, slender body, thin legs. She was always surprised to remember that he wasn't old, though he had old mannerisms. Perhaps too many years under the thumb of his domineering mother. Now his eyes were bright, a slight pink flush stained his long face. He was stylish in a white guayabera shirt, beige linen trousers, and sandals.

"Annie Darling told me you have some insights on Alex Griffith and—"

"Oh, my dear, yes." He took her elbow and his hand was clammy against her bare skin. "Do come this way. We'll have daiquiris—my dear, I make the very best daiquiris—and I'll reminisce. You can bring me up-to-date on what those stalwart policemen are doing. I can't wait to hear." Sniff sniff.

The Harley was tucked deep into the shadows of the pines. Hyla, too, would be indistinct in the shadows. As the manager had indicated, she had a clear view of Cabin 8. The lights were on.

She waited patiently.

Gnats buzzed. No-see-ums swarmed. She swatted away several mosquitoes. Her patience was rewarded twenty minutes later. She recognized Neil Kelly from his driver's license photo. He no longer affected a disguise, appeared trim and athletic and in a hurry. He rattled down the front steps, jumped into his red Mustang. Hyla was on her Harley and ready to roll as the car reached the end of the tourist court drive. She waited until she wouldn't be noticeable in his rearview mirror, set out in pursuit.

Dust plumed behind the red Mustang as it bucketed ahead on an infrequently used road that didn't boast a sign.

Hyla stayed far enough behind to avoid the choking cloud; in a corner of her mind she added *wash Harley* to her to-do list. The road dead-ended at the northern tip of the island where an eroding bluff overlooked the water. Gurney Point. She didn't spare time to think about the name. She wasn't an island native but she knew the area.

They'd staked it out a few times for drug busts. The point was named after somebody. Who knew, who cared? But so far as she was aware, Neil Kelly was a stranger to the island. Maybe he'd Googled a map on his cell. Whatever, he must be seeking solitude.

Pines crowded thickly on either side of the dirt road. She remembered a narrow overgrown lane that led to an abandoned cabin about a hundred yards from Gurney Point. They'd picked up some off-island smugglers at that cabin last winter . . .

She slowed, swerved, followed a faint path into the woods, aiming to reach the point without alerting Kelly. Her 500 wasn't designed for off-road so she took her time, watching for fallen branches, ignoring the whip of encroaching ferns. Clouds of insects swirled and curved and zoomed around her. She reached the clearing that held the cabin, stopped, rested the Harley on its kickstand. She waited to be sure the Mustang wasn't headed for the cabin. The only other open area was at the end of the road. She opened a front storage compartment, pulled out a pocket camcorder, slid it into a back pocket. She skirted the cabin ruins, then plunged into the woods, heading for road's end. She had a good sense of direction though the thick overhead canopy blocked a view of the sun, surrounded her with murky dimness. The onshore breeze stirred the tops of the pines. Birds chittered and cawed and twittered. Her head jerked at a crashing noise to her left and she glimpsed a tawny doe followed by a gangly fawn.

Hyla heard the rumble of surf before she reached the edge of the pines. At this end of the island, ocean butted hard against the headland. Bent trees dangled seaward as earth eroded beneath them. Water swirled over and around reddish-brown boulders at the base of a ten-to-twelve-foot bluff.

Hyla scanned the open area past the pines. Not much cover. She hesitated, then ducked across an open space, plunged beneath the branches of an enormous live oak. She pulled herself up onto a low limb. In a few minutes she was high above the ground with a clear view of the bluff, the surging water, the spume from the rocks, but well hidden in the thickly leafed middle of the tree.

She pulled out the camcorder, checked it, waited.

The red Mustang nosed out of the woods, came to the end of the road, stopped.

Hyla began filming.

Neil Kelly got out of the Mustang. Tousled brown hair, narrow bony face, well built, not tall but muscular. His face was clear in the bright sunlight on the point. He gazed all around. He looked smart, scared, uneasy. The wind tugged at his polo, whipped dust around his feet. He walked to the point, moving cautiously. A misstep would see him crashing down into the water.

Hyla shifted on the branch, steadied the camcorder in her hand. Excellent side view.

Abruptly he yanked up his shirt, pulled a gun free from the waistband of his trousers.

Hyla's hand on the camera never moved despite her shock. She had only seconds to see the weapon before he raised his arm and threw, putting so much force into the effort that he almost lost his balance. The gun arched in a high trajectory, then curved down and down to splash into roiling water and disappear.

Kelly turned and ran to the Mustang, flung himself into the driver's seat. The motor roared, the car swung around.

Hyla pulled her cell from her pocket. "Subject of interest in red Mustang departing Gurney Point. Pick up at exit onto Larrimore Road." Hyla kept her eyes on the area where the gun had entered the water, some fifteen feet east of a craggy boulder. "Subject disposed of handgun in water. Suggest search and retrieval. Remaining here until backup arrives unless instructed otherwise." She listened, then clicked off. A cruiser would be waiting when the car reached the main road. Surveillance would continue. Wasn't it time to put out a pickup order for Neil Kelly?

Warren tipped the crystal flute, eyed the contents critically. "Not enough for a mouse, much less a man." He downed a remaining inch of golden liquid, reached for the silver cocktail shaker on the end table, refilled his glass. He gave Marian a pitying look. "Another time when you aren't working, I will make daiquiris especially for you. But"—he gave a delicate shudder—"it wouldn't do to chase Dr Pepper. Your palate is ruined for now." He took an appreciative sip. "Oh, my dear. Delicious." He lifted the flute. "Here's to crime. Definitely the high point of the summer, don't you think?" Sniff sniff.

She kept her face pleasant, unrevealing. A toast to crime and Alex twisted in death on a sofa. She ached to tell Warren he was loathsome, but she didn't have that luxury.

He leaned back, crossed his feet. "The high point of the summer. Up to now. But perhaps it will get even better."

"Better?" Her tone was sharp despite her intention to remain impassive, blotting up fragments of lives as he prattled.

His face was now more flushed. His eyes glistened, long thin fingers drummed on the arm of the white couch. "I know more than anyone realizes." He nodded portentously. "I know where all the bodies are buried. Joan's little affair. George's wild night. Lynn's windfall from insurance. Of course, Heyward had to die before she got the pile. And there's Eddie, a hulking creature. I knew who was who the minute I read the novel. And here we are, Alex dead and somebody did the deed. Ring around the rosies, who plucked the posies? I think I can flush out our partridge. Dear Mother, she taught English, you know. She'd scold me—'Warren, don't mix your metaphors'—but you get my point. I have a little plan. What would you think if I brought you a picture tomorrow of Alex's murderer?" Sniff sniff.

Marian felt the hairs on the back of her neck stir. There was something repellent in his excitement.

"A picture?"

Slow emphatic nods.

"Be careful, Warren." She blurted out the warning. "If you know who killed him, go to the police. Right now."

His smile was huge. "Got your attention, didn't I? You know the cable news shows are running things about Alex day and night. They love murders of someone famous. If I get that picture, I'll be on all the programs."

Marian felt the burn of nausea in her throat. Alex dead and this malicious man talking about murder as if it were fun, as if it were a game. She came to her feet. "Alex shouldn't be dead." She had a wisping memory of coming into strong, enveloping arms, the warmth of Alex's body, the wild elation of passion. "He shouldn't be dead." No matter what he'd done, no matter anything and everything, he'd been alive and vital and once she'd loved him. She turned away, moved blindly toward the hall, her eyes filmed with tears.

"Why, Marian"—Warren's voice followed her, like an old dancer on mincing feet—"I haven't had a chance to ask about those years in Atlanta. You and Alex worked on the same newspaper, didn't you?" Sniff sniff.

8

George Griffith rose from behind his desk. A dark blue Tommy Bahama shirt with a light blue floral pattern emphasized the brightness of his red face. Loose lips spread in a smile that didn't reach pale brown eyes. "Annie." His voice exuded warmth and eagerness. "Are you and Max looking for a new house? Girl, you look wonderful." His chubby hands outstretched.

Annie pulled away from his sweaty handclasp as soon as possible. She didn't know which she found more insulting, the odious use of "girl" or his utter lack of awareness that the term was offensive. She kept a smile on her face. "Actually, I'm looking for information."

George gestured toward a small sofa. "Come sit down and talk to me."

She dropped into a chintz-covered chair that faced the sofa, said cheerily, "Much nicer if I can see you. You are looking very well." On a par with a regular perched on a barstool: bleary eyes, droopy red-veined cheeks, unmistakable paunch of a bloated abdomen against the stylish shirt.

George smoothed his slightly too long black hair. "Good of you to say so. What can I do for you?"

"How did you persuade Lucy to let you drive that night?"

George stared at her, reddened eyes glazed, mouth slack, lips twitching. Perhaps he'd started his morning with a shot of bourbon. The hands lying on the sofa trembled.

"I don't know"—the words came with struggling breaths between them—"what you are talking about."

"Oh, George." Her tone was chiding. "Of course you do. Alex wrote about you and yesterday he came to see you. He told you that he was going to describe that night and everyone would know what happened to Lucy."

George wrapped his arms tight across his paunch.

"He said he hadn't told anyone."

Annie shrugged. "I don't think many people know."

George pressed his trembling hands together. "Anybody can have an accident. He laughed at that." George's voice shook. "The fog was really thick and getting thicker. Lucy kept tugging at my arm. She wanted me to slow down but I thought I had a straight run. She jerked real hard and I pulled to keep going straight. That's why the car went left. That's what happened. All of a sudden there was a jolt. She screamed. I held on to the wheel, then it was all up and down and Lucy screaming and I was in the water. I came up, spitting and choking. There wasn't any sound anywhere. I kept going under and then I was clawing through the reeds and I fell face down on the ground."

"Did you try to find Lucy?"

His gaze slid away. He pushed up from the couch.

Annie tensed, ready to clamber behind the chair, shove it in his way, scream.

George stumbled to his desk, yanked out a drawer. He lifted out a bottle of whiskey, unscrewed the cap, took one hefty drink, another.

Annie was at the door.

He put the bottle on the desk, braced himself with both hands. His face suddenly took on a cunning, careful expression. "Was I talking to you? I don't remember. Sometimes I imagine things. If I said anything, it was all gibberish, didn't mean—"

Annie stepped into the hallway, closed the door behind her.

The breeze tugged at Billy Cameron's shirt. He shouted, "Keep the rope taut. There's a twenty-foot drop-off west of the rocks."

Hyla Harrison shaded her eyes. "Lou's in the right spot." She'd shown him as clearly as she could, estimated the space between the rock and the entry point of the handgun.

The motorboat rocked in swells. An officer in the stern kept a rein as the thick Manila line slowly played out.

Billy squinted against the glitter of the sun off the surging water.

Hyla knew he was concerned about Lou fighting a tricky current, staying clear of the rocks, using an underwater light in his search. Lou was like an eel. No one on the island was more at home in the water. "He'll be fine."

"Yeah." Billy kept his gaze on the murky green water with irregular whitecaps.

Hyla watched, too. "Are you continuing surveillance?"

Billy understood the point of her question. "For now. We can always pick Kelly up. We can figure he's the widow's boyfriend, but we don't have any evidence there's been any contact between them even though, convenient, yeah, he got a room right next to the Griffith suite, plus he used an assumed name when he checked in. If we're right, if he was the voice on the Griffith phone to room service, if he killed Griffith or if she did and he came in a little while later to make the call when she was out on the terrace to give her an alibi, we need to be able to prove they were in contact. Counsel could always claim, 'One of life's coincidences . . . Broward's Rock is a popular vacation destination . . . prosecutor has no proof Mrs. Griffith and Mr. Kelly were aware the other was on the island.' We'll catch them together at some point and then we'll have some questions."

They stood in silence for a few minutes, crows cawing, seagulls circling near the boat.

Hyla cleared her throat. "Why throw the gun away? Griffith wasn't shot."

Billy's smile was grim. "Does Kelly usually carry a gun? We'll find out. Does he have a license? Maybe he—or she—picked the gun up somewhere on the sly, an estate sale, a pawnshop that doesn't care where firearms come from. Maybe the original plan was to shoot Griffith. We may never know. I only know one thing. Neil Kelly is scared as hell or he'd never have tossed the gun into the ocean."

A nnie settled on the porch swing after a delectable supper—it was supper without Max—of local shrimp, tiny and pink, with her own homemade cocktail sauce, and her favorite nachos: tortilla chips topped with black beans, green chilies, jalapeño jack cheese, and sour cream.

She pulled her cell from her pocket. There was a call she had to make, which she dreaded.

"Hello." Rae Griffith's voice was thin, tight. Scared.

"Annie Darling. I went all around the island today. I talked to several people. I wish I could say I found something out. But I can't."

"Can't? Or won't?" There was an edge of hysteria.

Annie knew suddenly that Rae had been at the Seaside Inn all day, perhaps pinning too much hope to Annie's promise. Waiting and knowing that only feet from where she sat, her husband had died. Waiting and imagining that the local police were conniving to ensnare her, perhaps coming at any minute. Waiting, alone, friendless, vulnerable.

"I tried my best. You have to believe that. I want to find out what happened. I'm going to keep looking. I don't know what I can do next, but I'll check out some other ideas tomorrow." Because somewhere on the island Marian was terrified, too. "Look, maybe you should move out of that room."

"No."

Again that abrupt refusal. The idea that Rae was nearer to Alex there was harder to understand now. She could take his things, move to any room in the hotel, be free of the brooding horror beyond the closed bedroom door. "Have you had dinner? I could come—"

"No." Now there was an urgency to her refusal. "I mean, you're nice to offer. I don't want to see anyone. Maybe tomorrow. If you know anything, maybe you'll tell me or go to the police. Anyway, thank you. Maybe tomorrow will be better." Rae hung up.

Annie slid the cell into her pocket. Tomorrow. Tomorrow, she would burrow deeper. Ask Joan about the passage in *Don't Go Home*. Find out more about the day Heyward Griffith died, find a way to pierce Lynn's composure.

Warren gave a delicate shudder as he stepped into the phone booth. Not a nice scent. Reminiscent of something dead washed up on the beach. The outer handle had been sticky to his touch. Had some grimy child devoured cotton candy, then used the booth for hide-and-seek? But the disagreeable odor and undeniable grubbiness added to the ambience of a phone booth. A phone booth, shades of Sam Spade.

Positively antediluvian. Thank heaven for the booth, a relic from a time that now seemed far distant. Did anyone ever use it? Perhaps only for clandestine calls. How thrilling to make a clandestine call.

He pulled the folding door as far as it would go. It was almost dusk, the figures passing on the boardwalk indistinct between tall lampposts. In July tourists wandered up and down the several streets that composed downtown, picnicked in Pavilion Park, watched the sunset from Fish Haul Pier.

He pulled a small card from his shirt pocket. He was rather proud of the numbers, all cell numbers plucked from this island directory or that. He had a very useful collection of directories from clubs, charities, churches. He lacked a cell number for the widow. That would require a call to the Seaside Inn. Cell phones almost always assured reaching the intended party. A message left on a cell would be heard by the chosen recipient. However, reaching the widow required calling the hotel. No matter. He could speak in a normal tone when he called and asked to be connected to Mrs. Griffith. The clerk would have no means of knowing his voice. Once he was connected, then he would affect a whispery voice. Of course an anonymous call must be made in a hoarse indistinguishable voice.

He pulled a handful of quarters from a pocket sagging with change, stacked the shiny coins on the scarred shelf beneath the cumbersome phone. The boy at the drugstore had given him an odd look when he asked for ten dollars in change, but he wanted to be certain he had enough to make all the calls.

Warren preened at his stroke of genius. He wasn't sure how the idea had come. As he'd pondered the undeniable truth that someone he'd seen that night at the Seaside Inn was fresh from the kill—had only moments before caught Alex unaware, struck him, held a pillow over his mouth and nose—he'd felt there had to be some way to flush out the quarry . . . and then in a rush of images, he'd known the answer. One of them certainly was guilty so why not call all of them? Absolutely a stroke of genius.

Now . . . which one should he contact first? He had his list. The widow. Joan Turner. Lynn Griffith. George Griffith. Eddie Olson. And, added at the last moment, Marian Kenyon. There had been something in Marian's face when he mentioned the newspaper in Atlanta. He wriggled with delight. Could Marian possibly be Louanne in the novel? Not a woman he would have thought appealing to Alex, but who ever knew in matters of sex? She certainly had a son the right age and there was something in her face . . .

Which one first?

Darkness was thickening outside the booth. The darker the better. Perhaps he'd invite his listeners to come at ten-minute intervals, starting at nine o'clock. It would be interesting if more than one came. One definitely would come, but the others, the innocents, would likely be tempted to find out who had called them and be ready to deny any visit to Alex's suite. He felt a moment's misgiving. He wouldn't know the identity of Alex's murderer if more than one responded to his calls. He shrugged. But he'd certainly have a more exciting evening than roulette in the back room at the country club. He lifted the receiver, picked up several coins. At the very least he'd get some pictures that would be proof of his venturesome night. He murmured aloud, "The wicked flee . . ."

Marian massaged one temple. Ever since Alex's death—Alex's murder—she'd struggled with a dull throbbing headache. She remembered the porch of a wooden cabin at Lake Chatuge, fog wreathing the panorama of the Blue Ridge Mountains, the feel of Alex's hand on her wrist. A slight tug and she'd stepped into his arms.

"Stop it." Her voice was harsh, loud in the silence of the house empty except for her. Remembering either the good or the bad was useless. Alex was dead. David was alive. David was coming home Sunday—

The ring of her cell signaled a call from a stranger. She had special rings for David and Craig, for the *Gazette*, for friends. She slowly took the phone from the pocket of her slacks, feeling dull, weary, defeated.

Unknown Caller.

The phone rang until it stopped.

Marian pushed up from the rattan sofa, moved like an old woman into the kitchen, poured unsweetened tea over ice cubes. She opened the cupboard, found headache tablets, drank one down with the cold tea. She knew why her head hurt. She was waiting for Billy Cameron to knock at her door or walk toward her desk at the *Gazette*.

She'd lie.

But Billy knew her.

She was afraid of Billy, afraid he would know from the way she answered, from the lack of inflection when she spoke. He might be suspicious, but there was no evidence linking her to Alex's murder. Her lips pressed together. Not unless they'd fingerprinted the remains of the hurricane lamp. But the lamp was broken Wednesday morning. She felt a flicker of dark amusement . . . "lamp was broken" . . . the passive voice. She avoided the passive voice when she wrote. Now she avoided remembering the weight of the lamp and the mad rush of fury when she grabbed the metal frame and flung the lamp at Alex. Nimble Alex. He'd gotten out of the way. *He always got out of the way, didn't he? Until now.* Alex was killed Wednesday night. There was nothing to link her to the room where he died. Still, if Billy named her as a person of interest, a judge might order a DNA test for David's paternity . . .

Marian picked up the glass and carried it into the living room. She'd call David. See what he and Craig were doing tonight, tell him she loved him, keep her voice light and cheerful. She sank onto the sofa, picked up the cell, turned it on. Voice mail. She flicked, tapped, ready to delete, then sat rigid, listening to a breathy whisper.

"I saw you slip into Alex's suite."

The whisper was soft and silky, insubstantial, unpleasant.

"We can talk about it tonight. I'll wait for you." Sniff sniff. "Widow's Haunt. Nine o'clock." Sniff sniff. "If you don't come, I'll tell the police."

The call ended.

Marian sat still, arms hunched, scarcely breathing.

Warren drove into the west lot of the Seaside Inn and pulled into a handicapped spot. He reached into the glove compartment for the handicapped placard that he hung from the rearview mirror. Of course he'd kept the placard, which had belonged to his mother. Handicap spots afforded more room. People were clods. And careless. The Bugatti deserved extra protection.

He rolled down the windows. In summer months, dim lighting in the lot made passersby shadowy figures and cars indistinguishable dark blobs. During the mating season for sea turtles, all lighting across the island was kept to a minimum. Although there was a swath of forest between the inn and the beach, the coastline was only a quarter mile distant and naturalists feared tall lampposts in the parking area would be hazardous for the sea turtles, encouraging hatchlings to head toward the woods instead of the water.

Everything was working out perfectly. He'd contacted everyone on his list personally except for Marian. Perhaps she'd pick up the message. In any event, she'd been an afterthought. The responses fascinated him. Joan Turner and Eddie Olson hung up without a word. Lynn Griffith's high voice was indignant. "You've made a mistake. It must be someone who looked like me." George Griffith sounded like he'd had too much to drink. "Who's this? What's this all about? It's a lie. Damn lie."

Warren picked up the camera from the passenger seat and got out of the car, scarcely taking time to appreciate the smoothness as the door lifted up, then settled back in place. He kept to the shadows, wondering if others he'd invited would also take advantage of the inn's dim parking lot. Of course, many islanders also had bicycles. There were a number of ways to approach Widow's Haunt unobserved.

He skirted the back of the terrace. When he reached the woods, he stepped softly in the center of the path, which curved around a lagoon, darker than the night. He carried a small pencil flash that he used every few feet.

He glanced at his watch. The luminous dial showed twenty minutes to nine. None too early. The insects would be a bother even though he was doused with repellent, but he wanted to be in place well before anyone came.

Pete Anderson sat in the patrol car, headlights and motor turned off. The car was hidden in the deep shadows of a line of pines at Mickey's Fish Camp. The young police officer watched Cabin 8. Golden shafts spilled through the uncurtained windows. The 2009 Mustang was parked by the front steps. He had his orders. This was his first stakeout. He sat tensely, shoulders hunched. He wanted to do everything just right. Should he get out, take a closer look, make sure the guy was still there? He should be. Unless he'd managed to sneak out a back window. But then he'd have to walk around and get in his car. Behind the cabins stretched dark woods thick with undergrowth. He'd need a machete to get anywhere. Pete took a deep breath, in through his nose, out through his mouth. You got more oxygen that way. Stupid to be uptight. He could handle this.

Abruptly the windows in Cabin 8 went dark. *Okay. Somebody turned off the lights.* The front door of Cabin 8 swung in. Although the lighting was dim, only a pale wash from the windows in the next cabin, he thought it was a guy who hurried across the porch, thudded down the steps, dashed to the Mustang. As the car door opened, Pete had a good look at a young, sandy-haired, medium-sized male as he slid into the driver's seat. The Mustang roared to life and the noise masked the rumble of the motor of the patrol car.

The Mustang backed up, headed up the rutted dirt lane.

Pete was cool now, steady, driving without lights, following. He spoke into his lapel mic. "Subject departing Mickey's Fish Camp, turning left on Farraday."

The dispatcher's voice was clipped. "Maintain surveillance. Do not lose sight of Mustang."

The Mustang was going a little fast for the curving, twisty road. Pete took care not to get too close even though he was taking a chance driving without lights; but this was a rarely used road. When the Mustang reached the main island road, Pete turned on his lights. The driver would have no reason to connect the lights behind him with the fish camp.

"Mustang speeding." The speed limit on most main roads was forty. The Mustang was edging near fifty.

"Other cars alerted to let him pass. Stay on his tail."

When the Mustang turned onto a familiar road, Pete was excited. "Looks like he's going to the Seaside Inn."

"Stay with him."

Confident his headlights were nothing more than beams in a rearview mirror, Pete closed the gap between the cars. He slowed as the Mustang turned. "Parking in the west lot of the inn. I'll cruise past, find another spot."

"Backup en route."

Pete drove past the Mustang, which was parked in the second row. He found an empty slot a few cars down, parked, slid out of the car. He watched as the young man hurried toward the terrace.

"On foot. Walking to terrace."

"Keep subject in sight. Do not alarm him. May be going to Suite 130 in east wing."

Pete slipped from car to car, trying to remain undetected. A busload of seniors drew up at the entrance to the terrace, blocking his view. By the time he got around the bus, the occupants were spreading out onto the terrace, loud, happy, looking for tables. Pete looked frantically on the terrace, toward the pool. "Damn." He dashed toward the entrance to the east wing.

M arian dimmed the VW's headlights as she turned into the Seaside Inn parking area. She found a spot at the far end of a line of cars. She rolled down the windows, turned off the motor. She made no move to get out of the car. This was the easiest, most private way to reach Widow's Haunt. A narrow dirt road branched off the main road, wound through heavy forest to the ruins, where the historical society maintained a nicely graveled parking lot. Parking there, however, was an admission that you were on the grounds, that you had come specifically to Widow's Haunt.

If she was a reporter covering the story and she received an anonymous call suggesting information about a murder, she would have alerted Billy Cameron. He had every right to know if a damn fool was poking into a murder investigation. Then she would have grabbed her Leica and set out to see what happened.

That's what she would have done if she were just a reporter, not the mother of Alex Griffith's son.

Marian stared blankly out into the dim parking lot. Cold reason suggested Warren was toying with her. She hadn't been there when Alex was killed so Warren couldn't have seen her . . . Oh. How like Warren to call people he connected to Alex, poke them, see what happened. How many had Warren called? Abruptly, she was sure of her analysis. She wondered if anyone else had picked up on his identity. Warren obviously was unaware that he interspersed sniffs in every conversation.

She had to decide what to do, what she could do, what she must do. If she went to Widow's Haunt, she needed some way to explain her presence. If she went . . . But if she didn't alert Billy Cameron, she had to do something, find out what Warren was doing.

She turned on the motor, backed, turned. She could be at Annie's in a couple of minutes flat. If Annie would come with her . . .

Warren heard the whine of a mosquito, swatted at his face. Truly it was a wonder early settlers survived long at all. They blamed yellow fever on bad air, had no idea what caused malaria. He felt a welt rising on his cheek. He almost swung around, fled back to the manicured lawn of the inn. But he'd come this far. It was only another thirty or forty yards. He walked as swiftly as he dared, occasionally using the flash. He reached the main oyster shell path. Enough moonlight spilled over the tops of the pines to illuminate the clearing and the dark broken walls that hulked up in the night, sinister and foreboding.

He strolled toward a slightly lighter shade of gray that indicated the empty window in the front side of the house. Oyster shells crunched underfoot. He reached the broken wall, humming a little. He was in good time. He wouldn't go behind the wall for a while yet. Besides, he'd hear anyone approaching. He turned to look back the way he'd come.

Behind him, a dark shape moved in the shadows beyond the empty window.

Annie put two scoops of pistachio ice cream into a red pottery bowl. She sat at the food island, slowly eating the ice cream. Between bites, she engaged in an imaginary dialog with Max in preparation for the message she would leave on his cell:

I promised I wouldn't do anything stupid. And I haven't.

She imagined Max's response: *You told George you didn't think many people knew. Is that supposed to draw a magic safety circle around you?*

Max, he'll claim he never said any of it. He's probably so drunk by now he doesn't remember what he said.

Max: *Yeah, sure, if he's a murderer, it's slipped his mind that Annie Darling knows the guilty secret he thought he'd deep-sixed with Alex dead. As for stupid— excuse me, I'll be tactful—as for taking center stage as Sitting Duck Deluxe, you've made it clear to Joan Turner, Lynn Griffith, and Eddie Olson that exposure is only a heartbeat away. Your heartbeat.*

Annie took another big spoonful of ice cream, though it lacked its usual soothing effect. *You don't have to be rude.*

Max: *Rude? I'd like to wring your neck but Alex's murderer will probably save me the trouble.*

A vagrant thump on the porch closed her throat. She drew in a quick breath. Her heart thudded. She sat quite still and listened.

Pete's young face was forlorn, anguished. "I lost sight of him for just a minute."

Hyla Harrison understood Pete's misery. He'd had an assignment. He'd flubbed it. Pete knew and she knew and the chief knew that this wasn't a small mistake. This was big. The whole point in following Neil Kelly was to connect Kelly and Rae Griffith, prove that each knew the other was on the island, the first block in building a case for conspiracy.

Billy Cameron gave no evidence of irritation. "We have the Mustang covered. We won't lose him." He glanced at the closed door to Suite 130. He raised his hand, knocked again. This was the third try. No answer this time either. He pulled out his cell, made a call. "Suite 130." He held for a moment, clicked off the cell. "If they're in there, they aren't answering." He pointed across the hall. "Pete, wait by the ice machine. You won't be visible to anyone in the hallway. Keep an eye on 130. Come on, Hyla. Let's take a look outside. Maybe he was too canny to come to her room."

M arian perched on a high stool at the food island. "I don't know what to do." Her dark eyes were huge in a wan face. She made an effort to sit straighter. "I shouldn't have come here this late, bothered you, but I got a call a little while ago and I don't know what to do about it."

Annie was shocked by Marian's appearance, dark hair windblown, cheeks prominent, one thin hand twisted tight in the other. Annie pushed away the bowl with the melting ice cream. "Who called?"

"Warren Foster. I went to see him after lunch. He kept hinting he knew more than anyone realized." Marian knew Annie was on her side, but sharing Warren's anonymous call would make Annie a coconspirator hiding a fact the police should know. There was no way she would ever ask that of Annie. But Marian hoped that Annie would come with her to Widow's Haunt. Marian knew she couldn't call Billy, spin the same explanation. Billy would contact Warren, and Marian would be in big trouble. "Warren called a few minutes ago and hinted he was going to find out a lot tonight. I couldn't make much sense of it, something about taking a picture and cable news. He said he'd set up the most delicious rendezvous at nine, very convenient for the grieving widow, absolutely a haunting locale. He said he'd tell me all about it tomorrow and then he hung up."

The cuckoo in the wooden clock above the sink poked out its head. Treble cheeps marked a quarter to the hour. Max had been enchanted with the clock, one of Laurel's trophies from a Savannah flea market, because the cheeps vaguely sounded like "Rock Around the Clock." "Clever, huh?" he'd said. (Annie had resisted replying, "Stupid, huh?")

"Set up a rendezvous?"

"Right." Marian brushed back a dark curl. "But why would the widow—I guess obviously he means Rae Griffith—go meet Warren anywhere? I doubt she's ever heard of him." Marian glanced toward the clock. "It's close to nine now."

"It sounds like he suspects her, plans some kind of trap. What do you suppose he meant by 'very convenient for the grieving widow'? A 'haunting—'" She reached out, gripped Marian's thin arm, tugged. "Widow's Haunt! It's next to the inn so it makes sense he'd pick that if it involves Rae. Come on, Marian." Annie jumped down from the stool, hurried to the counter, pulled out the catchall drawer. "Here's a flashlight. We'll go through the woods. It's much quicker."

Marian remained at the counter. "What's much quicker?"

"We can walk more quickly than we can drive. There's a path through our woods to the inn. We go past the terrace to the east wing. There's an entrance into the woods very near the patio to the Griffith suite. We take that path to the ruins and we can approach without anyone knowing. I did a book event there last fall. Ghost stories. Everyone loved it. Come on, we'll find out what Warren's up to."

9

Billy Cameron flicked off his cell. "No one's approached either car. Rae Griffith and Neil Kelly have to be in the area. Lou checked the cabanas; Pete's been through the lobby and the bar. No sight of them."

Hyla could dimly see him in the shadow of the wall where they stood on the patio to Rae Griffith's suite. "Kind of interesting they've ducked out of sight."

"Very interesting."

Hyla was glad she wasn't Rae Griffith. Billy Cameron had Alex Griffith's widow in his sights as clearly as mallards against a November sky. Billy was a superb shot.

"Almost as good as a confession. The fact that he came here and she's nowhere to be found indicates they are together. I want to find them together. Then I'm ready to make a move."

Hyla ignored a whir of no-see-ums. "When I talked to her this morning, she was scared. You know how people hurt when they're torn up because somebody they care about got killed?" Her voice was gruff as she pushed away memories of the night her partner got out to check an alley and bullets ripped across his chest. "Well, she wasn't thinking about him. It was all about her. That doesn't mean she killed him, but she wasn't hurting."

Annie slowed. "There's an alligator in the pond. Let me make sure he isn't lolling around on the path." The fearsome creature was at least seven feet long and Annie had no intention of stepping on his tail. She flicked the beam down, lifted it enough to illuminate the area near the pond. "All clear." Reassured, Annie hurried ahead. Broken branches littered the path. Ferns poked out feathery fronds, slowing their progress. Nearby an owl hooted. Undergrowth rustled. Annie hoped the passing creature was a deer, not a wild boar. "The ruins are about twenty-five yards farther—"

A ragged scream rose, drowning out the rustle of the trees, the whine of insects, the rasp of cicadas in full summer chorus, the distant bark of a dog.

Annie drew in a quick breath, stopped. Marian bumped into her.

A desperate cry rose not far away. "Help, help! Neil, where are you?"

Annie plunged ahead, skidding a little on pine needles, pulling free of vines.

Marian yelped, "Annie, wait, we don't know what's up there."

Annie slowed. But the sound of that scream filled her mind, piteous, terrified, someone in bad trouble.

Marian's strong thin hand clamped on one arm. "Wait. Listen."

A woman sobbed. A man's voice was uneven, shaky. "Oh my God. Look at his face."

"We have to get out of here." The woman spoke in jerky breathless bursts. "Hurry."

"I'm going to be sick. Oh God." His voice was muffled.

"Neil, get up." Her voice shook. "Please get up. We have to get out of here."

Marian spoke again. "I'll call 911. Damn, where's my cell? Got it." Marian flashed the light down, tapped a number. She talked fast. "Woman screamed at Widow's Haunt. Somebody's hurt. Send help." The strength of her grip on Annie's arm never eased. "Marian Kenyon. Annie Darling and I are on the path between the inn and the ruins. We heard a woman scream. There's a woman and a man and it sounds like somebody's hurt."

Annie tried to pull free. "We have to see."

Marian clung harder. "Help's on the way. They said Billy's at—"

It was as she spoke that running feet thudded toward them on the path from the inn. Billy Cameron, despite his size and weight, came around the curve in the path first, a brilliant beam from his Maglite turning the path bright. Hyla Harrison was close behind, hand on her holster.

Billy's light settled on Annie and Marian. He gave them both a searching stare. "What's going on?"

Annie knew they made an odd tableau, both of them half turned toward the path to the ruins, Marian holding tight to her arm.

Marian jerked her head toward the ruins. "We heard a scream. A woman yelled for help and a man told her to look at somebody's face." She kept her voice steady with obvious effort. "Something bad's happened."

Billy was already moving. "If there's shooting, get back to the inn. Otherwise wait here." The last was flung over his shoulder.

Hyla Harrison didn't spare them a glance as she slipped past. She looked calm and cool, ready for any eventuality. Now she had her gun free. The two of them moved fast but cautiously around the curve.

Marian started forward. "Come on—"

Now it was Annie who clung to Marian's arm. "Let them see. We don't want to be in the way."

Marian resisted. "Got to find out what's happening. You can stay here." She yanked free, grabbed the flashlight from Annie's hand, and started around the curve.

Annie started after her. Marian always pushed barriers. Being told to stay back assured she'd keep going. Annie hurried to catch up, keeping the gleam of light in view.

Ahead she heard the sounds of Billy and Hyla and Marian on the path, twigs snapping as they moved forward.

A woman's voice, edging toward hysteria, rose above the rustling on the path. "Somebody's coming. We have to get out of here."

Abruptly the trees thinned. Annie and Marian were only a few yards behind Billy and Hyla. The stark beam from Billy's Maglite swept the clearing, stopped, framed Rae Griffith, wild-eyed, trembling, staring down at a slender young man on hands and knees, retching miserably onto the rough ground.

Billy's shout was emphatic. "Do not move. Stay in place. Police."

Hyla came around Billy, stood, braced, gun raised, aimed.

Billy shouted again. "Hands up. Do not move. Both of you."

Rae Griffith raised trembling hands. She wavered unsteadily. The man on the ground, still on his knees, managed to lift his arms.

Annie and Marian stopped at the end of the path. Marian muttered, "Why didn't I bring the Leica?" She held up her cell phone, began to snap pictures.

The Maglite revealed Rae and the man on the ground and a still figure slumped against a wall, a camera lying near one hand. Annie struggled to breathe. She reached out blindly, clung to Marian. She knew they both saw the same horror: a man's body half propped against a wall of the ruins—Warren Foster's body. Warren was braced against the wall where a patch of darkness marked the existence of a long-ago window. Warren's head tilted to one side near that open space. His face looked bloated in the moonlight, swollen, distorted.

Warren's eyes bulged, his tongue protruded.

Annie understood Rae's scream and her companion's nausea.

"Strangled." Marian shuddered.

Annie jerked her eyes away, knew that image would rise in the night, turn her sleep into nightmares.

"Hold on." Marian steadied her, but Marian, too, was keeping her gaze away from the wall. "Don't look. Damn." Her voice was deep in her throat, shaky.

Billy stepped to within a foot of Rae. "What happened?" The words were sharp, demanding, suspicious.

The night breeze stirred her dark hair. Her eyes were huge, beseeching. "I don't know." She stared at him, her mouth quivering. "How would I know?"

"You're here." Billy's voice was like the crack of a whip. "What happened to Warren Foster?"

"I don't know," she cried again. "I don't know him. I found him. Neil and I—"

Billy took a step nearer. He glanced from her to the man now struggling to his feet.

Hyla turned the gun toward the slender man with a green-tinged face. "Hands up, Kelly."

Annie was bewildered. Who was Rae's companion? Somebody

named Kelly? Neil Kelly? Billy and Hyla seemed to know all about him. Beside her, Marian looked from one to the other, her expression intent, wondering.

Hyla spoke into her lapel mic. "One-eight-seven. Three-nine. Two-six. Seven-nine. Widow's Haunt. Dispatch all available officers."

Billy looked down at Rae. "What are you doing here?"

Arms still partially raised, Rae gave a desperate look at her companion.

He was struggling to breathe. A dark frown twisted his narrow face. "You better tell them. I knew we shouldn't come. I told you we shouldn't come." His light tenor voice was tight with anger.

Rae stood silent.

"Like he said"—Billy jerked a thumb at Neil Kelly—"you better tell us. You're here; a man is dead. What happened?"

Rae dropped her hands, clasped them tightly together. "I got a phone call. A little after eight. Somebody whispered, said they saw me going in the suite during the time Alex was killed. That wasn't true. I didn't come back to the room until Alex was late and I went to see why and he was dead. But this voice whispered I had to come here or they'd tell the police. I said it was a lie, it wasn't me, it had to be somebody else."

"You're here." Billy flung the words at her.

The faint wail of a siren sounded in the distance.

Rae stared at Billy, eyes wild, lips trembling. "I was afraid not to come. I called Neil—"

Annie saw a look of satisfaction on Billy's face. If she were Rae, that look would terrify her, but Rae, her body shaking, kept on talking, faster and faster.

"—and told him what happened. Neil didn't want to come. He said I should ignore the call, that it was some kind of crank. But I was scared. This whispery voice went on and on. I thought I had to come and see because you're all against me. I was afraid if someone called the police and said they'd seen me come back to the room, you'd arrest me. I told Neil we had to come and talk to this person and tell them it wasn't true."

Neil was sullen. "We shouldn't have come. I told you we shouldn't come."

Rae turned one trembling hand toward Billy. "Please believe me. I don't know that man." She kept her eyes away from the wall and its grisly burden. "All I know is someone called and threatened me. I thought I had to come. I called Neil—"

Running steps sounded on the path. Lou Pirelli and two other officers came around the curve.

Lou gave Annie and Marian a quick look as they stepped out of the way, then he and the other officers spilled out into the clearing.

Billy held up a hand and they stopped, waiting for instruction.

Billy prodded Rae. "How'd you call him?"

Rae gave Billy a blank stare. "On his cell phone."

"You know his cell phone number?" Billy spoke as if the question was innocuous.

Rae's hands twisted around and around. "I . . . Yes. I know his number."

Annie knew the question was as terrifying to Rae as anything that had happened.

"What did you say to Mr. Kelly?"

Rae swallowed jerkily. "I told him to come to the hotel."

The sirens sounded louder, nearer.

"Where did you meet?"

Rae's eyes flickered. Now her shoulders hunched and her hands were still in a tight grasp.

Marian leaned close, whispered in Annie's ear. "She's afraid to tell the truth. Whatever it is."

Annie knew that she and Marian waited for her answer with a sense that they were observing disaster unfolding.

Neil Kelly wiped the back of a shaking hand across his mouth. "I should have got the hell off the island. I don't want to sneak around and hide from the cops. She said I had to meet her behind the cabanas by the pool. I didn't want to come back here—"

Billy pounced. "Was this your first time back to the inn since you checked out of Room 128?"

Neil's shoulders tightened. Fear stirred in the moonlit clearing, as unmistakable as the sudden flash of headlights. Cars squealed to a stop in the parking area on the far side of the ruins. Police spilled out of the cruisers, came hurrying, Maglites illuminating the clearing, settling on the woman with dark curls and a gaunt face, the man with a petulant expression.

Billy again held up his hand. He looked from Rae to Neil. "We'll have time to discuss Room 128 when we get to the station. Now I want to know about your plans tonight. Mrs. Griffith, you called Kelly, told him to come to the inn. Where did you meet?"

"Behind the cabanas." She sounded drained, defeated. "He was"—she gave Neil a helpless, desperate look—"ugly. He didn't want to come with me. I told him I was afraid to go by myself. The voice had told me where to find the path. We didn't have a flashlight. It was awfully dark in the woods and we kind of had to feel our way to stay on the path. It seemed to take a long time. Finally, it was lighter ahead. I saw glimpses of moonlight and I thought we must be getting close to the clearing. The voice had said to come to the clearing and walk across to the ruins. I thought maybe Neil should stay out of sight. He said I could yell if I needed him. I kept on going—"

"You went on alone?"

"Yes. I came out of the woods and there were the ruins. I didn't see . . ." She shuddered. "I called out, but nobody answered. I thought maybe it was just an ugly joke and we could go back. I stopped to listen. I didn't hear anything so I called out again."

Billy turned toward Neil. "Could you see her?"

An odd expression slid across Neil's face. His gaze flicked toward Rae. "I kept back a ways. I thought it was all stupid." His voice was thin. "I couldn't see her."

Uncertainty, panic, and fear flitted across Rae's face.

Billy looked at Rae. "You went ahead by yourself."

"The whispery voice told me to come to the wall with the missing window, that it was the front of the old house, the main part of the ruins."

Billy spoke quietly. "You walked to the front of the ruins. What happened?"

"I walked across the open space and as I got nearer to the wall, I thought somebody was resting on the ground, kind of sitting there. I called out kind of softly, 'Who's there?' Nobody answered. I kept on coming. I didn't know until I got right up to the wall. I looked down and I saw that horrible face in the moonlight. I screamed. Neil came running."

Billy rocked back on his heels. He looked formidable, well over six feet tall, muscular, powerful. His broad face furrowed in thought. "You came to the clearing to meet Warren Foster—"

"I don't know him." Rae's voice shook. "I only came—"

"Because a caller threatened to inform police you entered the room where your husband died at a time when you claimed not to be there, an eyewitness placing you at the scene of his murder. You came into the clearing alone, walked to the walls. We only have your word for it that Foster was dead when you got here. Maybe you found Foster here, spoke with him, perhaps asked him if he heard a sound behind him, and when he turned away—"

"I didn't. I didn't!" Her voice rose. "I've told you the truth. I swear."

Billy looked at Lou Pirelli. "Take these two into custody, suspicion of murder. Hold them at the station."

Lou and several other officers came up on either side of Rae and Neil.

Rae struggled between two officers, her screams rising.

Marian took a deep drink from a mug. "The coffee here's about as lousy as *Gazette* coffee."

A patrol officer had driven them to Annie's, permitted them to follow him to the station in Marian's car, brought them to the break room, offered coffee or soda, and said the chief would appreciate it if they'd wait there to have their statements taken.

Annie nodded. "But it's hot. And we aren't out there." Or in cells like Rae and the man named Kelly.

"Out there" would be the ruins in the moonlight and Warren's body. Doc Burford would have arrived by now and once he officially deemed Warren dead, the slow, careful, thorough crime scene investigation would begin: photographs, sketches, a search for physical evidence.

Marian's narrow face was somber. "Yeah. Looked like he was strangled. Billy can tell us what Burford says." Marian pulled her cell out of her pocket, flicked to an image. "Warren had a thin neck. At the angle he was resting, you can see something's embedded in the skin even in a cell pic. I'd guess a wire. Not a rope."

Annie didn't want to think about Warren's neck. But she had to ask. "Wire?"

"Simple, effective. Sneak up behind him. Have to move fast. Drop the wire over his head, yank against his neck, cross it behind him, pull hard. Very little noise. Maybe a kind of grunt or harsh whistle. Warren probably was standing with his back to that empty window. Somebody could have hidden there and strangled him before he had time to react."

"If it was wire," Annie said, thinking out loud, "the murder was planned."

"You can't trace a hard piece of wood and I'd guess it will be the same with wire." Marian's face furrowed. "Wire's thin. Does that sound stupid? But the thing is, I'll bet there isn't enough surface to pick up fingerprints. Might not be fingerprints anyway." Marian held up her hand, curled her fingers tight. "The wire would be gripped as the fingers folded against the palm."

Annie pushed the coffee mug away. Did an ordinary person usually have easy access to wire? Did someone go to the hardware store today and make a purchase? That would be easy to trace. She tried to remember if she kept a spool of wire anywhere in the house or at the store. Not that she recalled. Why would Rae carry wire with her when she traveled? Billy could deal with that question. It was now up to him to dig out what needed to be known about Rae Griffith. And her companion, the slender young man who unwillingly met her behind a cabana and came with her into the woods.

Annie looked at Marian. "Who do you suppose the guy is? Billy seemed to know all about him. Neil Kelly. Where did he come from?" It seemed obvious to Annie that Neil had to be someone Rae knew well. Why was he on the island? Why had Rae called on him to go to the clearing with her?

"I'd guess he's a boyfriend."

"Why was he on the island?"

Marian shrugged. "Maybe he always tagged after Rae and Alex. Billy will find out. What I want to know is when they got together tonight."

Annie was puzzled. "What difference does the time make?"

"It could make a lot of difference." Marian spoke slowly. "Maybe Rae killed Warren before she met up with Neil and said she wanted him to come with her—"

Annie shook her head. "I don't think so. If she killed Warren earlier, why not slip out of the woods and go back to her room? She'd stay as far away from the ruins as possible. I think she was telling the truth. She got a call from Warren and was afraid not to go meet him alone."

Marian's dark eyes were intent. "When they got to the ruins, she told Neil to stay back. She could have killed Warren then."

Annie frowned. "Why bring Neil along?"

Marian was thoughtful. "Who knows? She wasn't expecting us or the police. Whatever she did, she thought she would come to the ruins, talk to the person who called her, and nobody else would be the wiser. Maybe she really was scared to go alone. That sounds like she's innocent."

The break room door opened. Hyla Harrison came in, carrying a tape recorder. She nodded at them formally. "I'm here to take your statements."

Annie stopped to look out at the marina. She'd managed only a fitful night's sleep but the tightness around her eyes and the dullness of fatigue eased as she breathed deeply of the salty air, heard the slap of water against pilings, watched gulls wheel against the brilliant blue sky. She was free of the struggle to help Marian and Rae. In a few minutes, she'd be in the store, busy with all the happy minutiae that made up her day. And some of it not minutiae at all. In fact, now was a good time to call Max.

She pulled out her cell, tapped Max's name in Favorites. Although it would be better, far better to hear his voice, this was next best. "I'm at the marina, thinking about you . . . Marian's fine . . . I have horrible news about Warren Foster . . . Rae Griffith was arrested . . . Glad you're coming home tomorrow. I hope—" What did she hope? That Max would understand her broken promise? That he would come home and something good would take the place of Confidential Commissions?—"I hope you'll understand."

She felt better when the call was made and now she was busy in her everyday world. No more murder. Except in Death on Demand. As she turned to walk toward the boardwalk, she tapped Messages. She read the message from Laurel and stopped, eyebrows rising in amazement: *Better a broken promise than none at all. Mark Twain.*

Annie smiled and shook her head in bemusement. How did Laurel manage to always align her stars with Annie's current activity? Obviously, her mother-in-law's ESP was in high gear.

The next message was from Henny: *The novelette Murder Goes to Market by Mignon G. Eberhart is priceless for its look at wartime Washington, D.C., and its description of an early supermarket. Probably you don't even remember the world before there were supermarkets!*

Henny was having fun with Annie, dangling intriguing bits of information about two obviously rare publications, Phoebe Atwood Taylor's *The Disappearing Hermit* in the earlier text and the book by Eberhart in this text. Where had she found these titles?

Finally—and Annie's lips quirked in a smile—Emma's dictum: *I've*

warned Marigold, stop sulking or I'll create a new heroine, an artist who sketches
people in random places and one day at a coffee shop draws the picture of . . .

Annie laughed and ran up the last few steps, eager for the start
of the day, leaving behind her the darkness of the night.

Hyla Harrison knew her place at the morning staff meeting. She
was an officer, she did her job, she didn't expect credit for doing
her job. She stood at parade rest facing a table in the small conference
room. Billy Cameron sat in the middle, Mavis to his right. Hyla's tone
was matter-of-fact. ". . . requested that the inn bar housekeeping from
128, which was rented to 'Robert Haws.' Checked for fingerprints.
Obvious effort had been made to wipe most surfaces. Found partial
prints on handle of lower portion of closet door, thumb print on bottom of commode seat, four fingers on interior handle of sliding glass
door. Subsequent match to Neil Kelly." She sat down next to Lou
Pirelli, who gave her a thumbs-up.

"Officer Harrison set this investigation off on the right track." Billy
was clearly pleased. "She was thorough, wanted to know why she
couldn't contact the guest in the room next to the murder suite. She
discovered he'd checked out, got the name, looked at the security film,
set out to find him. And she did. She also turned up a witness who will
testify the widow and Kelly were on intimate terms. Good work."

At Billy's admiring nod, Hyla knew her face was turning pink.
"Thank you, Chief."

Billy leaned back, expansive now. "Here's how I see it, and the
circuit solicitor agrees. He's drawing up the charges. We have conspiracy to commit murder; a wife and her lover planned the husband's
murder, fixing it so she wouldn't be a suspect. Rae Griffith killed her
husband before she went out to the terrace. Kelly's job was simple.

Come in through the sliding door to the Griffith suite, call room service—man's voice orders two drinks, slips out before room service arrives. We didn't pick up any of Kelly's fingerprints in the Griffith suite but obviously he'd be careful, probably wore gloves. The call to room service sets it up that Griffith was alive when his wife was in public view, but dead before she left the terrace and discovered the body. The next morning Kelly or"—Billy glanced at a sheet of paper—"'Robert Haws,' the name Kelly used when he registered, checks out. He goes to a fish camp, rents a cabin, assumed name again, pays cash again. And"—now Billy's satisfaction was evident—"the search of his car turns up a blond wig, a pillow, a straw hat that matches what Haws wore when he arrived Tuesday. We've got him."

Mavis, Billy's wife, was not only the dispatcher and crime tech specialist, she was his sounding board. Mavis had a slightly old-fashioned appearance, long blond hair that curled softly around her face, a grave expression, eyes that were deep pools of intuition and experience. "I'm puzzled about the gun Hyla saw Kelly throw over the bluff."

"More good work there," Billy said quickly. "Hyla kept him under observation; Lou got out in those currents and brought the gun up."

Lou's round face looked pleased. "Sometimes you get lucky. The gun landed between a couple of rocks, wedged there, easy to spot. Once I got it back to the station, I ran a check. Reported stolen last year from an acreage out by Alpharetta. My guess is Kelly bought it at a garage sale."

Mavis turned her serious gaze toward Billy. "Griffith was smothered, not shot. Why throw the gun away?"

Billy's eyes narrowed. "Could be he knew or guessed the gun was stolen property. In any event, he didn't have a license. There's another possibility. How about the widow and the boyfriend originally planned to shoot Griffith? Say she were to persuade him to go out on a sailboat, shoot him, push the body overboard. Lots of possible scenarios. But maybe there was some urgency that he had to die that night at the inn. A gunshot could have raised an alarm. But after Rae smothered him, Lover Boy got worried, decided he didn't want to be picked up with an unregistered gun. Whatever, we've got 'em cold."

M arian Kenyon carried a big white mug of coffee to her desk. She was used to the murmur of activity that was the forever background to the newsroom: phones ringing; sports editor Eddie Abel grousing about that loused-up play at the Braves game last night where . . . (and here listeners could take their pick—the call was wrong, the strike was high, the outfielder smothered the ball, dammit, he didn't catch it); lifestyle editor Ginger Harris caroling into her phone, "Will you spell that name for me, please?" Everything was as it should be. Except that it wasn't.

Marian dropped into her chair, turned on her computer, noted the brief e-mail from the public information officer of the Broward's Rock Police Department, which was another title and duty managed by Mavis Cameron: *Press conference 10 a.m. Griffith/Foster murder investigations.*

Marian leaned back in her chair with a notepad in her lap. She always used soft pencils. She liked the rich dark lines better than the anemic, to her, ink in most ballpoint pens. She didn't need to check her notes. She had no difficulty remembering each and every moment of that week.

Especially last night. Warren's call. She sipped the coffee, could not have said whether it was hot or tepid, too strong or vapid. No one knew what Warren said to her. That was critical. She must remember exactly what she said in the statement she'd signed last night. That

Warren's call reiterated part of their conversation earlier in the day, his boast that he could get a picture of the murderer. In the evening call, he again made that claim and told her the rendezvous was very convenient for the grieving widow, absolutely a haunting locale. That was what she'd told Annie and that was what she must continue to tell everyone, especially Billy.

In the night, she'd lain sleepless, worrying that perhaps she might have saved Warren's life if she'd immediately notified Billy after she received the call from Warren. But, finally, that burden slipped away. Warren was dead by the time she and Annie arrived. Rae claimed he was dead when she and Neil came. If so, there would not have been time enough for Billy to close in on Widow's Haunt. That would have required calls, a quiet approach.

No, her inaction hadn't doomed Warren.

But she had another fear now. If she had to testify, those few words, which she had carefully devised to prompt Annie Darling to identify the meeting place as Widow's Haunt, would be another piece of evidence to help convict Rae Griffith of murder. She'd felt so clever putting the words into Warren's mouth: " . . . very convenient for the grieving widow . . ."

Annie restocked Louise Penny titles. Which was her favorite? Maybe *A Rule Against Murder*. But *Still Life*, the first in the series, was terrific. Hey, they were all good. Ingrid's favorite Canadian writer was Peter Robinson, but, of course, his books were set in Yorkshire. Lots of super Canadian authors—Vicki Delany, L. R. Wright, David Rotenberg, Gail Bowen.

"Annie, could I speak to you for a moment?" The cultivated voice was uncertain, diffident.

Annie came to her feet and turned. She was shocked at the paleness of Joan Turner's slender face. Annie's reply was swift. "Let's go back to my office."

When the door closed behind them, Joan rushed into speech. "I saw the news on TV. It's dreadful. I never liked Warren but it's hideous that he's dead. And to have Alex's widow arrested with another man . . . The news said you and Marian Kenyon were there last night. Why were you there? Oh, I know you must think this is strange, my coming here and asking. But I have to know." This morning her face was gaunt, strained.

"It's complicated. Rae Griffith came to see me yesterday. She was afraid of the police, thought they were going to blame her and weren't really looking at anyone on the island. I told her I'd help. Marian Kenyon and I were trying to find out more about Alex and people he knew on the island." Annie realized Joan was listening intently, absorbing every word. "Marian went to see Warren Foster because of something he said to me that night on the terrace, so Warren knew Marian was trying to figure out what happened. Warren called Marian, hinted that he was going to get a picture of the person who killed Alex, but he didn't say where he was meeting this person. Marian was worried and she came to see me and together we figured out he might have been talking about Widow's Haunt. So we went there." Quickly, she described the scream and what they heard and what they found.

Joan's voice was sharp. "You were there. You saw Rae. And the man. Do you think they killed Warren?"

Annie saw desperate hope in her violet eyes. Annie was back in that moonlit clearing with the horror of a dead man; a woman with wild, terrified eyes; her companion retching onto the sandy ground. "I don't know. That's what the police think. But I don't know."

"Why do the police think they killed him?" Joan's stare was intense.

Annie blurted out, "I think mostly because they were there. Rae admitted Warren called her, threatened her. Of course, she claimed she didn't know who called her. She said the voice was a whisper and she was afraid not to respond to the call."

Joan lifted long thin fingers to grip the silver chain that shone against her blue silk blouse. "They arrested them because Warren called her?"

"Don't you see?" Annie was sure she understood Billy Cameron's reasoning. "Warren Foster called Rae because he saw her going into the suite during the time when Alex was killed. Rae swore she didn't go back to the suite but stayed on the terrace."

Joan's fingers tightened around the chain, held so tight the skin of her knuckles blanched. "There's no proof Warren saw her."

"He called her. Rae said that he called."

"He called her." Joan's tone was heavy. Her hand fell away from the necklace. She took a deep breath. "That's what I needed to know." She turned away, plunged to the door, pulled it open.

"Joan—"

The door closed. Joan Turner was gone.

10

Print and TV reporters clustered near the front steps of the station. Off-island media included three blond on-air reporters, all female, one a well-known local-news star from Savannah. Each was accompanied by a cameraman. The TV reporters were uniformly slick with perfectly coiffed hair, very short skirts, and good legs, the cameramen uniformly casual in sport shirts and jeans. Slow-moving cars clogged the street, holidayers curious about a crime that promised to have lurid details. Customers from nearby shops, even a couple of fishermen from Fish Haul Pier, jostled for a place in the growing crowd.

Marian stood on a slight rise at an angle to the steps, her Leica hanging on a strap around her neck. She'd get good shots from there.

The TV star from Savannah strode to the front door, opened it. "Anybody home? The clock struck ten." She stood with her head poked inside, then withdrew, closing the door, and turned to face the audience. "I'm advised the presser will start shortly." Satisfied, she moved down the steps, but turned at the base, planting herself right in the middle of the sidewalk.

A moment later, the door opened. Uniformed officers Hyla Harrison and Lou Pirelli stepped outside, Hyla trim, Lou a little pudgy but obviously athletic. Both stood on the second step. Billy Cameron followed, closed the door behind him. Cameras flashed, videocams whirred. Billy wore his usual short-sleeved white shirt, khaki trousers, and brown loafers. Despite a long night, he looked fresh, intelligent, capable.

Marian lifted the Leica. Three good shots.

Billy was brisk. "Police Chief Billy Cameron. With me are Officers Hyla Harrison and Lou Pirelli, who contributed to a successful conclusion of our investigation into the deaths of Alex Griffith Wednesday night at the Seaside Inn and of lifelong island resident Warren Foster last night at Widow's Haunt. Rae Griffith, the widow of Alex Griffith, and Neil Kelly, who is known to Mrs. Griffith, were apprehended last night at the scene of Foster's murder. The circuit solicitor will formally charge them as co-conspirators in both murders. They will be transported to the mainland Monday for arraignment at ten A.M. in the Beaufort County Courthouse. They are currently in custody on the island."

The Savannah star called out, "Have they been Mirandized?"

"Both suspects have been read their rights and have contacted attorneys."

Marian flipped open her notebook: *Arraignment 10 a.m. Mon.*

"Autopsy reports available?" The balding reporter who asked this looked pugnacious.

Marian recognized him as a print reporter for AP. There had been past struggles in South Carolina when officials refused to release crime autopsy reports. Good question. She held her pencil poised to write.

"We will make those reports available. Griffith died as a result of asphyxiation after being stunned by two blows to his head. Foster was also asphyxiated but he was strangled with a wire. The killer looped a sixteen-inch length of green plastic-coated garden wire around his neck, pulled the ends back, crossed them with enough force that the wire was embedded a quarter inch into neck tissue, resulting in a crushed windpipe."

The words repeated themselves over and over again in Marian's mind . . . *green plastic-coated garden wire* . . . *green plastic-coated garden wire* . . . "Chief"—she knew her voice was thin and high—"what about fingerprints?"

"No useful prints were found on the piece of wood that struck Griffith, the pillow used to smother him, or the wire that choked Foster. The portion of wire embedded in Foster's neck was free of prints altogether and the extended ends were too narrow to retain a distinct impression."

Marian asked with a catch in her voice, "Has the garden wire been linked to Mrs. Griffith?"

Billy folded his arms. "Garden wire is easily obtained."

Marian persisted. "Was a search of her belongings made?"

Billy's face was stolid. "After obtaining warrants, Mrs. Griffith's car and her suite at the inn were searched. No wire was found."

A small TV reporter, who made up for size with a loud voice, shouted over several other questions, "How about motives?"

"It will be the State's contention that Mrs. Griffith and Kelly were involved in an intimate relationship. The State will contend that Mrs. Griffith killed her husband before she came out to the terrace at approximately a quarter to seven. Mrs. Griffith then remained in public view until she, accompanied by island bookseller Annie Darling, went to the Griffith suite to check on the author, who was late appearing at the gazebo. Mrs. Griffith ostensibly discovered her husband's body, professing shock and horror. It will be the State's contention that Kelly entered the room while Mrs. Griffith was on the terrace and that Kelly called room service and ordered two drinks. The call was intended to indicate the author was still alive. The State will contend that the crime was planned in advance and that Kelly, using an assumed name, checked into the room next to the Griffith suite in order to enter the suite unobserved and make the call to room service, thereby providing Mrs. Griffith with an alibi."

The AP reporter shouted, "Why tab the widow as the killer? Couldn't the boyfriend have entered the suite, killed Griffith, then called room service?"

Billy was judicious. "That is a possibility, but our investigation places Mrs. Griffith in a leadership role throughout. Mr. Kelly appears to have responded to her directions. Last night at the scene of Warren Foster's murder, Mrs. Griffith said she came to Widow's Haunt in response to a phone call from Foster in which he claimed to have seen Mrs. Griffith re-enter the suite during the time when Griffith was killed, that Mrs. Griffith insisted Kelly accompany her because she feared Foster's threat to notify police would incriminate her. It is the State's contention that Mrs. Griffith disposed of Foster's threat by strangling him with a length of garden wire. It will be the State's contention that we have only Mrs. Griffith's word for the contents of the call, that Foster may have made another threat that she thought too dangerous to ignore."

Marian frowned. She remembered Warren's call quite clearly. She knew she hadn't entered the suite so she had assumed Warren was playing a game of "who's left standing," calling those he associated with Alex—Joan Turner, George Griffith, Lynn Griffith, Eddie Olson. She'd also assumed Warren whispered the same accusation in each call. Warren had no way of knowing Rae and Neil were involved or that Neil was in the room next door. Right now Billy obviously thought Warren had made a single call—the one to Rae. Certainly Billy would have read the statements Hyla Harrison took from Marian and Annie. Billy apparently believed Marian's claim that Warren's call was related to her earlier talk with Warren. Billy didn't associate her with Alex. He knew her as Marian Kenyon, *Gazette* reporter. Billy knew Warren as well, knew him to be a gossip, knew him to revel in being a fount of information, assumed Warren had called Marian because she was a reporter, because he sought attention. If Billy knew Warren had called Marian and tried to lure her to the ruins with the same accusation, it would redirect his investigation. Quickly she shut off that thought.

The case sounded strong. She never doubted Billy had homed in on the squalid truth that Rae Griffith's companion was her lover. A jury would likely be convinced as well. Lovers might think their secret safe but someone always knew. There would be proof offered. That was a strong motive—a woman who wanted to be free of her husband, a man who was quite wealthy. Divorce was easy but the payoff was not nearly as high. Nothing new there. Then Rae was found at the scene of a second murder. One plus one equaled two. Stamp the case closed.

Marian wished mightily that she could believe in Billy's case. If Rae was guilty, Marian was safe, Marian and those she loved. But truth was truth, even when truth hurt. She followed facts. These facts seemed undeniable: Warren's murder was in response to his taunting phone call so a weapon had to be found quickly. Warren was killed by a length of plastic-coated garden wire. There was no store open on the island at that time of evening where garden wire could be purchased. Last night at Widow's Haunt, Rae Griffith screamed.

Annie scanned the mugs on the shelving behind the coffee bar. She reached up, chose the title *Calling All Suspects* by Carolyn Wells. She fixed a cappuccino with a dash of caramel and extra whipped cream. The Death on Demand coffee bar believed in customer rights. What you wanted was what you got. She smiled, thinking of an obituary of an islander who had created a fabulously successful high-end women's shop and the instruction she gave new clerks: The first rule of sales—the customer is always right. The second rule of sales—the customer is always right.

Annie carried the mug to a corner screened from the main aisle by Whitmani ferns, sank into the embrace of a softly cushioned wicker chair, took a satisfying sip, and thought about Joan's unexpected visit. Why had Joan come? Why was she upset? Joan wanted to know—appeared desperate to know—if Warren had called Rae. When Annie confirmed the call, Rae's admission of that call, and Billy's conclusion that Rae came to the clearing because she was afraid Warren might call the police, there was no relief in Joan's face.

Instead, before Joan turned away, Annie saw a woman grappling with despair.

What difference did it make to Joan whether Warren called Rae?

Annie was afraid she knew. Billy thought only Rae had been called. What if Warren called Joan? And others. Like Marian, who said he called to gloat about the picture he intended to take. Had that really been the reason for his call? But maybe it was true. Joan hadn't known the identity of the whispering caller. Surely if Warren called

Marian to accuse her, he would also have whispered. Annie felt quick relief. She didn't want to think Marian had lied to her. If Marian lied about a call, what else might she have lied about?

Annie turned the mug in her hands, looked at the red letters of the title. Had Warren called all the suspects, those he'd watched with malicious glee that night on the terrace? Joan Turner. George Griffith. Lynn Griffith. Eddie Olson. Rae Griffith.

If he had, that changed everything.

Annie drank more cappuccino, but the hot sweet coffee didn't lift her spirits. If Joan remained silent, Rae and Neil faced prosecution, likely conviction, possibly the death penalty. If Joan went to Billy Cameron, told him she, too, had received a call—had she responded? did she go to the clearing?—then Billy's entire picture of the case would have to shift. He might well still believe Rae and Neil guilty, and they might be guilty, but an honest investigator would consider who else might have known Warren was at Widow's Haunt. Billy was an honest cop.

Annie pushed away the mug. She could go to Billy. If she did, Joan would face questions: *Why did Warren call you? Did he threaten to reveal something you wanted kept hidden? Where were you last night at nine o'clock?*

There might be another way.

Marian clicked Send. Press conference covered. Story done. She sat for a good fifteen minutes, too tired to move, drained. Finally she pushed up from her desk, walked across the newsroom, stopped by the city desk. Before she could speak, the cherub-faced city editor, whose hair was three strands of pale blond over a balding dome, barked, "Good job. I can smell the seaweed."

That was Walt's highest praise when he liked a story. He could smell the seaweed. Usually that would be a boost even though she knew she wrote good stories. Still, everybody liked a ribbon. Today the accolade didn't matter, but she managed a smile. "Thanks. Think I'll go out and look over Widow's Haunt."

His pale blue eyes gleamed. "Got a hunch?"

"Maybe."

She stepped outside, wished the pulsing heat could warm the chill around her heart. It was about fifty yards to the parking lot rimmed by occasional palmettos and a couple of weeping willows. Even the drooping fronds of the willow looked hot. She'd left the windows in her VW down. She slid behind the wheel. It wasn't far to Widow's Haunt, perhaps a half mile. Hot air rushed through the windows, blowing her hair. But nothing pushed the refrain from her mind . . . *plastic-coated garden wire, plastic-coated garden wire, plastic-coated garden wire . . .*

A half dozen cars were parked in the visitor lot. She found a patch of shade beneath a live oak, walked briskly to the clearing. She shaded her eyes and studied the ruins, the broken wall that was attached to the remnants of a sagging front porch only partially supported by columns of tabby bricks. A knobby-kneed tourist crouched, snapping pictures. Another fun memento? Add a caption: *They found a body on the other side of the broken wall . . .* Several women watched from the shade of a willow.

There was no crime scene tape. That meant Mavis and her crew had covered the area, made meticulous drawings, videos, and photographs, felt that everything had been found that could be found. Now tourists were free to clamber where death had waited the night before.

Marian cut across the dusty ground. She stopped a few feet from the tabby wall where Warren had slumped in death. She had a good memory. She remembered exactly how his body, half sitting, half lying, sagged below the wide-open emptiness where a window once had existed. She walked closer to the wall. The windowsill was almost chest high. The long-ago window had opened onto a porch that had been gone for many years.

She stood on tiptoe, peered over the sill. Magnolia leaves had drifted against the base of the wall. Below the opening, the leaves mounded. As clearly as if it had been she who waited here for Warren to arrive, she knew a foot had brushed aside the leaves, made a clear patch where a killer waited, standing firmly without fear of a betraying crackle. Possibly Warren, too, had scouted out the ruins, studied the surroundings, decided cleverly that he could stand behind the wall near the opening and observe anyone arriving in the clearing. Warren no doubt arrived in what he felt was good time to take his place and was surveying the clearing before he followed the path beyond the porch to take his place behind the wall.

But a killer had arrived earlier.

This was the chilling reality. If the killer came and knew the way to seclusion behind the wall, the killer was familiar with Widow's Haunt.

Warren would have made no effort to be quiet, to keep his arrival unannounced. He may have sauntered toward the wall, possibly reached the opening, and turned to congratulate himself again on an excellent choice for a rendezvous.

Silently, a loop of garden wire slipped over his head, pulled him down, choked out his life. When Warren no longer posed a threat, the ground was smoothed over, leaving no visible mark behind, and leaves were pushed back in place.

Despite the morning heat, Marian felt hollow coldness.

◆ ◆ ◆

Olson Marine didn't waste money on amenities. The boatyard was a model of neatness, with boats in varying stages of repair, but the small sign that said OFFICE hung askew on one side of an unpainted wooden shack. The door stood open.

Annie stepped into the doorway.

Eddie Olson looked up from a battered old desk. He looked sweaty; his face was reddened by the sun. He saw her. "You again?" His dark eyes held dislike, irritation. No fear.

Annie crossed the few feet to stand in front of the desk. It, too, appeared tidy, an open folder and papers neatly aligned in stacks. A computer sat on a stand behind the desk. A ceiling fan did nothing to lessen the heat, feebly stirred hot, heavy air.

Annie met his gaze with equal dislike. "What time did Warren Foster call you about Widow's Haunt?"

For an instant, nothing moved in that heavy face, then, slowly, his large lips spread in a grin. "Jesus, was that Warren? I should have known. Just like the little bastard to whisper like a girl." Now Eddie Olson was laughing. "Got his, didn't he? Wish I'd been there."

"Weren't you?"

Olson stood, rocking a little on his heels. "Anybody ever tell you to keep your nose out?" He came around the desk, stopped only inches from Annie, leaned forward.

She saw flecks of red in his eyes, maybe too much sun, maybe too much whiskey. She smelled sweat.

"He called you, said he saw you going into Alex's suite, told you to come—"

"I hung up on him. Wish I hadn't. I wouldn't have minded watching Warren do a little dance."

Annie felt a churn of nausea. "You didn't see his face." Her voice shook. "His face was awful."

Olson folded his arms. "Bad, huh? Maybe you should think about his face." Hot dark eyes stared at her. "If you want to keep your face pretty."

Marian Kenyon stood at the end of Fish Haul Pier. She loved the pier, loved feeling the breeze against her face, the taste of salt spray, the distinctive cry of the gulls, the glimpse of a dark smudge on the horizon, a ship bound for faraway ports. She came here when she was happy. She came when she was troubled. Now she came and found no peace. If she climbed the railing and dove into the surging water and swam as hard and fast as she could, she couldn't get away. Some things you can't outswim, outrun, leave behind. They are what they are. She was here and she knew too much. It was even more bitter to accept because last night she'd believed she was safe, she was safe and David was safe and Craig was safe. She and Craig . . . The last few times they were together, there had been a special feeling between them. Not just pride in David. Something more, a rekindling of the affection and caring they'd once felt for each other. There had been the beginning of an understanding; maybe the past didn't have to die, maybe they could be Marian and Craig and David together.

That was what she'd thought was almost hers after last night, a new life with Craig. Together they'd care for David. She'd been freed from the terror that the investigation into Alex's murder would destroy the world she had so carefully built. When Rae Griffith and Neil Kelly were led away from the ruins, Marian had been almost weak with relief. She was safe. They were safe.

But now she knew. Green plastic-coated garden wire, a scream, and the ruins where Warren died. Now she had to decide who she was. She'd spent her life believing truth mattered. She'd always been ready to battle fat cats and bullies. She took up for the underdog, knowing some people had not one deck but maybe a dozen decks stacked against them. That was who she was. Marian Kenyon, poor but honest. Marian Kenyon, bright, smart, acerbic, hiding pain and emotion beneath flippant smart-ass cracks. But she'd always come down on the side of the lost, the hurt, the hopeless.

The breeze caressed her cheeks, tugged at her blouse.

What about now?

M avis Cameron stepped into Billy's office. He looked tired. Of course he was tired after the two hard nights he'd spent dealing with murders, but his broad face was relaxed. The circuit solicitor was pleased.

Billy looked up with a smile. "Just sent off the last of the files to the solicitor. They're expecting the prisoners about ten Monday. We'll take the early ferry." His expression was suddenly quizzical. "What?"

Mavis closed the door. He knew, of course. He always knew when she had a concern, whether it was Kevin's grade in chemistry or the flushed look when their little girl came home from preschool with a virus or something out of kilter at the station. Years ago Mavis had brought her little boy to the island to escape an abusive husband, and Billy, no glimmer of white then in his short-cut blond hair, had become her champion. She knew him to be always fair, always honest, always reasonable.

"That girl, Rae Griffith." Mavis slipped into a straight chair.

Billy's gaze was affectionate. "I know. She's young, doesn't look mean, swears she didn't do anything wrong."

Mavis wasn't deterred. "Billy, will you talk to her?"

He leaned back in his chair, surprised. "She didn't make a peep after we read her her rights."

Mavis brushed back a strand of blond hair that had a tendency to droop down across her forehead. "I was in the cellblock. She begged me to let her talk to you."

Billy's broad mouth eased into a wry smile, but his tone was gentle. "Swore she was innocent, right?"

Mavis nodded, but continued to gaze at him.

"Honey, perps lie."

Mavis's tone was equally gentle. "It won't hurt to talk to her."

Annie knew the way to George Griffith's office, but this time she didn't want to be announced. She doubted George would be eager to see her. She smiled at the pleasant-faced woman at the reception desk. "George is expecting me."

Denise Fowler nodded agreeably. "Slow morning. Nobody seems pining to buy a house. Guess it's too hot to look."

"Up to ninety-five already." Even with the sea breezes the island was baking. Annie moved past the desk and into the hall. She went to the third door on the left, didn't knock.

George Griffith looked up as the door opened. The beginnings of a welcoming smile froze in place, making him look like a ventriloquist's dummy, with too much curly dark hair, a fleshy face, eyes bulging, lips stretched wide.

Annie closed the door. "George"—her tone was warm—"I'm glad I caught you. I know you want to help find out what happened to Alex." It was as if they'd never spoken of Lucy Galloway and the car that went airborne and the lone survivor from the lagoon. Without an invitation, she settled in the cushiony chair that faced his desk, leaned forward. "I told Billy Cameron I knew you would be the right person to help us out."

His light brown eyes watched her carefully. "Billy Cameron?"

Annie knew she was taking liberties, but she'd promised Max she wouldn't be stupid and surely a claim to be working with the police offered some protection. Her smile was bright. "Since the bookstore was involved with Alex's appearance, I've been in close touch with Billy."

George's thick black brows drew down. "They arrested that woman. Apparently she has a boyfriend. I don't know anything about them."

"Of course not." Annie was reassuring. "But now we're trying to figure out the timing of what happened last night at Widow's Haunt." Was there a glint of fear in those pale eyes? Certainly she had his attention. One pudgy hand that was limp on the desk tightened into a hard fist before the fingers slowly, stiffly loosened. "What time exactly did Warren call you?"

"Warren?" He blinked in apparent surprise.

Annie watched him coolly, knowing he was scrabbling to decide what to say, what to admit, what to deny. If it was he who had carried a length of garden wire to the ruins, he would well know now that the caller was Warren.

"Didn't you know it was Warren who called up and whispered that he'd seen you go into Alex's suite?"

"I told him he was wrong." The words tumbled out, fast, hot, scared.

"George, we're asking everyone about the time he called."

"Everyone?"

Annie nodded. "Yes. We know he called several people and we're trying to find out exactly when he contacted each person."

George's relief was obvious. "Oh yeah. I don't know what the hell he thought he was doing."

"The time?" Annie's tone was patient.

After a moment's pause, George said cautiously, "It was about eight fifteen."

Annie stood. "That's a great help. Billy will be pleased."

When she was once again outside, she, too, was pleased.

Marian pushed through unmarked doors that led to the kitchen on the second floor of the Seaside Inn. She walked directly to a small office, poked her head in the open doorway.

A dark-haired woman with an oval face, dark eyes, and smooth skin looked up from a neat desk. She was trim, dressed in a white blouse and black slacks. She had a competent aura. She cupped a hand over the receiver on the phone. "Be right with you." Then she spoke to the listener in a pleasant, well-modulated voice. "That will be one chicken salad sandwich on wheat, coleslaw, and fruit, and one hamburger with mustard, onion, lettuce, no tomato, French fries, and two iced teas? Sweet teas? . . . Your order will be delivered in twenty minutes." She hung up, swiveled to a computer, typed rapidly, hit Send, faced Marian. "I'm sorry but the kitchen is off-limits to everyone but hotel personnel." She came to her feet, ready to shepherd Marian back to the main hallway.

"Marian Kenyon from the *Gazette*. I'm covering the story about the murder of Alex Griffith in Suite 130. It would be extremely helpful if I could speak to the person who took the order received from Suite 130 at seven seventeen P.M. Wednesday evening."

A faint line creased the smooth face. "I'm not sure I'm authorized to release that information—"

181

Marian was swift. "I can obtain the name from police records but it will save time for me if you can give me that contact information. I'll wait in the hall." Marian jerked her head toward the double doors. She expected that Ms. Rodriguez, whose name she'd noted on the tag pinned to the white blouse, would be relieved to have her offending presence removed from the kitchen; and maybe her matter-of-fact manner—and mention of police records—would yield a good result.

Five minutes passed. Marian frowned. Her next stop would be the manager's office. Maybe she should have started there. She was about to turn away when one panel of the white doors opened. A gangling young man with a nose peeling from sunburn stepped into the hall, walked toward her. Likely he was a college student working on the island for the summer, loving being a beach bum in his free time.

"Ma'am?" His accent was Southern-soft. "I'm J. T. Lewis. I took the call that night from the man that got killed."

"Hi, J. T. I'm Marian Kenyon with the *Gazette*. Since you may have been the last person to speak to Alex Griffith before he was killed, I'd like to find out exactly what he said." More than that, how he said it. God, it mattered; it might make all the difference to her, and to Rae Griffith.

J. T.'s short brown hair was cut in a crew. His face was spare with a thin nose and sharp chin. He gazed at her with wide eyes. "It was just an order. I wasn't paying a lot of attention. I mean, I was careful to get it right, but it was just another call. I answered, 'Room service. How may I help you?'" His face squeezed in concentration. "He said, 'This is Suite 130. Need some quick service, a gin and tonic, short on the tonic, and a rum collins.' He muffled the phone for a minute, said something to somebody, then came back on. 'And some peanuts, okay?

Thanks.'" He looked at Marian doubtfully. "I mean, that's all there was to it."

"What kind of voice did he have?" And what kind of question was she asking, what was she hoping for? Or not.

J. T. squinted. "Smooth. A guy used to people snapping to. He sounded"—a pause—"like he was having a good time." Another pause. J. T. swallowed hard, perhaps grappling for the first time, in a happy young life, with unexpected death. "He sounded like he was on top of the world."

A fine line marred the perfection of Lynn Griffith's smooth face. "Annie, honey, there must be some mistake." Her sweet voice was kindly. "I didn't get a call from Warren Foster last night. Why, I haven't talked to Warren in forever."

They sat again on the apricot sofa. This morning the sun glinted through louvers, throwing a black-and-white pattern on the wooden floor.

Lynn shook her head but not a strand of silver blond hair was disarranged. "I'm so sorry about what happened, but Warren really wasn't very likable." It was as if she confided a difficult but uncontested truth. Again that headshake. "I guess it's clear that awful young woman killed Alex and then Warren. Now"—she arched her eyebrows—"why are you asking?"

Annie again resorted to Billy as her shield. "I told Billy Cameron I'd ask around. Apparently Warren called several people last night."

Lynn looked puzzled. "I guess I'm confused, honey. I thought from what I heard a little while ago on TV that he called that woman—"

Annie knew she referred to Rae Griffith.

"—and told her he saw her go into the suite. The TV didn't say he called anyone else. Why do you think he called other people, too?" Her soft voice rose in a query.

"We know he called several people."

Lynn was placid. "He didn't call me."

Annie stared at the smooth, unlined face. Abruptly, she felt confident Lynn had indeed received a call. But her answer to Annie was consistent with her claim that she and Alex had had a lovely visit about old times.

Annie smiled. "In any event, I can tell Billy I checked with you." She rose.

Lynn walked with her to the hallway and opened the front door, murmuring, "Well, I'm glad it's all behind us. Dreadful, of course, what happened." A shudder. "Poor Alex. And a shock about Warren. But we have to be thankful the police have done such a good job."

As Annie walked toward the car, she carried with her a certainty that Lynn Griffith had indeed received a whispery call from Warren Foster. Lynn's smooth voice was untroubled and her smile bright as she bid Annie good-bye. Who said being somewhat obtuse didn't have advantages? Lynn simply refused to admit she had any reason to fear Alex or, consequently, any reason to fear Warren. Whether she was innocent or guilty, it was a stance that saved her from explaining anything to anyone.

11

Rae Griffith sat stiffly in the wooden chair facing Billy's desk. Short dark hair tangled, no makeup, thin face pale and drawn. "I swear to God I didn't have anything to do with Alex being hurt or that man in the woods."

Billy kept his face expressionless. Like he'd told Mavis, perps lie. He wondered what Rae Griffith wanted, what she hoped to accomplish. Did she think he would be swayed by a pale face, by eyes that were pools of fear? She'd find out that his role was done. Now her future was the responsibility of the circuit solicitor. Billy had one simple aim. Not to mess up the case. "Mrs. Griffith, anything you say may be used in court against you. You have a right—"

She lifted a thin hand. "I know. You told me all that."

The recorder on the desk whirred. Billy had refused to speak with her unless she agreed to a recording of their conversation.

Billy sat back in his chair, folded his arms, waited.

Rae clasped her hands tightly together. "You said you aren't taking us off the island until Monday."

Billy nodded. "The seven o'clock ferry. Arraignment's set for ten. As I understand it, your attorney, Brooks Clark, will meet us there. You will have time to confer with her—"

"I know." Her tone was dismissive. Monday was clearly unimportant to her at this moment. "I want to talk to someone here on the island."

Billy was puzzled. "You want to see about a lawyer—"

"Not a lawyer. I'll talk to Brooks tomorrow." At his flicker of surprise, Rae looked almost amused. "We went to school together. She's coming from Atlanta. But a lawyer can't find out who killed Alex. Or that man in the woods. I need somebody who knows people here, somebody who read Alex's book and knows where to look. I was scared after that cop talked to me yesterday. She asked all these questions. Like, what did I drink? Why did she care? But I could tell from her eyes that you people were going to come after me—"

Billy maintained a stolid expression. He didn't feel defensive. Hyla Harrison had coon-dog instincts and she'd treed a mighty nice coon. Besides, he always knew to *cherchez la femme*. Yeah, the dictum was trite but phrases became trite because they were nuggets of truth. *Cherchez la femme.* Round up the usual suspects. Look before you leap. He'd learned a few others in his time. Beware the man who smiles all the time. Scared people do stupid things. If it isn't sex, it's money; if it isn't money, it's sex; if it isn't sex or money, it's fear.

"—and you think all these things." Just for an instant her green eyes didn't meet his.

Billy watched her dispassionately. *Right, lady, we think these things because your boyfriend checked in next door with a hat, wig, sunglasses, pillow belly, and Hawaiian shirt. And a gun that he later disposed of in the ocean. Just a few hints that maybe all wasn't sunny-side up in your marriage. A man threat-*

ens to inform police you were where you claim you weren't and, surprise, he's dead, and you're on the scene.

"But I didn't hurt Alex." Now she gazed at him again. "If I could talk to that woman who owns the bookstore—"

Billy felt a quiver of surprise.

"—she said she'd try to help me. Please, will you let me talk to her?"

"You want to talk to Annie Darling?" He frowned.

Rae was animated, nodding her head quickly. "Just for a few minutes. Could you call and ask her to come and see me?"

Billy considered the request. He didn't want to mess up his case. Rae Griffith had been Mirandized. She didn't have to answer anybody's questions. At this point, building the case would depend upon facts and suppositions that they unearthed, not a confession from Rae Griffith. If she spoke to Annie . . .

"Mrs. Griffith, a lawyer would advise you not to speak—"

"Annie Darling promised she'd help me. She knows people on the island. She knows who wanted Alex dead. If she'll tell me, I'll have somewhere to start."

Start? Somewhere to start? Billy studied the thin, frightened face. "Look, if you talk to her, you understand that it won't be a privileged communication?" At Rae's blank look, he continued, "If you talk to her, I will interview her and she has to tell me what you said."

To his surprise, Rae Griffith brightened. "That's all right. She can tell anyone she wants to tell."

Annie slid her cell out of her purse as she hurried on the boardwalk. She wished she were a tourist with nothing to worry about except getting too much sun or twinging her back from staying too long on the driving range or trying to decide between key lime pie and apple cobbler for dessert.

She unmuted the phone, saw she had a text. She stopped short, drew in a deep breath. Max. The message began: *Back early. Got voice mail. See you shortly.* Annie clicked off the phone. Oh. And oh. No "Luv U," "Can't wait 2 C U," no hearts. Nothing but three crisp sentences. Should she reply? And say what? *Talking to possible murderers, no harm intended?*

She pushed through the door and saw a double line of restive customers stretching all the way back to the coffee bar. For once, she was glad to see people impatiently waiting in line. She was grateful for anything that kept her thoughts at bay, the decision she had to make about said possible murderers, and the impending arrival of a husband with an angry glint in his eyes. Annie plunged around the cash desk, opened up the second register.

As she started to ring up a stack of titles, she skimmed them, agreed with the purchaser's choices: Cara Black, Bill Crider, Sue Dunlap, Miranda James, JoAnna Carl, Mary Jane Clark, Naomi Hirahara, winners all. And much nicer to think about than an irate husband who might arrive at any moment.

Ingrid took a breath between customers. "Marian's in your office waiting for you. She looks like hell."

Carrying a folder in one hand, Hyla Harrison knocked on the door to Billy Cameron's office. She turned the knob and stood in the doorway. The chief was always open to seeing anyone at any time, no need to call and ask.

He was standing at the window looking out at the bay. The view was always the same, always different: the boardwalk, the shops that fronted on the water, the pier for the *Miss Jolene*, empty now, the marina filled with tethered boats, and, beyond, the richly green water, brimming with nutrients and sea life, gulls circling overhead, a V of pelicans skimming the whitecaps, shrimp boats trawling, sailboats, a distant catamaran, a windsurfer out a bit too far for Hyla's liking.

"Chief, can I talk to you for a minute?"

He turned and the flood of sunlight behind him made his hair shine like ripe wheat. His broad face was furrowed in thought, but his nod was immediate and he walked to his desk and settled into his chair.

Hyla sat down, wondering what had happened to worry him. That morning at the press conference he'd been relaxed, the department's job done, crimes solved, the machinery of justice in motion. She didn't want to add to his concerns, but the little burr of unease wouldn't go away until she spoke out.

"I've been thinking."

Billy waited, his expression grave.

The slight twitch of the chief's lips didn't escape her. Lou Pirelli's nickname for her was Serious Sal. But she'd seen what she'd seen. "I got to thinking about Widow's Haunt. I made a copy of Mavis's sketches and took them with me." She opened the folder, stood to spread the sheets on Billy's desk. She tapped the sketch showing the body propped against the uneven sill of the long-ago window. "You'll see that his head is hanging back on his left shoulder. The body stayed upright because the forearm rested against the sill. Since we figure the murderer stood behind Foster, there are two possibilities. Foster and his killer were standing together on the clearing side of the partial wall. The killer induced Foster to turn away, looped the wire over his head, yanked, choked him. At this point, for the body to settle where it did, the murderer had to pull him almost up against the wall, then let the body sag to the left and slump into the position where it was found. Could have been done, but why? Or Foster was standing with his back to the ruin. The killer was hidden on the other side of the wall. Foster stopped with his back to the open window. The killer leaned forward, dropped the wire, pulled. The body would naturally collapse into the position where it was found. On balance, it seems likelier the murderer was behind the wall, Foster was facing the clearing, and the body ended up where it did because he was yanked from behind."

Billy's eyes narrowed. "Your point?"

"I think"—the words came slowly—"the killer had to know the ruins. So far as we know, Mrs. Griffith had never been to the site."

"So far as we know."

"You have to be familiar with the ruins to get to the back side of that wall. There's a path on the far side of the porch. There's a stand of bayberry on the other side. You have to go a good ten feet back then climb over a broken sundial to get into the patch of ground on the far side of the opening. Last night, Kenyon and Darling stated they heard a scream and that's why Kenyon called 911. We were on the terrace so we got there in maybe two minutes. When we arrived, Mrs. Griffith was standing on the near side of the wall and Kelly was on his hands and knees, throwing up. If she screamed right after Foster was killed, there wasn't time to come around to the front side of the wall before we got there. Now, I guess they—she—could have swung over the ledge but that would likely have moved the body."

Billy leaned back in his chair, face furrowed, fingertips pressed together. "We don't know how long Griffith and Kelly were there before she screamed. Foster may have been dead for several minutes and there was plenty of time to come around the wall."

"Why did she scream?"

Billy looked more comfortable. "She's smart. She heard someone coming, knew they were going to be seen, screamed to make it look like she'd just found the body."

Hyla frowned. "I guess that's possible." She hesitated, then continued. "There's one more point. I looked behind the wall today. I know it's exactly how Mavis pictured it. There's this hump of leaves, really smooth, up against the base of the opening as you face the clearing. I think somebody moved leaves out of the way so there wouldn't be any crackles, waited for Foster, killed him when he came, then smoothed those leaves up against the bricks. Now, it could be that Griffith and Kelly got there before Foster. Griffith waited behind the wall. Kelly stayed back in the woods on the other side of the clearing. She killed Foster, prettied up the leaves, came around the wall. They were going to leave and then she heard someone coming and screamed."

Billy's face gave no hint to this thoughts. An eyebrow quirked up. "Doesn't explain Pretty Boy throwing up, does it?"

Hyla was judicious. "Maybe he hadn't seen the body until just before Kenyon and Darling arrived. What worries me more is how she knew to find her way behind the wall if she'd never been to Widow's Haunt before. Plus, we didn't find a flashlight on either Griffith or Kelly. The two routes to get behind the wall would be heavily shadowed despite the moonlight." She reached for the folder, gathered up the sheets, rose. "When I got to Widow's Haunt, Marian Kenyon was looking around. I'd say she's wondering, too."

She was at the door when Billy spoke. "Officer." She turned, a little apprehensive. Had she taken too much on herself? Was she out of line?

"Good work. Again." His face creased. "You picked up on Kelly's phony registration, saw him throw the gun away. We built a solid case from there. Do you think he and the widow are innocent?"

"I think"—she spoke deliberately, making a judgment—"the wife and the lover planned on killing Alex Griffith. I'll never doubt that. But maybe somebody beat them to it."

Annie took one look at Marian's face, wan, strained, somehow defeated, and bit back the words she'd been rehearsing, the words that would link the phone call Marian had received from Warren to the other calls he'd made, implicitly suggesting that Marian had lied to her. Instead, she said crisply, "Did you have breakfast?"

"Coffee." Marian's voice was dull, exhausted.

"No lunch?" In fact, it was almost one and Annie hadn't eaten either. "Stay right there. I'll get us some food." At the coffee bar, she quickly made two ham and cheese sandwiches on croissants, added a mound of potato salad, mustard based, not the overmayoed style that was too rich. A couple of dill pickles. Sour cream and onion potato chips, Annie's secret vice at the store. Max preferred crisp thin white corn chips that were admittedly delicious; but sometimes a girl wanted her sour cream and onion fix. Two tall glasses of plain iced tea, unsweetened. She carried the tray carefully, working around oblivious customers.

She brought the tray in, pushing the storeroom door shut behind her. As she placed a plate in front of Marian and the glass of tea, she said, "Not a word until we've eaten."

Marian started to speak. "We have to—"

Annie shook her head. "Eat."

Marian slowly picked up half of the sandwich, took a bite, and then, with a faint look of surprise, ate fast, almost gulping the food.

Annie was puzzled. The night before, when she and Marian parted, Marian had been hugely relieved. The crimes were solved.

No one would have any reason to pursue Marian's past. But ever since Joan's visit, Annie had been afraid. And now, looking at Marian, she knew there was more to come.

Marian finished first. She took a last gulp of tea, faced Annie. "Last night I thought I was sitting pretty, Rae Griffith and her boyfriend in jail. It got even better at Billy's presser this morning. Kelly's her lover. He registered under a false name. She and Kelly were found near Foster's body. But Billy kept on talking. You know how Warren was killed? Green plastic-coated garden wire." She stared at Annie. "I asked if they found garden wire in her room, in her car, in Kelly's car? Nada. Where'd she get garden wire? You carry garden wire around in your purse? In your car? I don't think so. I'll bet if we check, she's never done a day of gardening in her life. If she didn't have garden wire, she didn't kill Foster. Foster's murder was last-minute. No time to go out and buy garden wire. And then I started thinking about Widow's Haunt. I went back out there today. Unless I'm nuts, the killer got Warren through the empty window. The killer was standing on the other side of the wall." Slowly, emphatically, Marian shook her head. "Nobody from off island could know the ruins well enough to plan an ambush there. And"—a heavy sigh—"she screamed. Sure, maybe she heard us coming and screamed to seem innocent as a lamb. That could be. But I lay awake most of the night. What if Rae's telling the truth? What if she had nothing to do with Alex's murder? Maybe she and Kelly just had the hots and didn't want to be apart. If they are innocent, then Rae didn't kill Alex and go out to the terrace and Kelly didn't slip into the suite and call room service to make it sound like Alex was alive. Instead, it was Alex Griffith who called room service. I went out to the inn and now I'm damn sure they're innocent."

Annie knew that now she would never have to ask Marian about the call from Warren. Maybe he called because he was pleased at his cleverness, wanted to show off, throw out tantalizing hints to Marian. Maybe he called and whispered he'd seen her enter the Griffith suite. What Warren said in his call to Marian didn't matter now. Marian would not be sitting across the worktable, looking at Annie with despairing eyes because she now was convinced that Alex's widow and her boyfriend were innocent, if Marian had killed Alex and Warren. Marian was here because she wouldn't stand by, even to protect herself, and let a false accusation stand. Marian was innocent.

Marian spoke rapidly. "Alex called room service. I talked to the kid who took the order. Alex was full of himself, sounded happy."

Annie felt a wash of disappointment. Was that all Marian had learned? How could she be certain the caller was Alex just because the voice was untroubled? She knew her face reflected her feeling. "That doesn't prove anything. If you were standing in the room with a murder victim and calling room service to set up an alibi, wouldn't you make it a point to sound upbeat?"

"Kelly threw up." Marian's dark eyes were bleak.

Annie had a sudden vivid memory of Alex Griffith's body twisted in death and blood seeping from beneath a throw pillow. Warren's swollen dead face had been grotesque but no more hideous than blood and Alex's gray hand trailing on the floor.

Marian was brusque. "Yeah. You got it. The odds Kelly could bring off a lord of the manor tone with a dead man just feet away from him are, like, seventy to one in my book. So, we have to find out who killed Alex. I went back over everything that happened Thursday night. When you and I were on the path, I'm pretty sure I heard some crackling up ahead of us. Billy will say I'm imagining it because now I think she's innocent. But if she and Kelly were just ahead of us, there wasn't time for her to strangle Warren before she screamed." Marian brushed back a lock of dark hair. "But she got a call from Warren.

She told us that. If she's innocent, that means somebody else, maybe several people, got calls."

"That's exactly what happened." Annie talked fast. "Joan Turner came here this morning. She wanted to know if Warren called Rae. When I said he had, Joan looked sick. She left without another word, but I know she must be struggling right now, too. If she got a call and Rae got a call, who else might have been called? I know the answer. All of them did. George Griffith admitted it. Eddie Olson thought it was funny, claims he hung up. Lynn Griffith said it never happened, but I'm sure she's lying. I think that's how she looks at life. If she doesn't admit something, it doesn't exist." Annie wanted to drive the fear from Marian's dark eyes. She gave her a steady look. "It's fortunate you went to see Warren yesterday. That explains why he called you, too."

Just for an instant, Marian's eyes closed. When they opened, she said quietly, so quietly Annie could scarcely hear, "From your lips to God's ears." She took a breath. "So now we know Rae Griffith's in a hell of a mess. We know—at least we think we know—that Alex was killed by one of four people: his sister, Joan; his brother, George; his sister-in-law Lynn; or Eddie Olson. Each one had reason to fear Alex, but I'm damned if I see what we can do to figure out which one is guilty. The killer left no trace at the inn or at Widow's Haunt." Marian's face squeezed in thought. "Maybe there's one thing we do know—" She looked suddenly alive, intent, the Marian Annie knew. "Come on, let's go see Billy."

Billy looked from Marian to Annie. "Speak of the devil." He added quickly, "Not meant literally, of course." A brief wry smile touched his face. He gazed steadily at Annie. "I was considering whether to call you."

Annie almost explained hurriedly that she hadn't meant to imply to anyone that she was asking questions on Billy's behalf, but stopped herself in time. Wait until the accusation was made. As Laurel often admonished in her husky voice, "Remember to be like angels—never rush in!" The advice was often aimed at Annie, though in the most dulcet of tones with only the tiniest hint of exasperation. "Angels," Annie blurted out.

Billy looked at her with a flicker of amusement, Marian with quick concern.

"I was thinking," she continued with as much dignity as she could manage, "that it was time for angels to appear at Rae's and Neil's shoulders."

Billy's face tightened. "Not sure either of them deserves an angel." He shook his head. "Strike that. We all deserve angels and," he said thoughtfully, "maybe an unlikely angel has already appeared. I gather you two are here on their behalf. Let's hear the rustle of your wings."

Marian set out the arguments.

Billy listened as Marian described her interview with J. T. Lewis. The basic facts were the same as those discovered by Hyla when she spoke with the director of room service but Marian's report gave an insight on the attitude of the speaker. He made notes on a pad. "Tell me again about the call. Is that how you remember it?"

"J. T. Lewis said the caller was buoyant. That's my word but that's the impression I got from the kid. College boy. Smart. Well spoken. Not embellishing. Seemed struck by Alex's upbeat manner and the fact that he was dead within a few minutes." Marian paused. "Kelly threw up at Widow's Haunt."

"Yeah." Billy leaned back in his chair. "All of this kind of reminds me of when I cleaned out my aunt's attic after she died. Nobody had been up there for years. Cobwebs like a witch's hut. Every time I turned around, I was enmeshed by these fine silky strands. That's what this seems like. All kinds of silky strands, nothing strong enough to hold on to. But"—he sat up straight—"there's enough here that I'm going to bend a regulation or two."

Max Darling leaned against the rail on the top deck of the *Miss Jolene*. The breeze rippled his polo shirt, slapped at his trousers. He'd just spent five ocean-happy days, basking in the sun, fighting tarpon, drinking beer, but he never tired of the smell of the sea, the spume that dampened his face, the joyful glimpses of bottlenose dolphins at play, surfing in a boat's wake or arching up and out of the water and down again. In another quarter hour, there'd be a gray smudge in the distance, the first glimpse of the low-lying tangle of greenery that was Broward's Rock. The ferry wallowed a bit in heavy swells. Far out at sea, a tropical disturbance sent light boats scurrying for shore, slammed and slapped freighters and cruise ships. The coming storm was the reason for the early return of the fishing boat. Once onshore, he'd picked up his gear and, as he drove north, listened to a very familiar voice on his cell's speakerphone. Max remembered the first time he'd taken the ferry to Broward's Rock, a guy in a hurry to find his girl. Not that Annie Laurance knew she was his girl at that moment. But he knew. He'd come to the island determined that she would be his.

His Annie, serious, honest, kind, hardworking—sometimes a sticky point of difference between them—positive, smart, funny, proud of being a Texan, quick to help anyone in need . . .

He gripped the railing, squinted. A thin gray bar lay on the horizon. He willed the *Miss Jolene* to go faster. He was in a hurry again.

◆ ◆ ◆

Billy Cameron stood at his office window. He liked to look out at the harbor when he was thinking. He was like a laughing gull diving for mullet, watching the surface, ready to pounce when the prey was in view. He'd felt pretty good about arresting Rae Griffith and Neil Kelly. Now he wasn't sure. He understood Hyla Harrison's reasoning and the deductions by Marian and Annie, but he still smelled murder when he thought about Rae and her boyfriend in the next room at the inn. Yet he would keep searching. Three folders rested on his desk, one for George Griffith, one for Lynn Griffith, one for Eddie Olson. Three more folders were stacked on the corner, one for the widow and her friend, one for Joan Turner, one for Marian Kenyon. They weren't inactive folders but, for the moment, those suspects were not in his sights. He'd added Joan Turner's folder when Annie reported Joan's visit to the bookstore and her worry about Warren's calls. Murderers did not worry about the innocence of others. The same reasoning now held true for Marian Kenyon. She would not argue for Rae Griffith's innocence if Marian was the murderer. He was well aware, though he doubted Marian realized, of her connection to Alex. People had a tendency to think cops didn't read. He read books, especially books about the island, and he'd grown up on the island. When Annie Darling described her talk with Warren Foster on the terrace Wednesday night, Billy already knew who was threatened. He'd also made the connection between the contents of Alex Griffith's briefcase and the characters in Alex's book. Now he had three names still on his list. He gave a short nod, turned, walked to his desk, leaned over to click the intercom. "Send Officer Harrison in."

12

Tears slid down Rae Griffith's thin face. "You came. Oh God, I'm scared." The clownish, too-large orange jumpsuit only emphasized the terror in her face.

Annie reached across the table, clasped a narrow hand. "I can't promise anything but we are trying to find out who killed Alex."

"We?" Huge eyes stared at her.

"Marian Kenyon, the reporter for the *Gazette*. Marian insists you are innocent." At Rae's uncomprehending stare, Annie continued. "Last night Marian and I thought Warren was trying to get a glimpse of the murderer. Something he said to Marian made us think of Widow's Haunt. That's why she and I came. We heard you scream."

Rae's hand turned, took Annie's wrist in a tight grip. She was excited. "You were there? Then you can tell them you heard us find that man. Maybe they'll let us go." The excitement drained away. The eyes that stared at Annie once again held dark visions, hopelessness. "That big policeman doesn't believe us. He looks at me and he's sure I killed Alex. I didn't. And now I know I never could—" She broke off.

Before Rae's green eyes skittered away, Annie understood an ugly truth. Marian was right. Rae and Neil had planned for Alex to die. Annie didn't know how or what they intended to do. But thinking of murder and committing murder were not the same. What they might be in God's eyes wasn't for her to know. Rae and Neil, if ever they were freed, could struggle with whatever reality they knew. But right now, she was here because someone else on the island had moved silently Wednesday and Thursday nights.

Annie remembered Marian's last words outside the station. "Rae, do you always drink the same thing?"

Rae loosened her grip. She lifted both hands, pressed them against her cheeks. "I thought you came here to help me, tell me—"

"This is important. If Alex were ordering drinks for you, calling room service, what would he order? Think carefully, tell me exactly what he would say."

Rae's hands dropped. "You and that policewoman. What did I drink? I told her. I'm telling you. Ask anybody who knows me. I always drink a margarita and I like for the rim of the glass to be salted. If Alex"—a sick, sad look crossed her face—"if Alex called room service or we were at the bar, it was always the same. He'd order a margarita for me with salt, and for him"—her voice put the words in quote marks—"'a gin and tonic, short on the tonic.' What difference does it make?"

"All the difference in the world. He didn't order a margarita. He ordered a rum collins. So you weren't there."

She gave a ragged laugh. "Can you find out who drinks rum collinses? I can see it now, go from bar to bar, get the names—'Everybody who drinks rum collinses hold up your glass.' Maybe on a resort island that might narrow it down to a few hundred." She sagged back against the hard straight chair in the conference room.

Annie spoke quietly. "Rae, close your eyes for a few minutes. Empty everything out of your mind. Breathe in through your nose, out through your mouth."

Rae blinked, then closed her eyes. Soon her uneven breaths were regular, deeper.

Annie watched the big black minute hand on the round clock move. One minute, two, three. She waited five minutes, said gently, "Keep your eyes closed. Picture Alex when you saw him Wednesday afternoon. He came back to the hotel late after he'd been around the island. Try to repeat exactly what he said."

Rae spoke in a near monotone. "He said he invited them all—"

Gold-plated invitations to Joan, George, Eddie, and Lynn. All of them came to the inn to hear what he would say.

"—to come to his talk . . . told them they didn't want to miss their razzle-dazzle turn in the spotlight . . . Joan begged . . . never thought the high and the mighty would be reduced to that . . . not sexy enough anyway . . ." She stopped. "I didn't hear much more. He was pleased with himself and talking about people I didn't know or care about. I thought it was boring—"

Not only, Annie thought, had Rae decided Alex's conversation was boring, she thought he was boring.

"—but he said he was going to knock 'em dead, he'd figured out what really happened with his brother, and he wished he'd talked to—and this is where I can't remember the name, I think he ran into somebody he used to know and the name was really odd—he wished he'd talked to her before he'd written *Don't Go Home* but maybe it was better this way. Now he had evidence in black and white. Then he laughed and said 'actually in color' but that didn't make any sense to me."

Annie was confused. "Knew what had happened about what?"

Rae looked uncertain. "About his brother. Alex saw this woman and found out something that changed everything."

"Which brother?"

Rae shook her head.

H yla Harrison showed her badge. "Officer Harrison to see George Griffith. Which door, please?" Hyla was accustomed to shocked faces. She was often wryly reminded of actors on TV commercials evincing huge amazement at how quickly computer cobwebs can be removed.

The receptionist stared at her with wide eyes. A hand reached toward an intercom.

"I'll show myself in. Which office?"

The plump woman nodded quickly. "The third door on the left."

When Hyla reached the door, she didn't knock, just turned the knob and stood in the doorway.

George was stretched out on a sofa. He jerked upright. "What the—" He saw Hyla and broke off, like he had no breath left.

Hyla stepped inside, closed the door behind her. "Mr. Griffith, I want an accounting of your movements last night." She took three quick strides, stared down at him.

"Thursday night? You don't have any right—"

"I am investigating the death of Warren Foster. If you prefer to answer questions at the police station, we can go there now."

George's reddish face looked scared. "I thought you arrested that woman."

"We are pursuing further leads. Can you explain your presence at Widow's Haunt at approximately nine P.M.?"

"Who says I was there?" He struggled to get the words out.

"You were observed. I suggest you accurately describe your movements, beginning with the receipt of the phone call from Warren Foster. Start with the time." Hyla kept her gaze steady, her demeanor official, saw panic flare in his eyes.

George tugged at the throat of his dress shirt. "It was a quarter after eight. It said 'Unknown Caller,' but it was my cell so I answered. I didn't know who was calling. If I'd known it was Warren, I'd have ignored it. It was a damn whisper, said he saw me go into Alex's suite. That's a lie. I had nothing to do with Alex's death. But I thought I'd better find out what it was about." He leaned forward, placed his hands on his thighs. "I got to the lot about five after nine. I had a flashlight with me. I walked toward the ruins." He took a deep breath. "I called out, 'Hey,' but nobody answered. I almost turned around and left but I was kind of mad by this point, so I kept on walking and I flashed the light all around the ruins." He stopped and looked half sick. "I saw this body propped up on the wall. The face was awful but I didn't look long enough to realize it was Warren. I knew something bad had happened. I turned and ran to my car and got the hell out." He leaned back against the cushion, expelled a whoosh of air, as if he felt better having told what he'd seen.

Hyla studied his flaccid face. Not a prepossessing face. Not a man you'd count on in a fight. But his expression of relief mixed with remembered horror impressed her. She nodded. "Thank you for the information. We'll be in touch about making a formal statement."

◆ ◆ ◆

Billy Cameron was skeptical. "Pretty indefinite. Just a nice general smear of anyone and everyone. Does she think we're going to go around the island hunting for a woman with an odd name?"

Annie knew she'd slammed into a wall. Billy thought Rae wanted her husband to die. But he could be wrong. "Rae said Alex always ordered a gin and tonic, light on the tonic."

"If Kelly called room service, you can bet he was primed. He wouldn't order a margarita."

Annie knew it was time to stop tugging on a dead horse. "What about the break-in at the suite late Wednesday night?"

Billy leaned back in his chair, looked thoughtful. "Rae could easily have staged the entire scene to make it look like somebody was hot to find something. She had plenty of time to get rid of the briefcase before she called 911. She says Alex claimed to have incriminating evidence of some sort when he made the rounds Wednesday. It's clear from your forays"—Billy's gaze was chiding—"that Alex saw his sister, his brother, his sister-in-law, and his old classmate. He took the briefcase along when he left the inn. It was in his car after he was killed so if one of them killed him, they could have come back late at night hoping to find the briefcase. Right after the crime, the killer could have tried to find the briefcase but it wasn't in the suite at that time. Maybe Alex carried the briefcase with him as he looked up people so the killer knew what the briefcase looked like and didn't see it in the suite. Or somebody else had something to hide and thought the suite would be empty and decided to take a look."

Breaking in argued someone was worried about papers. "You and Rae checked the briefcase. What did you find?"

Billy scooted his chair forward, reached for a folder. He flipped it open. "Mavis cataloged the contents, took some pictures, and scanned the contents. A bunch of clippings." He paused, skimming the pages. "The football game where Michael Smith was hurt. The drowning of Lucy Galloway. Heyward Griffith's disappearance. Clippings about his body washing ashore." His face creased. "The brief in the divorce column for Marian and Craig Kenyon. Birth notice for David Kenyon. A letter—"

Annie listened intently.

"—from Heyward Griffith. Innocuous message: 'Alex—looking forward to lunch Tuesday. I'll bring you up-to-date. It's time to cut my losses.' And"—Billy was expressionless—"a picture of a big blond guy in swim trunks. No ID. Scrawled on the back: 'Midsummer madness.'"

It seemed obvious which memento was associated with which figure out of Alex's past. Annie wondered how Alex had gotten the picture, if the man in swim trunks was the lover Joan had taken. Joan herself had revealed that Heyward kept in touch with Alex, possibly vented his displeasure with Joan and George. Joan had come to Death on Demand and when she learned that Warren had called Rae, Joan looked despairing. If Joan killed her brother, she would not have come, would not be concerned about Rae's fate, would in fact be delighted that Rae and Neil had been arrested.

Billy leaned back in his chair again. "That's the sum total of the famous missing briefcase. I don't see it gets us anywhere."

"Did Rae see you photograph the contents of the case?"

Billy shrugged. "She was there. She appeared to be in shock. Maybe she did. Maybe not. Maybe she still thought a fake break-in was a good idea, divert attention from her."

"I don't think so. Rae was half drugged. She'd taken a sleeping pill. I think someone did break in. But"—and now her face squeezed in thought—"it wasn't the killer."

Billy raised an eyebrow. "Looking in your crystal ball?" But his tone was genial. "Why so?"

"The killer would have checked out the suite after killing Alex. So the killer knew the case wasn't there. That means someone else came, figuring the suite was empty and hoping to get whatever Alex had mentioned that day."

Billy shook his head. "Maybe the killer had to hurry. Maybe room service knocked and the killer got the hell out, not sure whether the case was there or not. So it could have been the killer who came or one of the others threatened by Alex or none of the above and Rae Griffith was looking for a decoy. As for Rae"—now he was fully intent—"exactly what did she tell you?"

Hyla Harrison was courteous but firm. "Mrs. Griffith, it is important that I speak with you."

Lynn Griffith's pale lips tightened for an instant. She paused to let her exasperation show, then spoke. "Nellie—that's my nail girl—is working me in. I've snagged one of my nails." She held up her right hand, displayed the nail on her index finger. "I have to hurry."

"Yes, ma'am." Hyla spoke quickly. "It will only take a moment. What time did you get to Widow's Haunt last night?"

That perfect face was utterly still, then blue eyes widened. "I beg your pardon?"

"You received a phone call from Warren Foster and he told you when to come to Widow's Haunt. If you can—"

Lynn shook her head impatiently but her silvery blond hair

remained in place. "Officer, I have been patient but enough is enough. I don't know what Annie Darling told you. She came here"—the voice lifted in outrage—"and asked me about Warren and I told her she was mistaken, and that's what I am telling you. I didn't speak to Warren. I didn't go to that place where he died. I know nothing about his death. Or Alex's. I do not wish to be harassed further."

Marian welcomed the dimness beneath the spreading live oak even though the shade did nothing to diminish the July heat. She leaned against a low branch, watched the harbor. The front steps of the station were in her peripheral vision. Would Annie learn anything that could help? Or would she learn only enough to clear Rae Griffith and Neil Kelly, turn the investigation onto others—like her—who were desperate to prevent Alex from speaking out?

Marian's shoulders tightened. If she'd kept quiet . . . But she couldn't remain silent. Not even for David. She felt a twist of pain deep inside. And, she knew another truth. She had to trap the person who killed Alex. Alex should be alive right now, causing trouble in his own bullheaded way. But Alex should be alive.

David's father . . . She owed Alex justice.

Tomorrow was the last full day of David's visit. He and Craig planned to spend the day at the High Museum. David had left a message on her cell. "Mom, there's a huge exhibit of art of the Old West . . ." Marian had loved the excitement in his voice. He sounded younger than fifteen. He sounded . . . oh God, he sounded so happy.

"Marian."

She recognized the familiar voice.

She turned and watched Max Darling stride swiftly toward her.

◆ ◆ ◆

Eddie Olson stood in the shade of an awning, gulped Gatorade from a cooler. He shot Hyla Harrison an amused look. "Like I told Annie Darling—and I don't know where she got her deputy badge—I don't know from nothin'. Yeah, I got a nutty call from the Whisperer, dire threats, I was to show up at Widow's Haunt at half past nine. Like hell. At nine thirty or thereabouts I was having a big tall cool one out by my pool. And no, I don't have a handy alibi. My wife's in Chattanooga visiting her folks. Now if you don't mind, I got to finish straightening out a propeller shaft."

Annie shaded her eyes against the midafternoon sun when she stepped out of the police station. She scanned the shade of a live oak. She'd expected Marian to be waiting there to hear if Annie had picked up any leads from Rae. If only Rae had listened more closely to Alex's ramblings about his morning. Alex spoke of something in black and white, no, make that color, that changed everything about his brother. Would that be his brother George, who drove a girl's car and made a deadly turn? Or his brother Heyward, who set out for a sail and whose body washed up three days later? Heyward was the brother everyone whispered must have committed suicide because he was much too expert a sailor to have an accident and he had an insurance policy to pay off his debts.

Annie thought for a moment about suicide to save a lifestyle. Was Heyward that crazy about Lynn? Or was Heyward the one who couldn't face being poor? She'd always felt certain that suicide reflected a morass of unhappiness that saw no brightness, only gloom and emptiness.

A figure came out of the shadows of the live oak tree, walked toward her. Max stepped into the sunlight, tall, tanned, his golden hair shining, a smile lighting his face. He strode toward her, his arms open.

She ran and the world was sunnier, brighter, better. Max was here. It didn't matter when or where she saw him, tousle haired and stubble cheeked first thing upon awaking, across the room at a cocktail party, a quick turn to observe his profile at early morning church, crossing the sand in swim trunks carrying cold beers, the lift in her heart was the same.

They came together, both talking at once.

"I can't go out of town for a minute and you're off on a tear." His voice was exasperated, but there was acceptance, too. "Annie, rescuer of orphans, homeless dogs and cats, and, of course, any creature in peril."

"I meant to keep my promise. I swear I meant to——"

He bent down. She stood tall. Their lips came together. In a moment she pulled away, breathless; they were making a public spectacle but she didn't even care. She looked up into blue eyes that scolded but said *I love you.*

Her whoosh of relief was huge and heartfelt. "I was afraid——"

He put a gentle finger on her lips, turned her about so that they were walking arm in arm across the dusty ground. "Time for a mea culpa. Mine, not yours."

Fish Haul Pier, as always in summer, was hot, smelled of bait, and played host to a motley array of fishermen, many creating small oases with umbrellas, chairs, coolers full of chicken necks and chunks of mullet, and smaller coolers with beverages of choice.

Max steered Annie toward the end, found them a spot some feet away from the nearest fisherman. They stood with their elbows on the railing and the fresh sea-scented breeze tugged at their clothes. Water slapped against the pilings.

Max's handsome face was thoughtful. He looked at Annie, not at the whitecapped harbor. "I did a lot of thinking as I drove north. I thought about when I first saw you. Remember that party in New York? I saw you and I knew I had to know you and the minute we talked I made up my mind. You were going to be Mrs. Maxwell Darling. I learned all about you over time and everything I learned was good. That's what I kept coming back to as I drove. You are Annie. When someone tugs at your heart, you don't think, you rush out to help. Of course I recognize that when you don your Saint Joan cloak, a gecko has a higher self-preservation quotient. But I knew that about you from the start." His eyes were soft. "That's who you are. Who the hell was I to tell you not to do the right thing, not to reach out when a friend is in big trouble? So if you're a gecko without any brains, I was an ass. I like geckos better than asses."

Annie started to laugh. It ended up midway between a laugh and a sob.

Max's warm, strong hand cupped her chin. "Hey, no gal from Texas worries about what a guy thinks. She does what she has to do. And you did." He dropped his hand and grinned. "You should have seen Marian when I walked up. She watched me like I was a cross between an ax murderer and a body snatcher, maybe with a little zombie thrown in. I told her what I've told you and I told her we were here for her and we'd do our damnedest to find out what happened to Alex and Warren and keep her out of it." His face changed. There was no more laughter. "I never thought I'd see Marian cry. I told her to mop up her face, you and I were officially part of Marian's army. I told her to get back to the *Gazette* and kick back in her chair and think. Now"—his eyes were intent—"what did you find out from Rae Griffith?"

◆ ◆ ◆

Hyla Harrison stepped into Joan Turner's shop. The elegance of the white desk, the splash of crimson against a black background in a painting that was the only decoration on one wall, swatches lying on a steel table might have daunted her if she were on a personal quest. She knew enough to understand that the spareness was a statement, that she would be amazed and more than a little bit put off by the price of Joan's services. But she was there about murder so she moved forward with an aura of command.

Joan looked up as Hyla came nearer. Joan remained unmoving behind her desk. Her face was empty of expression but her shoulders tensed.

Hyla ignored the red molded chairs, remained standing. "I'd like an explanation of your actions at Widow's Haunt Thursday night."

Joan remained silent. Her thin face was stiff and still. The phone rang. Joan ignored the peals and finally there was silence.

Hyla's gaze never left Joan's face. "If you prefer we can go to the station."

"I'd rather not. I was afraid you would be coming. I suppose Annie Darling told you I wanted to know if Rae got a phone call from Warren."

Hyla made no response. When witnesses started to talk, let them keep on talking, never let them know they're telling you something you didn't know.

"I should have come and told you. I got a call, too. A little after eight. I didn't know the caller was Warren. I suppose it should have occurred to me. Poor Warren. He was always a fool but so sure of himself. I suppose he thought he was being clever. I didn't go into

Alex's suite that night but I was afraid to ignore the call. I didn't know what I was going to do but at least I wanted to know who called me."

"What time were you supposed to come?"

"At nine fifteen." She took a shaky breath. "I was there, right on the minute, but I never got to the ruins. When I pulled into the parking lot, I saw a car parked there. I never stopped. I turned around and drove home."

"Can you describe the car?"

Joan's face was empty. "I can't. It was just a car. I decided maybe I was being stupid trying to find out who called up and claimed something that was a lie. I drove home."

Can't identify the car, Hyla wondered. Or won't?

The break room at the *Gazette* had all the charm of wadded-up, day-old socks. It had dirty brown walls that likely last felt a paintbrush in the nineties; a warped, uneven wooden table, the Formica top marred by long-ago cigarette burns and time-immemorial stains; a vending machine that grabbed unwary quarters, burped, and resisted yielding its lukewarm cans until kicked.

Marian dropped in two quarters, kicked, the machine shuddered, out came a Dr Pepper. "What can I get you?"

Max poured coffee that had the consistency of molten asphalt, looked at Annie.

Annie approached the vending machine with an aura of confidence, kicked. Before she could plunk in her quarters, out slid a Mountain Dew. She carried it to the table, pretending the can was cool, but, hey, it was sugar.

Marian eyed her with amazement. "You figured out the magic charm. Kick first, no quarters needed. I'll take that as an omen." Her voice was determinedly light, an echo of the old Marian, but her face was ashen. "Tell me"—there was only the slightest quiver to indicate how much the answer would matter—"that the widow knew something we don't."

When Annie finished, Marian popped to her feet. "Hang on. Enjoy the amenities." A wave of one hand around the dingy room. "Back in a heartbeat. Or two."

When the break room door closed behind Marian, Annie took a sip of Mountain Dew, wished she hadn't. Cold, the taste was great. Warm . . . not so much. She pushed away the can, looked up at a wall clock whose minute hand moved in jerks.

Max looked, too, gave her an understanding glance.

Time, as it always did, was moving inexorably forward. Monday morning would come and the ferry would leave for the mainland with two prisoners aboard. They had so little time to fashion a rescue for Rae and Neil. And not much information. Little more than Rae's vague recollection that Alex talked to a woman with a funny name and something in color told him the truth about his brother. What was Billy doing? If anything? What could they—

The door opened. Marian carried three folders. She settled at one end of the table, slid one folder to each of them. "We know all about gallant George and the girl in the lagoon, but I looked up the stories about Heyward Griffith's death. Six years ago he went sailing on a Monday afternoon, an overcast day with a freshening wind. He left the marina at shortly after one o'clock in *Summer Song*, a thirty-two-foot Sabre. He was expected back about four, told Jody Carson at the dock house he was going to be off to Atlanta the next day and wanted the boat serviced while he was gone. At six the dock house got a call from Lynn Griffith. She told Jody she was just home from a round of golf and was surprised Heyward wasn't home. She asked if *Summer Song* was back. Jody checked. The slip was empty. He tried the radio. No answer. Jody raised an alert. A search got under way, but the weather was deteriorating. The search was called off when it was too dark to see. Overnight there were heavy rains and wind but the weather cleared by daybreak. A shrimp trawler found *Summer Song* capsized shortly after six A.M. the next morning about a mile south of the marina. The boom was loose, nobody on board. His body came in to shore on Thursday." Marian riffed through several sheets. "The autopsy report: Death by drowning. A head injury to the right temple consistent with a sailing accident." She put down the sheet. "He was an expert sailor but everybody makes mistakes. The wind was gusting that afternoon. Maybe he lost control of a crossover, the boom cracked him, and he went over the side. Anyway"—she straightened the sheets—"he went out and he didn't come back. So is he the brother Alex was talking about?" She looked from Max to Annie.

Annie hunched forward on the uncomfortable wooden chair. "Rae said Alex saw someone he used to know, a woman with a funny name, and something she told him made all the difference."

Max picked up a pen, sketched a car, shaded in lines of rain. "Let's suppose Alex was talking about George. George picked up Lucy Galloway in the lobby of the theater, went out and drove her car, heading out to an area where kids liked to race. But it was raining, he was driving too fast, she yanked on his arm, the car went into the lagoon. He got out. She didn't. That's bad but it wasn't deliberate. Maybe this woman knew something to indicate the car in the lagoon wasn't an accident, maybe George and Lucy had a history, maybe she claimed to be pregnant, maybe he decided to get rid of her."

Annie said slowly, "Alex may have learned something dangerous to George. The facts seem to be clear about Heyward's drowning. He went out by himself. He didn't come back. It seems the only question could be whether he committed suicide. That could make a huge difference to Lynn Griffith but I don't see how it could ever be proved, one way or the other. Nobody was out there with him."

"So . . ." Max frowned. "We're right where we started. Which brother was Alex talking about?"

Marian was crisp; now she sounded like Marian going after a story, sure if she asked the right questions, kept on looking, she'd find out what she needed to know. "Look at the sheets stapled together."

Annie and Max both pushed aside the printouts about Heyward Griffith, picked up the attached sheets.

Marian talked fast, gamine face squeezed in concentration. "The *Gazette* runs the list of high school seniors every spring, a full-page tribute."

Annie looked at Marian in concern. Had Marian, smart, cogent Marian, channeled Max's mother? The remark seemed wildly irrelevant.

Marian saw her gaze. For an instant amusement glimmered in dark eyes that for days had held nothing but fear and misery. "Alex's friend has to be among those names. Alex left the island after high school, never came back for any extended period. If he saw an old friend, I think it would be someone he knew in high school. Let's look for 'funny' names."

They came up with seven: Twila Tullis, Sydney Morris, Clarinda Smith, Viola Graham, Ginevra Hill, Cairo Ainsley, and Storm Porter.

Marian tapped the sheet. "Twila James is the dental technician for Dr. Forbes. I'll bet she was Twila Tullis. She's about the right age."

Max made a checkmark by Cairo Ainsley. "Cairo Richards sells real estate. Ditto and ditto."

Annie had a quick memory of an elegant woman with coal black hair drawn back in a chignon and a Mona Lisa face. "Viola Hunter's a tech at the vet's. She's the right age, too."

Marian popped to her feet. "I'll run the list past Ginger Harris, see if she knows anything about the others."

When she was gone, Annie looked at her notepad. They needed to be careful how they approached Alex's former classmates. Possibly start with the simple question, "Are you one of the old friends Alex talked to on Wednesday morning?"

She glanced at Max. His expression was . . . interesting. "Are we being silly?"

He shook his head. "No. It's as good a lead as we have. But there's something surreal about ferreting out a witness—if there is one—because of an odd name. Only in a small town."

Annie began to feel restive, but finally the door opened. Marian returned with a bemused expression. "If you ever want to disappear, don't even think about it. Ginger Harris knows all, sees all, remembers all. She told me where all seven of the girls are, their marital history or not, children, political persuasion, and hair color. She gave us a gold star, said those three we know are the only ones still on the island. Then she asked me—I swear she's a barracuda with blue eyes and a white perm—if she could have first dibs for a color story on the heart-tugging moments Alex spent with an old friend on the last day of his life. I won't go so far as to say she was licking her lips but it's only because she's always a lady and ladies do not."

13

Marian pushed back a lock of dark hair. "I have phone numbers. We'll each call one. Any preferences?"

Annie chose Viola; Max selected Cairo; Marian took Twila.

Marian glanced at Annie. "You first."

Annie held for a moment until Viola Hunter picked up the call. "Is Dorothy L having more trouble with her paw?" The venturesome cat had ended up with a thorn in her back left paw two weeks earlier.

Annie put the cell on speaker. "She's fine, Viola. I'm calling about a classmate. You were in school with Alex Griffith—"

"Golly." Viola's sweet voice was shocked. "I can't believe what happened to him."

"When you saw him Wednesday—"

"Me? Must have been someone else. I haven't seen Alex since the high school prom. I hoped he'd ask me to dance. But he didn't."

When Annie's call ended, Marian nodded at Max.

He put his cell on speaker: ". . . tracking down people Alex Griffith spoke to on Wednesday."

"Are you calling for the police?" Cairo Richards's deep voice was wary.

Max answered carefully. "If we learn anything that would be helpful to the police investigation, it's our duty to inform them."

"We?" It might simply have been an inquiry but the query suggested reserve, hesitation.

Annie pictured Cairo's face: eyes dark and deep, high cheekbones, full lips, a firm chin.

"Annie and I are trying to put together a complete picture of Alex's activities Wednesday."

Marian pointed at herself, then at the phone. Her narrow face was intent, her glare demanding.

Max placed his forefinger briefly on his lips, mouthed, "Later."

Cairo was silent, then said slowly, "Perhaps I should talk to you. I've been debating what to do. I'll be in my office for a few more minutes before I leave for an appointment. If you can come—"

"We'll be right there." Max clicked off the cell.

Marian's expression was fierce. "*You and Annie* are trying to put together his day? What about me?"

Max was already standing. "We'll fill you in. But some people, especially someone like Cairo, don't want to be in the *Gazette* in connection with a murder case. She's always dressed to the nines, drives a Mercedes coupe, and butter won't melt when she's trying to sell a beachfront property for a couple million."

Marian tensed like a cheetah ready to spring, then slowly relaxed. "Gotcha. I'll walk over with you, wait on the pier."

◆ ◆ ◆

As they followed Cairo Richards down the hall, Annie glanced at the closed door to George Griffith's office, wondered if he was here or out showing a property. Cairo led the way to a corner office that overlooked the harbor. She gestured toward a brocaded sofa. A white leather album lay open on the oak coffee table. As they settled on the sofa, Annie admired superb photographs of a Mediterranean mansion overlooking the ocean.

Cairo's white linen jacket emphasized the midnight darkness of her ebony hair. A heavy linked gold necklace added richness to a pale lime blouse. Tall, slender, and elegant, she walked across the heart pine floor and sat opposite them in a chintz-covered chair, crossed linen-clad legs to display green stiletto heels. She placed fingertips together, spoke in her distinctive deep voice. "There was a knock on my door about ten Wednesday morning. I called, 'Come in.' The door opened and Alex stepped inside. I was delighted. We dated a bit in high school. He said he'd dropped by to see George and saw my name on the door and wanted to give me a kiss." There was a flash of sadness in her eyes. "I was glad to see him. He sat on the sofa." She nodded toward Annie and Max. "I'd seen the story in the *Gazette* about his talk. I told him I'd definitely be there. And then he was expansive, the old Alex. He sprawled back against the cushions and said he intended to pull the draperies off some old statues, but that was enough about him. I'd find out everything Wednesday night. Then he looked at my wall"—a graceful hand gestured to her right and a wall with more than a dozen paintings, all obviously by the same artist—"and asked if those were mine. I'd just said yes when my phone rang, I went to my desk to answer. Alex got up and wandered over to look at my watercolors. The call—well, it doesn't matter but it was complicated, a problem with a second mortgage. I finished and when I turned to Alex, he was staring at one of the paintings in the first column. I could tell even from his back that he was shaken. He looked back at me and I knew he was excited. He asked, 'Can I take a picture of that painting?'" She pointed to the third watercolor.

Annie was the first one to reach the wall. She looked at the third painting. She could hear Cairo's deep voice saying, ". . . plein air . . . absolutely made the painting . . . took a photograph so I had the image clearly . . ."

The watercolor had a brooding quality, showing a narrow inlet between thickly wooded banks, the spartina grass dull beneath scudding gray clouds, the water dark as well, with the only points of light its rising whitecaps. A long wooden pier jutted out from the marsh to deeper water. A wet figure climbed the ladder's pier, pulling off a white swim cap to loose a cascade of silver blond hair. Her body was lithe and strong in a full-body stinger swimsuit, black with pink stripes down each arm.

Annie gripped Max's arm, pointed at the bottom right of the watercolor, the artist's name and the date.

The jukebox blared—Annie always felt a sense of comfort when she heard Bob Wills's "Deep in the Heart of Texas"—but the booth was a pocket of tension. Max's face furrowed in a tight frown. Marian's small jaw jutted in determination. Parotti's Bar and Grill was packed with boisterous vacationers and querulous sunburned kids who were too tired to eat. The holiday aura emphasized the grim divide in their booth.

Max was adamant. "Once Billy sees that watercolor, he'll know what happened. Lynn Griffith's a master swimmer. We all knew that. Now we know she was out for a distance swim the afternoon Heyward's sailboat capsized."

Annie chimed in. "That's what Alex meant when he was talking to Rae. He said he had proof in black and white and then he laughed and said in color. He was talking about Cairo's painting."

Marian nodded energetically. "The watercolor places Lynn in the right place to plan a swim out to intercept Heyward. I agree—"

Cairo had described the mansion for sale that summer on an inlet north of the marina and how on Mondays, which she always took as her day off since she worked weekends, she'd take her portable easel and set up on the second-floor balcony. "The Browns were in Europe and I was showing the place and I knew no one was ever there. The pier was part of their property. That day was perfect for a brooding, dark painting. But the swimmer added depth, power. I always have my camera along. I got a half dozen shots and that's how I was able to get the figure at the top of the steps just right."

"—this is terrific evidence. But it isn't enough. What do you think Billy would do?"

Max finished his last bite of grilled flounder. "He'd know there were three murders. He'd go see Lynn Griffith—"

"Exactly." Marian was dismissive, aggressive. "She'd gaze at him with that perplexed dumb-blonde look and say he was mistaken, she can't imagine what he's talking about, and she has a meeting so if he'll excuse her. And that will be that."

Max said again, firmly, "We need to alert Billy."

Marian pushed away her half-eaten grilled cheese. "Max, what difference does it make whether we go to him now or tomorrow? Here's what I want us to do . . ."

Annie moved her hand below the tabletop, gripped Max's knee.

His gaze slid toward her, saw the plea in her face. His hand came down on top of hers, squeezed. "Okay, Marian. We'll do it your way."

Moonlight streamed across the bedroom. Annie slipped her arms around Max's bare back. "I'm glad you're home." Glad for love, for care, for warmth, for touch and passion.

His lips were soft against her throat, her cheek, her mouth, his hands warm and seeking, and then there was no thought, only feeling, dizzying, tumultuous, incandescent.

When they were lying quiet in the moonlight, hands clasped, he said, "Me, too. Some things beat fishing."

She laughed. "I'm glad I outrank a tarpon."

"Outrank? On a scale of . . ."

She snuggled against his side, listened drowsily as Max made clear his priorities. Nice to know she was a billion light-years more desirable than a fishing trip. As she drifted into sleep, she felt a poignant wish that Marian could be as happy as she was, but perhaps at least she was resting better tonight, knowing tomorrow they might bring a sad chapter in her life to a close.

Marian glanced in the mirror. Black turtleneck, tight black jeans, black sneakers. No wonder this was the style for cat burglars. Even in bright moonlight, she'd be hard to see and she intended to make certain no one saw her. She'd recently watched *To Catch a Thief.* Thankfully she wouldn't have to scale a chateau roof. But she still felt dryness in her throat, the parched discomfort that fear brings. She was afraid.

Her mouth twisted in a wry grimace. Not being an utter fool, of course she was afraid. Lynn Griffith was a tall, imposing, ruthless killer.

Lynn had murdered her husband, moved swiftly to kill Alex when he posed a threat, waited unseen to choke the life out of Warren. Surely any killer, Marian thought, is preternaturally alert to danger. Perhaps especially this one. There would be no mercy if Marian got caught.

Marian stood still, breathing shallowly. She didn't have to do this. She didn't have to take this kind of chance. Instead, she could fix a drink, take a hot shower, let the police send Rae and Neil to prison. And if she did, she'd never be at peace.

She slowed her breaths, made them even. She had to do whatever she could, whatever it required, to make sure Lynn Griffith, not Rae Griffith and Neil Kelly, faced a jury. She knew the ways of police and the courts. There wasn't enough evidence to convict Lynn. Not nearly enough. Lynn Griffith was a triple murderer. Marian had to see her brought to justice, even if she put herself in danger.

She glanced at the clock. Almost midnight. She'd studied a map of the bike trails that webbed the island. She knew precisely how to ride from her house to Lynn Griffith's home, not more than a half mile distant, and from the Griffith house to Widow's Haunt.

In the kitchen, she took a last sip of water, slid a small LED flashlight into one pocket. She wore soft, supple leather gloves. She turned to a cabinet, lifted down a box of quart-sized plastic bags. She pulled out several bags, selected one that had been in the interior and never touched, folded the plastic, tucked it into the other pocket. She turned off the lights, moved in darkness across the kitchen, stepped out the back door. Probably no neighbors were watching, but she was now a part of the substratum of society that moves in the night and does not wish to be observed.

She hurried across the hummocky ground to the shed that housed the lawn mower, leaf blower, David's bike, and hers. Almost every island home had a similar shed. She pulled and the door creaked. The rasp could be heard above the whir of the cicadas and chirp of the crickets. She waited until her eyes adjusted to the darkness, stepped carefully to avoid the dark lump of the mower, reached her bike. She flipped up the kickstand, rolled out the bike, closed the door.

Once on the street, she pedaled fast. She used the bike's front light on the streets. A dark bike might seem sinister. She was simply an eccentric islander out for a midnight ride. Again, her mouth twisted wryly. She'd have to do a survey, write a feature about midnight riders. She imagined Walt's reaction: *Who the hell would do that?* It was comforting to think about Walt and the newsroom, bright lights and sharp minds, no connection to her foray into the night and the terrifying task that lay ahead.

She felt safer when she turned off into the woods and onto an asphalt trail. She followed the winding trail through tall pines. Thick undergrowth flourished on both sides. A crashing sound off to the right might have been a deer. She slowed as she skirted a lagoon, watching for alligators. She saw a fork. If she went left, she would reach Widow's Haunt. She veered right. She kept the headlight on until she was about a quarter mile from Lynn Griffith's home. She turned off the light, managed with occasional brief bursts from the flashlight. The trail here ran about twenty yards behind the houses.

She caught a faint scent of cigar smoke and immediately braked. She waited, listening. Although it was late, some smoker, likely forbidden to light up in the house, must be on a patio.

Marian rolled the bike forward.

Deep ferocious barks shattered the silence.

Marian stiffened, stood still.

Shrubbery rustled. A dark, moving shape hurtled toward her, stopped a foot away. Deep-throated barks rose to a crescendo.

"Sinbad."

The smell of cigar smoke was stronger.

"Sinbad, you damn fool." The deep male voice was aggravated. "The last time, you got twenty quills in your hide. Come back here, idiot dog."

Marian blinked back angry tears. She had to get past this. Hoping her instinct was right, she reached down, flicked on the light, called out, "Hey, sorry. Do you mind asking Rover to let me by?"

The red tip of the cigar appeared, then a heavyset man in a tee and shorts. "He's a big blowhard. He'll roll over on his tummy for you in a minute."

The German shepherd's fangs were near enough she could see yellow from tartar. Saliva drooled as he continued to bark.

"Damn sorry." The deep voice was apologetic. "Stay, Sinbad." He reached the dog, bent down, fumbled for his collar.

"Thank you. At the inn, they said it was all right to take a late bike ride. I couldn't sleep—"

"Night owl, huh. Me, too. You ride on now, I'll take him in."

Marian swung onto the bike, turned her face a little as she wheeled past the man and the dog, hackles still raised. Her heart thudded. Around the next bend, she slowed, turned off the headlamp. The Griffith house was the sixth past the fork in the path. Not this one, the next.

Marian coasted to a stop. She hadn't thought about whether Lynn owned a dog. But barking dogs were never unusual. The night forest held many creatures that excited dogs—porcupines, squirrels, raccoons, foxes, deer, occasionally wild boar.

Marian propped the bike on the kickstand, stepped lightly through the thinning woods. Moonlight illuminated the back of the house and the swimming pool. The layout was simple: a wooden enclosure for trash pails, a small greenhouse, a shed. Marian pulled the leather gloves from her pocket, slipped them on. She looked for a long moment at the trash enclosure, shook her head, slipped through shadows to the shed. A lock hung from the hasp. For an instant, she couldn't breathe. She reached out, her hand trembling.

The lock wasn't engaged.

Marian breathed again. She edged the shackle free of the hasp, pulled the door open slowly, stepped inside. A brief flash of the LED flashlight revealed an expansive, concrete-floored storage shed. Her eyes went directly to a red bike. She felt a flicker of triumph. She'd been sure there would be a bike.

She moved the bike out of the shed, taking her time. Sweat slid down her back and legs. Once out of the shed, the door closed, the lock carefully rehung, she kept to the shadows. She reached the bike path. She waited until she was past Sinbad's house—likely the dog was standing with nose pressed to a sliding patio door—to turn on the light. Then she went faster, gloved hands light on the steering grips so as not to smudge fingerprints. She was startled at how quickly she reached the fork and made the turn to Widow's Haunt. This portion of the path plunged through woods. Another few minutes and she was at the deserted parking lot. She turned off the headlamp, waited. Nothing stirred in the night but creatures of the woods. An owl hooted. Mourning doves called. Cicadas rasped. Crickets chirped. High above, a plane moved through the night sky.

She exhaled slowly. No door slammed, no voice rose, no footstep sounded. She had Widow's Haunt to herself—to herself and whatever ghosts might be abroad, the emaciated woman who grieved herself to death, the unavenged spirit of Warren Foster.

Marian wasn't worried about ghosts. A part of her watched askance. Fabricating evidence . . . she'd done a series once exposing fake invoices in a city office. She'd despised an official for cheating, for betraying trust. She'd always tried to play it straight. But she knew that Lynn's bike had been at Widow's Haunt and a man died horribly. Bike tracks had been erased or avoided. How fair was it to make that piece of evidence available for a jury? Marian didn't subscribe to the modern whatever's-right concept but she had a clear memory of Rae's haunted face and of Alex with all the life and vigor and strength drained away. There had been tire tracks from this bike. She set her jaw. There would now be tracks again.

She felt pressure to hurry, to get her task done, to get the bike back into the shed and no one ever the wiser. But she had to do it right.

She turned on the headlamp, used the flashlight as well. The paved parking lot was no good for her purposes. At the end of the lot, one path led to the front of the ruins, another cut a sharp left to curve through willows behind jumbled bricks. Marian shone the flashlight on the ground. Tufts of johnsongrass. Drifted pine straw. And there, about eight feet ahead, was a mushy area left from the last tropical storm, a low-lying depression that didn't drain well.

Marian smiled, swung onto the bike, pedaled slowly and carefully straight ahead.

She rode the rest of the way behind the ruins, keeping close to the path. She found another low muddy patch.

She stopped a few feet behind the remnants of the wall, saw the paler oblong that marked the empty space where there had once been a window. She flicked the light around the area behind her. A stand of cane. Perfect. She rolled the bike across the ground, careful not to step on any dusty or damp patches. She wedged the bike into the cane. In a moment, she pulled the frame free, trampling a bit of cane, perhaps leaving marks there as well. She swung onto the seat, rode across the ground, regained the parking lot.

The journey on the bike path was dreamlike, silent except for the sounds of the night and the whish of bike tires. She found her bike where she had left it, a few feet off the path. She turned off the headlamp of Lynn's bike. She rolled Lynn's bike through the shadows to the shed, opened the door, replaced the bicycle precisely where she had found it. When the shed door closed behind her, she hung the lock on the hasp, then turned to look toward the trash enclosure.

Again she slipped from shadow to shadow until she reached the concrete stoop of the enclosure. She lifted the wooden bar. The gate swung in. She cringed at a deep melancholy creak. She didn't dare take a chance of being trapped within the garbage area. She stood on the step, pressed against the post, listened with an intensity that magnified every sound: the rattle of magnolia leaves, the soughing of the pines, calls and cries and chirps. She watched the back of the house. A minute passed. Two. Five. One part of her urged *hurry, hurry, hurry.* The other warned *be careful, be careful, be careful.*

The windows remained dark.

Marian stepped into the enclosure. Now she had to use her LED flash. She cupped one hand over the beam, located three trash cans. She stepped to the first one, unbuckled the straps that prevented foraging raccoons from retrieving late-night snacks. She glanced over her shoulder, felt queasy. She couldn't see the house now. She had no way of knowing if there might be a light or a door opening. She lifted the lid; the sweet scent of spoiled fruit struck her full in the face. She wrinkled her nose, peered over the side, aimed the beam down. She pulled on the tie of the first trash bag, loosened it, spread the bag wide.

Perfect, perfect, perfect. She reached down, plucked up the object she sought. She pulled the plastic sandwich bag from her pocket, opened it, slipped her trophy inside. She retied the trash bag, slid the lid in place, buckled the straps.

She edged to the gate, looked out. No lights in the house.

It took only a moment to cross the backyard, darting from shadow to shadow, but her shoulders ached from tension. She reached the trail, safe now in the darkness of the woods. She started to get on her bike, then paused. She stepped away, shielded the light with her body, ran the beam along the ground. Damned if there wasn't . . . She thought for a moment, then bent and used her gloved hands to smear away a print from her front tire. Now she moved foot by foot, finding tracks, obliterating them. And then she was on the bike trail and around the curve, turning on the headlamp and flying through the night.

When she reached the house, she hurried the bike into the shed, stumbled, exhausted, across the yard, climbed the back steps and was in the kitchen.

She was home.

She was safe.

She turned on the kitchen light, not caring now who saw and knew there was movement in her house. She leaned back against the door, rested for a long while, then, legs leaden, walked to the kitchen table, sank onto a wooden chair. She pulled the sandwich bag from her pocket, laid it on the table.

She was trembling. She must move, take a hot bath, fix a drink, get to bed. Tomorrow she must play her cards right. She held a good hand now. The woman who killed Alex had no inkling that a trap had been fashioned. It was as if Lynn stood there, confident, untroubled, serene in her safety. But the trap must be sprung.

Marian slumped in the chair, too weary to stand. Tears streamed down her face.

S un splashed into the kitchen. The smell of good strong coffee mingled with the scent of freshly squeezed oranges.

Max slid a plate with a waffle in front of her.

Annie added three strips of bacon. Maybe that was piggy but Max's bacon—actually it was good Arkansas bacon—practically danced its way onto a plate. And, she sighed happily, Max had fixed whipped cream and fresh strawberries. "It is nice to have you home."

Max's smile was wry. "Hmm. I recall murmuring sweet some-things to you last night, proclaiming that frolicking with you was much grander than fishing. Am I to understand you are glad to have me home to cook?" Great emphasis on the last verb. His eyes were telling her how much he remembered of their moments together in the night.

Annie grinned. "To frolic." A pause. "And to cook."

"On a scale of one to ten—"

But her mouth was full of crisp, succulent waffle with a bite of bacon. "I'm not any good at math."

Max joined her at the table, grumbling. "Serves me right for being such a good cook. Maybe I'll take a sabbatical."

"Ten," she said hastily.

"Which is a ten?"

"You."

"That's better."

Annie enjoyed breakfast. Most of all she enjoyed looking across the table, talking, laughing. How lucky was she? It wasn't simply that Max was handsome, sexy, and fun. When he was beside her, her world was right. As simple as that. As complex as that. They never ran out of things to talk about, though this morning they were avoiding rehashing Marian's early morning call and her plea that they meet her at Widow's Haunt.

Annie glanced at the clock. "We'd better hurry."

Max's face creased in a frown. "We should go straight to Billy and tell him about Lynn Griffith in the bay the day Heyward died. That's what matters. Going to Widow's Haunt won't accomplish anything."

"I think," Annie said slowly, "Marian has a hunch."

"Ah, feminine intuition." He had the long-suffering-male expression. "Annie, they've done studies. It doesn't exist."

Annie was short on studies to cite, but statistics could prove whatever anyone wished to prove. She didn't need a study to recognize the utter conviction in Marian's voice. Marian said she had a feeling something had been missed, she'd waked in the night, knew they'd find something, they had to look.

"Marian's really upset—" She heard three rapid pings. Annie pulled her cell from her pocket, smiled at Max. "My morning uplift from the Incredible Trio." She looked down. "From your mom: 'Life does not consist mainly—or even largely—of facts and happenings. It consists mainly of the storm of thoughts that are forever blowing through one's mind. Mark Twain.' Max, that's exactly what Marian was describing, a storm of thoughts!"

Max laughed. "Why am I not surprised when a woman has a storm of thoughts? Men, of course, arrange thoughts in an orderly fashion."

But Annie was already reading Henny's text: " '*The Corpse Was Beautiful* by Hugh Pentecost describes the home front and the work of civilian air spotters. The moral is: Careful observation makes all the difference.' " Annie looked meaningfully at Max.

He raised an eyebrow. "So it's our duty to carefully observe Widow's Haunt?"

Annie glanced at the final text, laughed. "The oracles have spoken. Emma's text: 'Marigold dared me to dump her, popped a title at me. *In Plain Sight*. What the hell does that mean? She wins. Have to find out.' " Annie grinned at him. "What more do you want?"

Marian Kenyon's untidy mop of dark hair had scarcely been touched by a brush. She'd added a dash of makeup but bright red lips emphasized the gray-white of her face. Billy Cameron prided himself on an ability to read body language. Marian Kenyon's posture—head poked forward, shoulders tight, arms tensed—told him she was defensive, desperate, determined. A wrinkled pale blue blouse half tucked into brown slacks told him she'd dressed hurriedly.

". . . came straight here." Marian held up a plain manila envelope. "I found this on my front steps. When I saw what was written on it, I got a dish towel to pick it up." She held the envelope with a Kleenex.

Billy saw an inscription in plain block letters: FOR POLICE.

Her small chin jutted. "I figured somebody left it at my place because of the *Gazette*. So it's like a tip. That's why I slid out the stuff inside." She pushed up from the straight chair, took a step, and held the envelope open. Out onto the desktop fell a quart-sized plastic baggy and an eight-by-twelve sheet of computer paper. She pulled a pencil from her pocket, used it to turn the sheet toward Billy.

He read the all-cap message aloud: "'Check fingerprints on butcher paper'"—he glanced at the white paper stuffed into the baggy—"'against any unidentified prints found at Griffith death scene. If a match, get prints George Griffith, Joan Turner, Lynn Griffith, Eddie Olson.'"

Billy leaned back in his chair, eyes narrowed. "On what basis do I ask people for their prints when we have suspects in custody for the murders of Alex Griffith and Warren Foster?"

Marian flung out a hand. "You can do it. Tell them it's a matter of protocol. Tell them the prints are necessary to prove they weren't present when Warren was killed. Tell them you know as good citizens they want to help finalize the case against the suspects who will be arraigned on Monday."

"People aren't stupid, Marian."

Marian's lips twisted in what might have been a smile. "No, they aren't stupid. But quite often they are credulous. And the killer will be delighted to aid the police in proving their case against Rae Griffith and Neil Kelly."

14

Max jiggled his car keys in his pocket. "Where's Marian? She insists we meet her at nine sharp and she's nowhere to be found." He slapped at his arm with his free hand. "I saw a mosquito the size of a 727. Five more minutes and I'm out of here. At least the golf course sprays. What's the problem with the historical society?" He slapped again, waved away a cloud of no-see-ums.

Annie answered absently. "It's the director, Jane Jessop Corley. She's an ecological nut. Insecticides are listed in the evil lexicon, right after *Exxon Valdez*." Annie shaded her eyes from a sun that was already scorching, but the Widow's Haunt parking lot was barren of cars except for Max's Maserati. She was turning toward the line of pines that screened the ruins when a screech of tires announced Marian's arrival.

The faded yellow VW skidded to a stop. The driver's door opened and slammed shut. Marian was out and jogging toward them, one hand steadying the Leica that hung from a strap around her neck, sandals slapping on the blacktop. "Thanks for waiting. Found a surprise on my porch." Quickly she described the manila envelope and plastic bag and Billy's reaction. "Who knows? Maybe it will amount to something." Her narrow face was pale. "Anyway, thanks for coming. Last night I couldn't sleep. I kept thinking about how Lynn Griffith came to Widow's Haunt. Did she drive? If so, she had to park in either this lot"—she jerked a thumb behind her—"or at the inn. She knew she was going to kill him when she came because she brought garden wire. So she knew from the get-go she didn't want anyone to realize she'd been anywhere near Widow's Haunt. She wouldn't park at the inn. Her MG is too distinctive. It might easily be seen and remembered by someone. As for the Widow's Haunt lot, the road dead-ends here. She'd be boxed in if anyone else came. Plus, again, everybody on the island knows her car. So I figured she didn't drive."

Max pointed vaguely to the north. "Doesn't she live a couple of miles from here?"

Marian nodded. "I checked the map. A bike trail runs right behind her house. It intersects a trail that runs into the parking lot. So we're going to hunt for bike tracks." She half twisted to reach into a backpack.

"Marian"—Max sounded exasperated—"don't you think Billy Cameron knows how to secure a crime scene? As soon as the ME certifies a victim's dead, they string crime scene tape a good fifty feet in each direction, then search foot by foot, looking for anything that could be physical evidence."

Marian's hand came out of the backpack, clutching a dozen or more darts with feathered tips held together by a sturdy rubber band. "Sure he knows how to secure a crime scene. And I'll bet Annie's told you everything that happened Thursday night. We got here right behind Rae Griffith and the boyfriend. I called 911. Billy and Hyla were already at the inn, looking for Rae and Neil, so they got here pronto. It looked like Rae Griffith was fresh from the kill. Everybody knew she and the boyfriend walked over here. No car. Whatever they looked for, it wasn't bike tracks." She slipped off the rubber band, handed Annie four yellow-feathered darts, Max five red-feathered darts, kept the blue ones.

She started walking. "I figure Lynn got here before Warren. She didn't want him to know she was here so she didn't leave the bike in the lot. She'd either ride it around to the back of the ruins to get to that opening in the front wall or she'd walk it there. Either way, that bike had to cover some ground. Okay, I'll take the segment that runs alongside the oyster shell path to the main clearing. Max, you veer off on the path that skirts behind the main ruins. Annie, you take a look just behind the wall . . ."

Hyla Harrison appraised George Griffith. Curly black hair needed a cut. Red-veined face was a whiskey marker. Pouchy middle, pudgy fingers. Too much pasta. She smelled a faint scent of garlic. But she gazed at him with false camaraderie. "Good of you to see me, sir. Chief Cameron said he was sure you would be glad to help out."

Pale eyes stared at her. "Help out?"

Hyla held up a small black vinyl case. "Fingerprints. Quick. Easy. As I'm sure you know, arrests have been made in the murders of your brother and Warren Foster. To complete our case against the accused we want to counter any defense allegations that we were slack in investigating unexplained prints at the scene of the Foster murder." She placed the case on his desk, popped it open. "There's a full hand-print on the back of the wall where his body was found." She lifted out the rectangular container with the fingerprint pad. "Taking your prints will prove that the unidentified print doesn't belong to you."

◆ ◆ ◆

R ed-feathered darts framed a clear print of a bike tire in a dusty
patch near the stand of cane.

Annie looked from the cane to the back of the wall with the empty
space for the long-ago window. She looked back at the cane stand, at
the square of darts, their feathers bright in the morning sun. The sun
fully illuminated the bare patch of ground. Annie pointed. "That
looks like a little punched-out spot for a kickstand."

Marian took a blue-feathered dart, placed it a few inches from
that impression. She stepped back, lifted the Leica, snapped several
times. With a satisfied nod, she edged away from the cane. "Prints in
four different places. Now we have something for Billy. He can send
Lou to make molds."

"To prove what?" Max ran a hand through his hair. "Okay, we
haven't had a rain for four days. But those prints could have been
made anytime since then. How many tourists come over here on
bikes? At least a few a week. You know what these bike prints prove?
Somebody rode a bike here."

Annie winced inside. She hated to see Marian disheartened, but
Max was right. What did bike prints prove?

Marian's face gave no hint of discouragement, looked tough,
determined, convinced. "The prints will prove Lynn Griffith rode a
bike here. Hey, you say that's not against any law. Of course not. But
the prints of her bike at Widow's Haunt will be evidence she was here
and when that evidence is added to everything else, Billy will find out
what he needs to find out."

"Like"—Max's tone was faintly sarcastic—"whether Lynn Griffith
owns a bike?"

Marian's retort was fast, sharp. "Yeah, like whether she owns a bike." Triumph flashed in Marian's dark eyes. Triumph and certainty.

Annie understood. Marian in her own mind had figured out what must have happened and, for the night to have unfolded as Marian believed, Lynn Griffith had to own a bike.

Time would tell.

M arian waved for Max to drive out first. As the Maserati curved into the narrow road lined by pines, Marian yanked her cell from her pocket. She swiped. As soon as Walt answered, a brusque "City desk," she said, "Marian. Gonna have a big story. Need a little help. ASAP. Go out to the boardwalk"—the *Gazette* offices were at one end of Main Street—"use the pay phone, call my number. I'll answer. We talk for a couple of minutes. You can read the tide table." Walt had a thing about tides, always knew the times. "Whatever. Just chat. Three minutes. When you leave the booth, you're in a somnambulist state, don't know where you've been, what you've done. Total amnesia." She felt uncomfortable using Walt to set up her plan, but she'd already crossed that bridge. She would do what she had to do to trap a killer.

She swiped End. She could count on Walt. He'd do precisely as asked. And no one else would ever know.

H yla Harrison neatly removed a strip at the top of a foil packet, handed the packet to Joan Turner. "Moist towelette, ma'am. Removes ink in a jiffy."

Joan's violet eyes looked huge in a pale face. Tight lines splayed at the edges of her mouth. "Thank you, Officer."

"Thank you, ma'am, for cooperating."

Joan glanced at the ink pad, still open, and the cards with her fingerprints. He cheekbones were sharp, prominent. "I will do anything I can to convict the people who hurt Alex." Tears glistened in her eyes.

M ax drove fast. Dust rose in swirls behind them.

"Don't asphyxiate Marian."

"Sorry." He slowed. "But I feel like we should have already reported to Billy, told him about the watercolor and Lynn Griffith coming up out of the ocean. We've known since last night."

Annie twisted a little in the seat. "I don't see the VW. I thought Marian would be right behind us."

Max relaxed a little in the seat, drove at a sedate thirty, though that pace still kicked up dust. "I know she wanted to have as much confirmation as possible for Billy but I'm afraid she's counting too heavily on those bike tracks."

Annie had one of those odd feelings that she usually attributed to spending too much time with Laurel, though maybe she should accept that the subconscious often reaches the right conclusion from a myriad of tiny, scarcely realized observations. But she knew what was going to happen. "Lynn Griffith will have a bike. Those tire prints will be from her bike."

Max gazed at her with a question in his eyes.

"I don't know," she said breathlessly, "how I know. But I know."

Max looked thoughtful.

Annie twisted again to look back. Despite the haze of dust, the VW was closing fast on their trail.

◆ ◆ ◆

Hyla Harrison stepped under an awning.

Eddie Olson was bare to the waist. He used a block of sandpaper on a strip of mahogany cap rail. His tanned back was sweaty.

"Nice boat." Her admiration was genuine.

He turned, saw her. His eyes narrowed at the uniform. "You looking for a boat?"

"I wish."

His dark eyes were friendlier. "Got a couple of good ones. I'll sell 'em on time, a couple of thou down."

"I'll check them out when I'm off duty. Right now . . ."

He listened as she explained. "Like I told you the other day, I wasn't there."

Hyla nodded. "I recall. So you have no reason not to help us out."

"Maybe not. What's in it for me?"

"A good citizen—"

Eddie laughed. "I wasn't a Boy Scout. I got no merit badges. As somebody once said, I don't give a damn. But what the hell." He held up a broad stubby hand in a mock Scout salute. "Maybe if I get stopped for speeding, there'll be a gold star on my record."

The call came as Marian expertly tucked the VW into a parking space a half block from the station. She let the cell ring twice to be sure the number logged in as a recent call. "Yeah."

"Humphrey Creek. Low tide one twenty-eight A.M. High tide seven forty-four A.M. Low tide one fifty-three P.M. High—"

"Hope you aren't frying in the booth."

239

"If it'll be above the fold, worth it. If not, you can scrub my kitchen this weekend."

"Lead story Monday."

"Hell, we've already led with the arraignment—"

"More. Better. Trust me."

"I guess I do. Or I wouldn't be standing here sweating up my best seersucker pants. Should have worn my usual khakis."

"I'll pay for the cleaning bill." Marian saw Annie and Max starting up the station steps. "Got to go." A quick breath. "Walt"—her voice was choking up—"you're a—"

"Got it. Peachy guy. Sweetheart. You can tell my ex-wife. There's a herd of tourists shambling by. I'm going to hang up, slip out as gracefully as somebody built like me can slip, and end up at the pier for a smoke. If anybody ever asks, I don't know from nothing. And I've held on to the receiver with my dandy handkerchief. Always knew it was good to carry one. Besides, I'll bet the receiver was sticky. Ditto the handle to open the door. Me, I don't like sticky." The connection ended.

Hyla Harrison pushed the doorbell for the third time, waited. No one came. She glanced at the drive and the red MG TD that made her think of dancing slippers and champagne. She didn't have any dancing slippers, had rarely tasted champagne, but that was what the car brought to mind. The car also suggested Lynn Griffith was at home. Unless, of course, she had been picked up by a friend.

Live oak leaves rustled but the faint breeze did nothing to lessen the midmorning heat. Hyla turned, followed a walk to her right. She came to a wooden gate on the other side of the garage and pulled it open. Was she trespassing? If challenged, she would simply say it occurred to her that perhaps Mrs. Griffith gardened. For an instant, her stride checked. A gardener would surely have green plastic-coated garden wire. But that wasn't her concern at the moment. She walked on flagstones the length of the garage.

She passed a hibiscus hedge in full bloom. A white picket gate was inset between hedges and beyond was a spectacular pool.

Pool water cascaded from a white cap as the swimmer rose out of the water in a powerful butterfly stroke. At the end of the pool, a flip turn, and a return lap freestyle, fluid and fast. The swimmer reached the end of the pool, stood.

Hyla opened the gate, walked across the patio.

Lynn Griffith's frown was quick. "I will not be badgered. I will ask you to leave—"

"Ma'am, I'm here with a special request from Chief Cameron." Hyla stood near the pool. "We've asked all the family members to help us. You see . . ."

Lynn stood in the sun, listened. Slowly the irritation faded from her face. When Hyla finished, Lynn pulled off her cap, her face thoughtful. "Let me be sure I understand. There's an unidentified full handprint on some wall at Widow's Haunt that Chief Cameron believes is important? Oh, very well. Certainly I'm willing to do whatever I can to build a case against Alex's murderers." She walked toward a glass-topped table, picked up a red-and-green-striped beach towel. "Let me dry my hands."

Annie sat in a shaft of sunlight shining through the harbor window in Billy Cameron's office. Max was in the middle straight chair facing Billy's desk, Marian to his left. Annie flicked an occasional glance at Marian's tense profile. Marian hunched forward, as if she had something more to say but was waiting, picking her moment. But what could she know that they didn't know?

Billy Cameron listened intently, made notes, as they marshaled all they knew: Cairo Richards's plein air painting on a brooding summer day, the rising from the sea of the woman both Annie and Max believed to be Lynn Griffith, the bicycle tire tracks at Widow's Haunt—he'd held up a hand then and barked orders into the intercom—and Annie's conviction that it was Alex who called room service.

Billy Cameron's tone was dry. "All of this is possible. But anything is always possible. If Cairo Richards painted Lynn Griffith in an inlet the afternoon her husband's sailboat was out in the sound, it raises serious questions. *If* she swam out, intercepted her husband's boat, how did she get aboard? Pretending she had a cramp? A happy chance? A couldn't-wait-to-see-you impulse? Let's say she swam out, got on board, cracked him on the head, pushed him overboard, left the boom loose, swam back to shore. If that's true, the watercolor would terrify her. So why didn't she go after the artist? Maybe Alex talked about a painting, gave no clue where he'd seen it. That would almost have to be the case."

Annie frowned. "Cairo said Alex was excited when he saw the watercolor. He must have been certain the swimmer was Lynn. He saw the date beneath the artist's name. He knew she was a powerful swimmer. When he talked to Lynn, who knows what he threatened? Maybe he said he'd do a new book, describe the wife swimming out to the sailboat, create a scene of murder. Or maybe he told her he was going to announce Wednesday night what she'd done and then he intended to go to the police, insist on an investigation."

"Maybe, maybe, maybe," Billy murmured. "We need facts. We can check Alex Griffith's cell, see if we find a picture of Cairo Richards's watercolor, see if she happened to keep the photos she worked from. The date on the watercolor is definitely suggestive." He tapped his pen on a printout of the investigation into Heyward Griffith's drowning. "If it gets to that point"—his tone suggested the possibility was light-years distant—"we could have a lineup with Lynn Griffith and some other blondes, see if Richards can pick her out. But even then, even if she admitted being out for a swim, that doesn't prove she intercepted the sailboat. Now, if she killed Heyward, she might think she had to silence Alex and then Warren Foster, but a watercolor doesn't prove murder. However, the painting puts her in the proximity of Heyward's drowning and she claimed at the time that she was golfing that afternoon."

Marian scooted to the end of the seat, placed her hands on the edge of Billy's desk. "Just before I got here, I got a ring on my cell. You know that butcher paper I brought you this morning?"

As Billy nodded, she turned briefly to Max and Annie and said, "That's what was in the envelope I found on my porch." Then she looked back at Billy. "The caller said the prints belong to Lynn Griffith. If you find a match at the hotel—"

Billy's face was abruptly hard. "Let me see your phone."

She took her cell from her pocket, handed it to Billy.

He looked, flicked on the intercom. "Mavis, trace this number." He read the number out; then, as he turned off the intercom, he swung back toward Marian. "Okay, give: Who called?"

Marian looked regretful. "Sorry, Billy. I couldn't do that even if I knew the caller. A reporter has to protect her source."

Billy looked grim. "Source?"

"This is a big story."

He studied her for a minute. "Man or woman?"

Marian shook her head. "Somebody who didn't want to be involved. There was no explanation of how they got the butcher paper. I don't know how they knew her prints might be in the hotel suite. All I know is what the caller said: 'Lynn Griffith killed Alex. Her prints are in the suite.' That's what I know."

"Yeah." His blue eyes were cold, suspicious. "How does some 'source' happen to have your cell number?"

Marian's expression was wary. "My cell number's all over the place. I know a lot of people. If somebody knew something about Lynn Griffith, but didn't want to come out in the open, the easiest way to get information to the police is to tip off a reporter. Whoever left that envelope at my house or called me a little while ago doesn't matter. What matters"—Marian's tone was urgent—"is whether there are any matches at the hotel. If there are, then you'll know."

Billy picked up his phone, dialed an extension. "Mavis, have you had a chance to finish checking the prints from that sheet that came in this morning?" He listened. "You're sure? . . . Where in the room? . . . Send me a report." He put down the phone. "It isn't much, but it's definitive. In the sitting room of the hotel suite, three prints match or partially match the index fingerprint taken from the butcher paper. I sent Hyla Harrison to get prints from Joan Turner, George Griffith, Lynn Griffith, Eddie Olson. She's asking for them on the premise that we want to foreclose any defense attacks about unidentified prints at Widow's Haunt. When she gets back, we'll have Lynn Griffith's official prints. Mavis can check those prints against the prints from the Griffith murder scene. That means we can bring her in—"

Marian pushed up from her chair, leaned on the desk. "No." There was desperation in her voice, intensity in every line of her thin frame.

Billy was exasperated. "If the prints place her in that room, she'll have to explain when and why she was there."

"That's exactly what she'll do." Marian's husky voice strained. "Lynn Griffith's smart. She has a dim-witted stare and she likes to prattle, but that's calculated. She'll flutter long eyelashes and talk in a sweet little voice about dear Alex and how could anyone possibly think she was involved and then she'll claim she dropped by to see him in the afternoon and she hadn't mentioned it, it was no one's business, they had a nice talk about old times, she's so glad she saw him before that dreadful attack. She'll smile at you and get up and walk away."

Annie came to her feet, too. "But we found those bike tracks at Widow's Haunt. If she has a bike"—Annie didn't doubt that there would be a bike; somehow Marian knew there was a bike; but that was a thought for another time—"and if the tracks match, how can she explain those?"

Marian was adamant. "She'll explain the bike tracks the same way. She'll claim she's been there many times on her bike. She'll say, 'Oh, did I ride my bike there? Oh yes, I believe I did a few days ago, but I didn't think to mention it since I wasn't there Thursday night. I often ride that way.' No one can prove differently, just as no one can prove she didn't come to the hotel Wednesday afternoon and visit with Alex." Marian's voice shook with intensity. "It won't work to bring her in for questioning. That would put her on alert and she'd probably decline to answer without an attorney. Instead, we need to have her say in front of other people that she was never in that hotel room, had never been in it. The only way to do that is to get her talking when she isn't aware she's under suspicion."

Billy was thoughtful. "You think if she sees us, she'll go on high alert?"

"Exactly."

His eyes narrowed. "Some kind of private showdown? I don't like that idea."

Marian shivered. "Actually, I don't either."

Annie looked at Billy. "You said Hyla's out getting fingerprints from Joan Turner, George Griffith, Eddie Olson, and Lynn Griffith?"

Billy glanced at his watch. "She should be back soon. Then we can certify the fingerprints—"

Annie shook her head. "I wasn't thinking about the prints. But Hyla's visit makes these people think they're on the side of the law, that they're cooperating. How about getting them together for a report on the status of the investigation?"

Max was skeptical. "If Lynn's as smart and tough as you think she is, she won't tumble to a come-into-my-parlor conclave. How can you get all the so-called suspects to show up? Why would they? And where?"

Marian ran a hand through her tangled dark hair. "There has to be some place where she'd come."

Max gestured toward Billy. "To a tête-à-tête with the police? If I thought I was getting away with a couple—no, make that three murders—I'd say, sorry, can't make it, have to wash my hair, bake a cake, play bingo. It isn't going to happen. You'd better pick her up and see what you can get."

Annie rushed in, talking fast. "I know a way." She hoped she did. She thought she did. Would Billy agree?

Billy looked at her inquiringly.

Joan Turner stood at the window overlooking the harbor. At the tinkle of the front door, she turned. She saw Annie and her face tightened. She walked forward, unsmiling. "I thought you would come. Yesterday morning I could tell from your face that you knew Warren called me. But you don't need to worry. The police know now. That young policewoman came and asked me. I told her I went to Widow's Haunt. But I didn't stay. There was a car there. I was afraid. So the police know Rae isn't the only person Warren called. I've been trying to think what to do. I told Leland I couldn't play golf this afternoon, that I had to come up with a redesign for a clubroom. I've been here all day. I haven't answered the phone. I haven't had lunch. I keep walking and walking and thinking." Her face was abruptly anguished. "What if the police come to the house, ask me in front of

Leland why I went to Widow's Haunt? Leland won't ask, but he'll look at me, wonder why Warren called me. Leland will realize Alex knew something about me that I was desperate to hide."

"Leland won't ever have to know you went to Widow's Haunt." Annie hurried across the shining parquet floor, took two limp hands in her own. "The police know who killed Alex and Warren."

"They know?" Joan pulled her hands free, clasped them tightly together. "Have they let Rae go? And that man?"

"Not yet. It isn't simple. The police know who killed Alex, but they don't have proof. Marian Kenyon and I think we know a way to trap the killer. That's why I've come to you. You can help us."

Joan frowned, fine dark brows drawn down. "I don't know any- thing"—but there was a flicker of worry in her eyes—"that implicates anyone."

Annie gestured impatiently. "This isn't based on what you know about anyone."

"Who killed Alex?" The demand was sharp.

Annie looked steadily into Joan's wide, worried gaze. "Let me explain what Marian and I want to do. If you agree to help, we hope to create a situation where the murderer will be publicly revealed."

"You know who killed Alex!" She leaned forward, her face strained. "Who?"

"I can't tell you—"

Joan's hands clenched. "That's unconscionable. To come here and claim you know who killed my brother and refuse to tell me. Damn you, who?"

Annie felt the moment spinning out of control. "Please hear me out. I know this is horrible for you. But tell me, if you knew who killed Alex, could you look at that person and keep the knowledge out of your face?"

Slowly Joan's hands opened. Tears glittered in her eyes. "If I looked at that person—"

"If you opened the door for Alex's murderer to walk into your house, could you stand there, **greet that** person, offer a drink?"

Joan whirled away, walked to the window. She stood, her back stiff.

Annie waited. What would Joan say? What could she say?

Finally, Joan turned. Her face was drawn, bleak. "What do you want me to do?"

"You are the oldest in the family."

Joan's face was still, quiet, watchful.

"If you invited everyone—"

Joan lifted a hand to touch her throat. "Who's everyone?"

"Your brother, George. Your sister-in-law Lynn. Alex's classmate in high school Eddie Olson."

"Invite them to do what?" Violet eyes were wide and doubtful.

Annie spoke slowly, carefully. One wrong word and Joan Turner might refuse. "Those close to Alex surely must wonder what has been discovered. They know what has been publicly announced. You could call each one, say you believe family and friends deserve more facts about the investigation so you contacted the police. The police chief explained that he wasn't at liberty to speak about the prosecution, that was the prerogative of the circuit solicitor, but he suggested that Marian Kenyon of the *Gazette* and Annie Darling, who was involved in setting up Alex's program at the inn, might be willing to share what they know. That you contacted both Marian Kenyon and Annie Darling and they agreed to be at your house at eight P.M. and will be happy to provide more background."

Joan walked to a red molded chair, sank onto it, buried her face in her hands. "I have one brother left."

Annie waited a moment, said quietly, "The circuit solicitor has a strong case against Rae Griffith and Neil Kelly."

15

Hyla Harrison rode her Harley as precisely as she drove a police cruiser: competently, unobtrusively, and intensely aware of her surroundings. She wore a pale blue tee, navy Bermudas, and sneakers with a soft cap and sunglasses, making her indistinguishable from ordinary vacationers who biked, swung golf clubs, sprawled on beach blankets. It was unlikely that anyone on the island, much less one of the three persons of interest listed by the chief, would know where she lived or have any interest in her Saturday afternoon activities. She'd studied the map carefully before she set out. She took a circuitous route from her apartment house. She was certain no one followed her when she turned off on the bike trail that skirted behind the home of Joan and Leland Turner.

She spotted the Turner house through the pines without slackening her speed, continued for a quarter mile, stopped, waited, listened. This was a less-frequented bike trail. The green tunnel beneath overlocking limbs pulsed with the hot high heat of midafternoon. In the thick humid air, whining insects and chattering birds were the only signs of life on the secluded path. A good time to be in a pool or the sudsy surf or lounging in the shade with a tall, cool drink. Sweat beaded her upper lip, slid down her back and legs. She turned the Harley, rode back to the Turner house. In a moment, the bike was out of sight behind a hibiscus shrub. She reached into the storage compartment, drew out two items, tucked them in the capacious pockets of her shorts.

Following instructions, she opened a tall iron gate between pittosporum shrubs, sniffed the sweet banana scent of their blossoms. She followed an oyster shell walk around a weeping willow. She carefully noted the features of a broad backyard, a tiled pool with a cabana, a terrace with bright lawn furniture and umbrellas, a discreet garden shed near a side gate. The two-story white house featured expansive windows. A small contingent of officers could be deployed unseen on the far side of the sliding glass door to the patio.

As she crossed the terrace, the sliding glass door opened. Joan Turner stood aside for Hyla to step inside.

Joan followed her, closed the door, leaned back against the glass as if for support. "I thought we'd sit in here tonight." Joan's face looked haunted, weary, despairing.

The room seemed dim after the blaze of the afternoon sun though lights shone from several table lamps. The family room was separated into two sections. A pool table and wet bar to the left; a comfortable grouping of two red leather sofas on either side of a fireplace and two large blue chairs facing it. An all-glass coffee table on chrome legs sat between the fireplace and the furniture. At the end of each sofa was a matching small side table with a lamp.

Hyla noted a painting above the fireplace. She wasn't knowledgeable about modern art, but she was struck by the power of the canvas, swaths of thick red paint that made her think of bubbling lava spilling over the rim of a volcano and streaks of coal black and canary yellow. The red and yellow were echoed in a strident pattern on the rug between the couches.

The coffee table held several pieces. Hyla didn't think of them as objets d'art. She looked at them from an entirely different perspective. Her eyes moved from a creamy porcelain bowl with assorted wrapped candies to a silver filigree box, perhaps six inches by four inches, to an ivory carving of a snake to an open printed silk fan.

Hyla reached into her pocket, pulled out a rectangular recorder as slim as the newest-model cell phone. She crossed to the coffee table, punched a button on the recorder, slid the case beneath the silver box.

Joan's face was somber.

Hyla was brisk. "The recorder will run for fifteen hours. That's more than enough time."

Joan glanced at the clock. A quarter to five. "I'm going to invite them to come at eight."

Hyla's gaze moved to one of the end tables. "You do crosswords."

Joan looked vaguely surprised, nodded. "Yes." She spoke as if talking about another time, another life.

"Perfect." Hyla withdrew a fountain pen from the same pocket. She slid the stylish black pen's pocket clip to activate this recorder, placed the pen atop a small pad next to a crossword magazine.

Joan's eyes fastened on the pen. Her face was tight with pain and fear.

Hyla said quietly, "Two people are dead, ma'am. We want the right person to go to prison."

Joan massaged one temple. "I wish Alex had never written that terrible book."

Hyla understood what Joan feared might be recorded on the small device. When Joan pulled into the parking lot at Widow's Haunt Thursday night, she saw a car. She claimed not to recognize the car. Hyla now had no doubt that Joan recognized the car very well. The car belonged to her brother, George. "Ma'am, wishing can't save lives. Doing saves lives. If you don't mind making the calls now, then I can report that everything is in place."

Joan slipped her cell phone from the pocket of her slacks, swiped, put it on speakerphone. "Hi, Lynn. Joan."

"Oh, Joan, I've been so upset. Poor Alex."

Joan swallowed, continued, her voice tight. "I'm glad I caught you—"

Hyla listened intently, her face impassive. Good. Exactly the right tone.

"—I hope you can come over tonight. I've been upset trying to find out more about what happened to Alex. The family should be better informed. I ran down that reporter for the *Gazette*. She and Annie Darling were at the inn that night. They've agreed to come over and fill us in on what's been happening and the latest on Rae's arrest. Can you come around eight o'clock?"

The next call was to Eddie Olson. After Joan spoke, there was a silence that stretched.

Hyla remembered his tough face, the sinewy arms.

Finally, "Deep background, huh? Yeah. I'll try to make it." Did he want to be sure no one was talking about that long-ago football game? Maybe. Or maybe he was curious.

After the call to Olson, Joan turned away so Hyla couldn't see her face. She called her brother. Her last brother.

When the call was completed, Joan dropped the cell phone into her pocket and walked blindly to one of the red leather sofas, sank down, buried her face in her hands.

◆ ◆ ◆

Officers arrived one by one, taking up posts among the pines that bordered the Turner backyard. Three figures, dressed in black, one of them carrying a large rectangular object covered in Bubble Wrap, crept silently from shadow to shadow to press against the wall on one side of the sliding glass door to the patio. The curtains were drawn, blocking out a view of the Turner family room.

Hyla Harrison pointed to the slight space between the glass pane and the frame. Joan Turner had done as she'd promised, leaving the sliding door open an imperceptible amount, enough that the door could be moved after the guests arrived, making it possible for them to hear what was said.

Billy Cameron nodded, turned a thumb up. Lou Pirelli's head moved slowly as he scanned the shadows. He kept one hand on the wrapped rectangle that was now propped against his right leg.

There were no lights on the patio tonight.

"It's good of you to come." Joan Turner managed the everyday social phrase though her eyes appeared sunken in her face and her cheekbones jutted. "Please sit where you wish. Everyone's here." She gestured toward the red leather couches and the blue chairs.

Annie glanced at Marian, nodded toward the fireplace. Max turned to join Leland Turner at the wet bar.

The guests watched in silence as Annie and Marian joined Joan and faced the couches and chairs.

Leland Turner, tall, thin, attractive in a professorial way, shook hands with Max, looked toward the fireplace. "It's very generous of you to take time to help us out." He appeared to be his usual genial self, his long bony face that of a welcoming host, his tenor voice pleasant.

George Griffith's fleshy, red-veined face was sullen. He slumped against an arm of a leather sofa. Eddie Olson lounged back in a blue chair, his expression quizzical. Lynn Griffith looked regal in the other blue chair as she arranged a fold of a patterned lime scarf that matched the color of her blouse. Her thin-legged white linen trousers were immaculate.

On any other summer evening, Joan would have been strikingly attractive in a beige pull-on top with a boatneck and finely stitched pattern in a center panel and slightly darker beige slacks cinched on one side near the ankles, a fashionable touch. A wooden replica of a sand dollar hung from a long shell necklace. Tonight she looked tight, tense, tormented.

Leland Turner smiled at Marian. "Let me fix everyone a drink before you start."

Marian looked appreciative. "Beer will be fine."

Annie didn't want a drink but this was supposed to be a quasi-social gathering. "White wine, please."

"Lynn?" Leland's tone was expansive. "What would you like?"

Lynn Griffith's silver blond hair was teased in soft ringlets that framed her heart-shaped face. Lashes dark as midnight made her large blue eyes look wider. She brushed back a curl. "Rum collins, Leland. Thank you."

"Rum collins coming up."

George was ready. "Bourbon and Coke."

"Scotch and soda." Eddie Olson's tight polo emphasized the strength of his upper body. His tan slacks fit him a little too snugly.

Max smiled at his host. "I'll take a beer, Leland, thanks. I'll serve while you bartend."

Leland glanced at Joan. She gave a slight headshake.

Leland selected bottles from the shelving above the sink. The small refrigerator door squeaked as he opened it. Ice clinked in glasses.

Max brought drinks to each in turn.

Joan stood stiffly a few feet from Marian, did not look toward her. "I very much appreciate"—Joan's voice was thin—"the willingness of Marian Kenyon of the *Gazette* and Annie Darling, who was helping Alex with the program at the inn, to come here tonight to bring us up to date on the progress of the investigation into Alex's death. Marian will speak first."

Marian had made an effort beyond her usual casual appearance. Tonight she was crisp in a white blouse and dark slacks. A plain gold link bracelet was her only adornment.

She reminded Annie of a ragtag wirehaired terrier who knew there was a bone to be found, her dark eyes alert and watchful.

Marian began in a clipped rapid voice. "Alex Griffith revealed in a *Gazette* interview that he based various well-known characters in *Don't Go Home* on real figures from his past. He returned to the island, announced plans to publicly name the inspiration for his characters Wednesday night. During the day Wednesday, he went around the island, spoke to several people, making it clear what he intended. His wife, Rae, left him in the suite at shortly before seven P.M. She went to the terrace to greet members of the media and make sure the audio was in place and working at the gazebo. After she left the suite, Alex called room service. He always drank a gin and tonic. He ordered one gin and tonic. He also ordered"—her dark eyes settled on Lynn Griffith—"one rum collins."

Lynn held her rum collins in her right hand. "Really?" There was mild curiosity in her voice. She smiled. "Rum collinses are very popular."

Marian looked disappointed. "We thought you must have been there. Alex knew very few people on the island after all these years. Of those he saw that day, you are the only one who drinks rum collinses."

Lynn's eyes glittered. "Drinking a rum collins isn't a crime. Obviously Alex knew someone else who preferred rum." She spaced the words. "I was not there. He did not order a drink for me. I never saw Alex that evening."

"Oh." Marian's face squeezed in a frown. "You weren't in the suite?"

Lynn was emphatic. "I was never in Alex's suite, not that night, not anytime."

Marian shot Annie a triumphant look. The lie had been recorded. Now Lynn Griffith could not explain away her fingerprints in the room where Alex Griffith died. Now the fingerprints could be admitted into evidence in a capital murder trial. Alex's murderer was going to be brought to justice.

Annie wanted to make sure. She asked, as if puzzled and a little unsure, "So you are claiming you have never been in the room where Alex was killed?"

Lynn was irritated. "I don't know how to be any clearer. I was never in the suite where Alex was staying. I don't know the room number. Besides, I had no reason to wish Alex dead." Her exquisitely sculpted brows drew down in a frown. "I don't see any point to your questions. The police have arrested the murderers. What more is there to know?"

"Oh, not much," Annie said carelessly. "Perhaps we could talk about the afternoon your husband drowned."

Lynn's face tightened. "Heyward's accident has nothing to do with you. It's very unkind of you to bring up that sad day. It certainly has no bearing on what happened to Alex."

"That day"—Annie spoke slowly, distinctly—"has everything to do with Alex's murder. Heyward's death was not an accident." She heard Joan's sharp intake of breath.

Joan reached out, gripped Annie's arm. "What are you saying?" Her voice shook, rose.

Annie put a consoling hand over Joan's, felt the tremble beneath her fingers, but she continued to look at Lynn. "Alex found out that you killed Heyward. You are a powerful swimmer. You swam out to intercept *Summer Song*. Alex had proof. He told you when he saw you that there was a painting of you coming up out of the water in a bay late that afternoon, a painting that was signed and dated. You had to kill him. You planned it cleverly. You found a heavy piece of wood, probably in the trees behind your house. You brought the weapon with you. You walked behind him and turned and struck the back of his head."

"I don't know what you're talking about." But Lynn's blue eyes were wide and staring, her voice grating.

The curtain billowed. Billy Cameron stepped inside. All in black, he was formidable, a big man moving with the grace of an athlete. Hyla Harrison followed, one hand on her holster. Lou Pirelli turned a bit sideways to maneuver his large wrapped burden.

Billy Cameron advanced toward Lynn, his heavy face tough and determined. "Lynn Griffith, I have a warrant for your arrest for the murders of Alex Griffith and Warren Foster. Anything you say may be used in evidence against you."

As Lou walked, he pulled free the sheet of Bubble Wrap, tucked the protective material under one arm. He held the framed watercolor out in front of him.

Joan Turner let go of Annie, stepped out, and stared at the painting. She looked. And looked. Then she swung around, faced Lynn.

"You killed Heyward. I should have known. He'd told me a few days before that he was going to leave you. He said you never cared anything about him, only for money, and you'd badgered him to take out a huge insurance policy, double indemnity if he died accidentally, but he had no intention of dying. He was going to leave the island, go to Atlanta, stay with Alex, get a divorce. He said he thought with what he had left he could pay off his debts, keep *Summer Song*. He said he would be free and he would sail forever. When he died, I thought what a terrible irony that he'd died sailing. But it wasn't irony. You killed him. You killed my brothers."

Lynn stared emptily at the watercolor, then her gaze slid around the room. But there was no way out. Her wide blue eyes moved back to the frame gripped in Lou's strong hands. Forever and always at the bottom of the painting that depicted her, strong, vital, alive, climbing from the water, was the date, the date her husband died.

16

Annie glanced at her watch. "Marian's being mysterious."

Max's face creased in concern.

"Happy mysterious. Not bad, sad mysterious."

"Good to know."

His relief was evident, which Annie found endearing. He truly didn't want her mucking about trying to find murderers. She almost volunteered that she'd keep all mysteries on the shelves in Death on Demand, but it was too beautiful a morning to make a promise she might not be able to keep.

He leaned against the railing that overlooked the marina. "Mysterious about what?" The morning sun turned his short hair to gold, made his blue eyes darker than a glacial lake. The breeze off the marina tugged at his shirt. She looked at him admiringly.

She saw that he saw the—okay, admit it—lust in her glance, not to put too fine a point on it. She hurried to speak before he suggested maybe it was a good morning to hasten home for some afternoon delight.

"About why she's coming to the store and wants us there at ten sharp. That's why I thought we'd better get here early since you want to drop by Confidential Commissions." This past week she'd been instructed not to glance right when she stepped into Death on Demand.

Max looked eager. He took her hand.

They started toward the boardwalk. Annie stopped as she heard three pings. "I'd better see."

Max shook his head. "Has anyone ever told you you're compulsive about texts?"

"I am not." But she spoke defensively. "Just their texts." She didn't have to explain whose. She pulled out her cell. "From your mom: 'In a good bookroom you feel in some mysterious way that you are absorbing the wisdom contained in all of the books through your skin, without even opening them. Mark Twain.' She added: 'Perhaps, dear Annie, immersion in mysteries accounts for your affinity for puzzles.'" Annie beamed. "Now, that's a nice thing for Laurel to say, isn't it?"

Max gave her an innocent glance. "Or maybe you're a sucker for trouble?"

"I like Laurel's interpretation better." She looked at the screen, read Henny's text aloud. "'Herbert Brean's *The Hooded Hawk* beauti fully captures the scarcity of new cars after World War II, an unusual background for murder.'" A quick frown. Where was Henny finding these books? Another ping. She skipped Emma Clyde's text for the moment. Another from Henny. She read quickly, "'You can find the books I've mentioned in *American Murders*, a fabulous collection of eleven short novels from *American Magazine* 1934–1954. The collection was edited by Jon L. Breen and Rita A. Breen, published in 1986 by

Garland Publishing.' " Annie's eyes narrowed. "That's a collectible I have to have. I'll trade with Henny. She's nuts about Colin Cotterill's books and I have a signed copy of *The Coroner's Lunch*."

"Better watch your step." Max had that told-you-you-were-addicted-to-texts smile.

Annie waited until they finished climbing the steps to the boardwalk before she flicked up to see Emma's text: " 'Marigold's off on a tear. Three bodies, a stolen emerald, invisible ink, a man in a Cossack's fur hat, and, if it's in plain sight, I don't know where the hell it is! According to Lauren and Henny, the Mississippi's awesome. I'm too busy to look.' "

Annie was laughing as they came to the end of the boardwalk.

The Gone Fishing sign no longer hung from the knob. An easel with a chalkboard sat to the left of the front door to Confidential Commissions. Printed in overlarge letters that had a happy tilt:

Confidential Commissions
Looking for answers? Lost a treasure map?
Searching for an old friend?
Puzzled?
Need an adventure?
Walk right in.

Annie beamed. "I like that last."

Max eyed the chalkboard judiciously. "I aim to please. I decided to expand the field. I'm good at finding fun things to do. Safaris, gold mines, romantic getaways. And speaking of . . ." He took her hand.

She gave a determined tug toward the front door of Death on Demand. "Later," she murmured.

Ingrid looked up from the counter with a smile. "Hey, Max, glad you're back." She tipped her head toward the coffee area. "They're waiting at the table beneath the watercolors. And there's going to be some treats coming. Barb's already cooking."

Max grinned. "She's the best secretary on the island."

"Barb's bringing over a platter of honey buns." Though thin as a rail, Ingrid had a weakness for sweets. "Barb said, 'When I got Max's text to come back, I knew he'd come to his senses. What are women to do if they don't take care of folks around them?'"

Max turned his hands up. "What's a man to do when he's outnumbered?"

Annie was already moving down the center aisle. She heard a murmur of voices. Ingrid said "they" were waiting. Who were "they"?

Marian met her halfway, her rapid steps a clatter on the heart pine floor. She grabbed Annie, gave her a huge hug, rattled in her raspy tone, "I wanted to bring you and Max all up-to-date on everything." She had Annie by the arm.

As they reached the coffee area, chairs scraped.

Marian gestured. "This is Craig."

Tall and muscular, Craig's big face creased in a smile. A shock of dark hair was threaded with gray. "And here's David. He's grown a lot since you last saw him." David was almost as tall as his father, with sun-streaked hair and blue eyes. "They've heard a lot"—her dark eyes looked carefully at Annie—"about the big story I was working last week."

Annie took her seat, glanced from David to Craig. "I'll bet Marian hasn't told you that if it weren't for her, two people would be facing trial for murders they didn't commit. Marian kept digging."

Marian still stood, hands on her bony hips. "We did it together. And I just wrote a story for this afternoon's *Gazette* that cinches the deal. The police confirmed that Lynn Griffith's fingerprints were in the sitting room where Alex died. Plus the treads from her bike match tire tracks found at Widow's Haunt. So they've got big-time physical evidence."

Annie started to ask Marian why she had been so certain Lynn Griffith had a bike.

Marian looked at her.

Annie saw a flash of cold satisfaction in Marian's dark eyes.

Oh.

"Anyway, Lynn Griffith was arraigned this morning. Rae Griffith and Neil Kelly are free and have left the island. And now . . ." Marian's voice was light and happy. "I—we—Craig and I—Craig and David and I—have great news. Craig and I are getting remarried at seven o'clock at Parotti's. Did you know Ben was once a ship captain and can marry people? Anyway, he's going to marry us and we want you and Max to stand with us."

Ingrid and Barb were standing by the coffee bar, clapping. Marian was crying. Craig looked both proud and embarrassed. David's grin was as big as a baseball diamond.

Annie grabbed paper napkins, thrust them at Marian. "No tears. Not even happy tears. Congratulations. Of course Max and I will do the honors. This will be one of the best nights ever at Parotti's Bar and Grill."

Marian reached out and pulled Annie close for another hug. Craig wrapped his arms around both of them. "Hey, gals, happy days are here again. We have some terrific planning—" He looked over their heads and up at the watercolors. "Neat idea. I know those early books. My dad ran a secondhand bookstore. And the new ones are three of my favorite authors. *The Puzzle of the Blue Banderilla* by Stuart Palmer, *Great Black Kanba* by Constance and Gwenyth Little, *Miss Dimple Disappears* by Mignon F. Ballard, *Out of Circulation* by Miranda James, and *Murder at Honeychurch Hall* by Hannah Dennison."